WATERS

'Kalki' is the pen name of Ramaswamy Krishnamurthy (1899–1954), whose career in writing and journalism began as activism during the struggle for Indian independence. He served as editor of the popular Tamil magazine *Ananda Vikatan* before launching *Kalki*. The magazine—and eventually its founder—was named for the mythological tenth avatar of Vishnu to symbolise a vision to 'destroy regressive regimes, express radical thoughts, take readers into new directions, and create a new era'. Kalki wrote several novels, including *Parthiban Kanavu* and *Sivakamiyin Sabadam*, as well as political essays, film reviews, dance and music critiques, and scholarly work.

Nandini Krishnan is the author of *Hitched: The Modern Woman and Arranged Marriage* and *Invisible Men: Inside India's Transmasculine Networks*. She has translated two of Perumal Murugan's works into English: *Estuary* and *Four Strokes of Luck*. She was shortlisted for the PEN Presents translation prize 2022 and the Ali Jawad Zaidi Memorial Prize for translation from Urdu 2022. She is an alumna of the Writer's Bloc playwrights' workshop by the Royal Court Theatre, London. Her novel-in-manuscript was a winner of the Caravan Writers of India Festival contest and showcased at the Writers of the World Festival, Paris, 2014.

PONNIYIN SELVAN BOOK 2

TROUBLED WATERS

KALKI

TRANSLATED BY
NANDINI KRISHNAN

eka

eka

First published in Tamil as *Ponniyin Selvan*

Published in English in 2023 by Eka, an imprint of Westland Books, a division of Nasadiya Technologies Private Limited

No. 269/2B, First Floor, 'Irai Arul', Vimalraj Street, Nethaji Nagar, Alapakkam Main Road, Maduravoyal, Chennai 600095

ISBN: 9789357768702

10 9 8 7 6 5 4 3 2 1

This is a work of fiction. Names, characters, organisations, places, events and incidents are either products of the author's imagination or used fictitiously.

Typeset by SÜRYA, New Delhi
Printed at Nutech Print Services, India

CONTENTS

1

'A ROYAL GUEST'

Once the poets had left, the royal physician brought a concoction for the emperor. Malayaman's daughter, the queen consort, received it from him and stood before her husband to administer it.

Chinna Pazhuvettaraiyar, who had waited patiently until that moment, walked up to the emperor without letting go of his grip on Vandiyadevan, dragging him along in the process.

'Prabhu! Has the new medicine shown any effect?' Chinna Pazhuvettaraiyar asked.

'The physician says it has, and Devi agrees. But, for some reason, I'm not able to put my faith in it. Truth be told, Thalapathi, all this seems a pointless exercise to me. Destiny calls to me. I think Yama has headed to Pazhaiyarai in pursuit of me. Once he learns I'm not there, he'll come straight here.'

'Prabhu! You must not speak with such a broken spirit. You shouldn't hurt us so. You come from a dynasty that ...'

'Ah! I come from a dynasty whose men had no fear of Yama, you mean. If I had the good fortune, as did so many of my ancestors, of dying in battle while leading the vanguard, I would have absolutely no fear of such a glorious death; I would not weaken in its face. I would embrace it with enthusiasm. My father's older brother Rajadityar lost his life even as he fought on his elephant at Takkolam, and immortalised the valour of the Chozha clan in that battlefield. He earned the posthumous title "Yaanai Mel Thunjiya Devar"—The King Who Ascended to the Heavens on His Elephant. What will my posthumous title be? "Noi Padukkaiyil Thunjiya Sundara Chozhan"—Sundara Chozhan, Who Ascended to the Heavens on His Sickbed. My father's other brother, Kandaraditya Devar, was free from fear of death thanks to his Shiva bhakti. He went on a pilgrimage to the various sthalams of Shiva, venturing into the kingdoms along the western shore. And he passed away on one such pilgrimage. He earned the title "Merkezhundaruliya Devar"—The King Who Graced the Western Shores. I'm no devotee of Shiva like he was, and I've lost my capacity to go on a pilgrimage anyway. How long can I lie on my sickbed like this, a burden to everyone around me … but something deep inside my heart tells me I'm not long for this world …'

'Chakravarti! The royal physician says there is no danger to your life. The astrologers concur. But this stripling saw fit to warn you of some danger …'

'Ah! This is the boy from Kanchi, isn't he? Yes, he spoke of some danger, said "abaayam". What were you talking about, thambi? The state of my health?'

Vandiyadevan's brain worked at lightning speed. If he admitted that he'd warned the king about impending danger, he would rouse suspicions that would put *him* in danger. He must escape that situation. Right, he could try a quick fix. With grammar for a friend, he would convert the long vowel to the short.

'O Chakravarti, my lord! Who am I to speak of "abaayam"? When our Thalapathi, the epitome of courage Chinna Pazhuvettaraiyar, the royal physician and our Maharani—as devoted as Savitri[1], who prised away Yama's hold on her husband's life—are with you, what danger could befall you? I surrendered at your feet, saying, "Abayam, abayam"—Refuge, Refuge! I, a naïve stripling, am all that is left of the ancient, venerable Vaanar clan. I serve the Chozha empire in a manner that pleases your distinguished son. You must grace me with a small portion of the ancestral domains of my clan. O king of kings! Abayam! Abayam! This stripling places himself under your care!' said Vandiyadevan, without taking a breath through this entire soliloquy.

Pazhuvettaraiyar's face drew itself into a scowl, and Sundara Chozhar's blossomed into a smile. The Maharani's features brimmed with compassion.

'It appears Saraswati Devi etched her words on this boy's tongue the moment he was born. He has an extraordinary gift for speech!' said the queen.

Sensing an opportunity, Vandiyadevan said, 'Thaaye! You must speak on my behalf. I'm a motherless, fatherless orphan. I have no one else at all, no one in the world. It is up to me to speak for myself. Just as Parvati Devi intercedes with Shiva Peruman and Lakshmi Devi with Mahavishnu, taking pity on their devotees, you must intercede with the emperor on my behalf. Even if I were to be given back just ten villages of my ancestral lands, I would leave a happy man!'

Sundara Chozhar was surprised and pleased by what he was hearing. He turned to Chinna Pazhuvettaraiyar and said, 'Thalapathi! I've become quite fond of this young man. Devi's face suggests she is contemplating adopting him as her third son. We can grant his request, can't we? That won't cause any trouble, will it? What is your opinion?'

'What place does my opinion merit in such matters? It is Prince Aditya Karikalar's opinion we must ask, isn't it?' said the commander of the Thanjai fort.

'Chakravarti! The crown prince tells me I must ask the king of Pazhuvoor, and the king of Pazhuvoor says I must ask the crown prince. And my request is lost between the two of them …' said Vandiyadevan.

'Pillaai![2] You don't worry! We'll sit the two of them down together and figure this out,' said the emperor.

Then, he turned to Chinna Pazhuvettaraiyar and said, 'Thalapathi! This boy brought me a scroll from the prince. As usual, Adityan has written to ask me to come stay in Kanchi. He has apparently built a brand-new palace of gold. I must spend at least a few days there, he says.'

'Your wish is our command,' said Chinna Pazhuvettaraiyar.

'Ah! I'm all too aware that my wish is your command, but my legs won't follow *my* command. It would be impossible for me to journey to Kanchi. I find the idea of climbing into a palanquin like the royal women, with curtains to screen me from the world, quite revolting. I must send a reply asking Aditya Karikalan to come visit me instead ...'

'Can the prince afford to leave Kanchi at this time? Our enemies in the North remain quite strong.'

'Parthibendran and Malayaman will take care of things on that front. Something tells me the prince must be at my side now. And not just that; a letter must be sent to Ilango[3], the younger prince, who is leading the war in Eezham, asking him to come here. I wish to sit the two of them down and consult them on a crucial decision I must make. While Arulmozhi is here, we can also convey your reservations regarding the shipping of provisions for the army from here.'

'Chakravarti! Do forgive my saying this, but it is not I who have reservations regarding the shipping of provisions for the Chozha army from these lands. Neither is it the Dhanadhanyadhikari, my brother, who has charge of the kingdom's finances and granaries. It is the subjects of Chozha Naadu who have reservations. The last harvest barely yielded enough for our people. Under such circumstances, the people find it objectionable that ship after ship of grain is being sent to Eezham. For the moment, they restrict their protests to muttering under their breath. In a while, their voices will get louder. Those voices will enter this very palace and affect your health …'

'Arulmozhi will never do something to which the people of this kingdom object. Anyhow, let him make a trip here. Once Periya Pazhuvettaraiyar arrives, we must have a man sent to Lanka. When does he return?'

'He will definitely be here tonight!'

'Let us send a response to Kanchi tomorrow. We can send it through this boy, can't we?'

'This young man has just blitzed his way from Kanchi to here. Let him stay here for a few days and regain his energy. We can send the scroll through someone else.'

'Please do. This boy can stay here until the prince arrives.'

As Malayaman's daughter, the queen consort, rose, Chinna Pazhuvettaraiyar said, 'I have troubled you greatly today and made you speak for too long. Please forgive me. Our audience has dragged on until Devi was forced to take it upon herself to warn me!'

'Thalapathi! This boy is a royal guest. Please take good care of him and make all the arrangements to ensure he has a comfortable stay. If only the emperor were well, we could have asked him to stay right here in our palace,' said the queen.

'I will take care of him, thaaye! You need have no worry on that account. I will take very good care of him!' said Chinna Pazhuvettaraiyar. Even as he said the words, one swarthy hand reached involuntarily for his moustache to give it a twirl.

2

THE CHITRA MANDAPAM

Chinna Pazhuvettaraiyar escorted Vandiyadevan to the royal court. He wasn't entirely satisfied with the young man's explanation about his words to the emperor. It struck Chinna Pazhuvettaraiyar that perhaps it had been the wrong decision to allow Vandiyadevan an audience with Sundara Chozhar. He was Aditya Karikalan's man, and it was but natural that he be subjected to suspicion. Yet, the fact that Periya Pazhuvettaraiyar had sent his signet ring along with this messenger placed him above suspicion. Aha! One could hardly presume to school Periyavar in circumspection. Yet, he couldn't help but relive the moment he had entered the king's chambers, and observed the young man's nervousness. Vandiyadevan had seemed to blink as if from fear. He remembered hearing the hiss of 'Abaayam! Abaayam!' clearly. If the young man had indeed said 'Abayam', was it likely that Chinna Pazhuvettaraiyar had misheard it as 'Abaayam'?

Taking everything into account, it would be prudent to not let Vandiyadevan go on his way yet. Once his brother returned, Chinna Pazhuvettaraiyar could figure out exactly who the messenger was and then act accordingly. A gutsy youngster would be a good fit in his personal army, he thought. Why, he might even consider giving Vandiyadevan a share of his ancestral property in return. Boys like him would be eternally grateful for a good turn, and would devote their lives to the service of a benefactor. And if it turned out he was working for the enemy, well, appropriate arrangements would have to be made to put an end to it. In any case, he would wait for his brother, and then see what course of action was best.

Once they reached the royal court, Vandiyadevan looked about him with seeming enthusiasm. He searched the surroundings with his eyes. He stared at the spot where he had handed over the scroll to the Thalapathi. Just in case the other scroll—that all-important scroll—might be lying about. If he failed to find it, there would be no greater fool than he! He would lose a chance to meet the young princess whose praises the entire world sang. And, he would be leaving the deed Aditya Karikalan had entrusted to him half-done.

Chinna Pazhuvettaraiyar turned to one of the attendants and said, 'Take this boy to our palace. Show him to the guest chambers and settle him in. Stay right there until I return.'

The moment Vandiyadevan and his chaperone had left, another man approached and deferentially held out a scroll to the Thalapathi. 'We found this on the path leading from here to the king's reception hall. It must have fallen from the person of the young man who just left,' he said.

The commander took the scroll and opened it eagerly. His eyebrows shot halfway up his forehead. His features underwent a terrible change.

Aha! A scroll from Aditya Karikalar to Ilaiya Piraatti. 'A warrior who will stay firm and true in carrying out secret missions, a determined man who will ensure that he completes the task at hand ... you had asked me for one such person, hadn't you? I'm sending the bearer of this scroll for this purpose. You can trust him with all your heart, and assign him duties of the highest importance,' writes the crown prince, in his own hand. There is some mystery behind all this. Nothing is quite as it seems. Does Periyavar[1] *know about* this *olai*[2]*? I'll need to be even more careful around this chap now!* the commander of the fort said to himself.

He signalled to the man who had brought him the scroll and whispered something to him; the man nodded and left right away.

Vandiyadevan was given a royal welcome at Chinna Pazhuvettaraiyar's palace. He was bathed, and given brand new clothes to wear. Vandiyadevan, who was partial to dressing up, was thrilled. He even forgot his worries about the missing scroll. Once he was dressed, the servants offered him a plate of royal dishes—arusuvai sitrundi, snacks suited to the six traditional tastes.[3] A famished Vandiyadevan put paid to them in no time. He was then escorted to the Chitra Mandapam of the palace.

'You can admire the extraordinary paintings here until Thalapathi returns,' the men said.

The escorting party then left, except for three guards who stationed themselves outside the door and busied themselves with a game of chokkattan—dice—even as they kept up their chatter.

The new capital of the Chozha clan, Thanjaipuri, was famous back in the day for its sculptures. Just as Tiruvaiyaru was the home of dance and music, Thanjai was home to the art of stone sculpture. Chinna Pazhuvettaraiyar's Chitra Mandapam had gained much renown for its artwork. Vandiyadevan had contrived to enter this hallowed place. He studied the murals of astounding colours and dimensions, and found himself enamoured. He forgot himself in this intoxication; he forgot the crucial mission on which he had been sent.

The paintings that illustrated the life stories of the various Chozha kings fascinated him. Incidents from the last hundred years featured prominently in the Chitra Mandapam. They were the ones that appealed the most to Vandiyadevan.

At this juncture, one would like to remind readers of the lineage of Chozha kings who had ruled the land from Pazhaiyarai and Thanjai over the last hundred years. This little refresher will prove handy in understanding the events that will unfold in our story from here on out.

We have already spoken of Vijayalaya Chozhan, whose skin bore the scars of ninety-six war wounds.

It was customary for Chozha kings to adopt the titles Parakesari and Rajakesari in turns. Parakesari Vijayalayan's son Rajakesari Aditya Chozhan inherited the crown from him. The apple did not fall far from the tree. He was his father's son in every way. First, he aligned himself with the Pallavas, beat the Pandiya king and expanded the Chozha empire. He then went to war with the Pallava king Aparajita Varman. Aditya Chozhan leapt up on to the elephant on which Aparajita Varman was seated during the battle in Ambari, killed him and brought Thondai Mandalam under Chozha rule. Kongu Mandalam, too, became part of his kingdom. Adityan was an exemplary devotee of Lord Shiva. He erected several Shiva temples along the shores of the Kaveri, from the river's origin in Hasya Malai to the point where it joined the sea.

Next in line was Parakesari Parantakan, who would go on to rule for forty-six years. He was the greatest Chozha king after Karikaal Peruvalaththaan who had flown the tiger flag from the Himalayas. His titular names included Veeranarayanan, Pandita Vatsalan, Kunjaravallan and Soorasigamani, along with 'Maduraiyum Eezhamum Kondavan'—He Who Conquered Madurai and Eezham.

Even as early as the era of Parantaka I, the Chozha empire stretched from Kanyakumari to the river Krishna. The tiger flag flew over Eezham for a while too. This was the very same Parantakan who had erected a golden roof over the Tillai Chitrambalam.

Towards the end of his rule, the Chozha empire was assailed by various dangers. The Rashtrakuta kings, who were the most powerful rulers in the North, decided to put down the rising influence of the Chozha empire. They waged war against the Chozhas over and over again, and saw some success too.

Parantaka Chakravarti had three sons. Of them, the most valiant was his eldest, Rajadityan. Given the constant incursions from the North, Rajadityan was stationed with a large army at Tirumunaippaadi for a considerable length of time. The Chozhas and Rashtrakutas clashed in a terrible battle at Takkolam, near Arakkonam. Having decimated the enemy's armies and etched his name in the annals of history, Rajadityan died a hero's death on the battlefield. Like Aparajita Varman, he too was killed while riding his elephant, and earned the posthumous title 'Yanai Mel Thunjiya Devan'—He Who Rode His Elephant to the Heavens—which is how he is remembered in stone edicts.

If only Rajadityan hadn't died young, he would have inherited the Chozha throne from Parantaka Chakravarti, and his offspring after him. But the prince died before he could wear the crown and produce heirs, and so it was his younger brother Kandaraditya Devar who inherited the title of emperor and the titular name Rajakesari.

Like his father and grandfather before him, he too was an ardent devotee of Lord Shiva. And a great patron of the Tamil language as well. To tell the truth, he was not particularly interested in ruling his empire. He was far happier praying at temples and reading Tamil literary works.

He followed the path forged by the Nayanmars and wrote devotional songs in honour of Shiva Perumaan. In the last of these songs, which are collectively known as *Tiruvisaippa*, he sings of himself in the following manner:

Seeraanmalgu Tillai sempon ambalathaadi thannai
Kaaraar solai kozhi vendan thanjaiyarkon kalanda
Aaraa insol Kandaradityan arunthamizh maalai vallavar
Pera ulagir perumai odum perinbam eyduvaare!

Those who can recite by rote
This garland of songs crafted in wondrous Tamil
Singing of He who danced in the golden hall of Tillai
Singing of He in whom indescribably great qualities reside
Singing in insatiable ardour, in the sweetest words
That poured out of the King of Thanjavur,
The Kozhi Vendan who rules over gardens
Blooming with so many flowers

That they attract such numbers of bees
As to appear entirely black
Will earn fame, praise, and joy
In the world that is yet to come

The Chozha kings who came after Vijayalayan might have ruled from Pazhaiyarai and Thanjai, but they always considered Uraiyur their hereditary capital. Uraiyur was also known as 'Kozhi', which is why the Chozha kings styled themselves as 'Kozhi Vendar'.

Although Kandaradityan ruled the kingdom in name, it was his younger brother Arinjayan who immersed himself in governance. He had accompanied their eldest brother Rajadityan to various battles, camping with him at places like Tirunavalur. He had waged a fierce battle against the Rashtrakutas. After the terrible defeat at Takkolam, he had ensured that the fortunes of the Chozhas reversed swiftly, confronting the invading Rashtrakuta army well before they reached Thenpennai.

So, Rajakesari Kandaradityar named his brother, Arinjayan, the crown prince and announced to the entire kingdom that the latter would inherit the throne.

There was another crucial reason for his making this decision. Kandaradityar's first wife had passed away before he had been crowned king. He did not remarry for a long time after. His younger brother, Arinjayan, had a son whose appearance, intellect and aptitude were so superior to others that one found it hard to decide which his greatest asset was. He had been given the name of his ancestor Parantakan by his parents, and the title of 'Sundara Chozhan' by the subjects of the kingdom. Kandaradityar wished for his brother to inherit the mantle of ruler from him, and for his brother's son to be second-in-line to the throne.

He held meetings with the most powerful heads of tributary kingdoms, army commanders and representatives of the commonfolk, and ensured that the decision was unanimous. He also had the announcement made public with great pomp and show.

Well after these arrangements had been made, Kandaradityar's life took a most unexpected turn. He happened to meet the daughter of Mazhavarayan, the ruler of a minor kingdom. The beauty, charm, poise, demeanour and Shiva bhakti of that icon of femininity left him besotted. In his twilight years, he married her, and a child was born from that union. They named him Madurantakan, and raised him with all the love they had to give. He was the apple of their eyes. Yet, neither the king nor queen wished to change the decision regarding the inheritance of the monarchy. The path they had chosen was that of ascetism and the worship of Lord Shiva, and that was the path on which they wished to set their son. How could an empire in this material world stand comparison to the empire of Shivalokam? Their son must prepare for a life in Kailash, not waste his time on earthly trifles. Kandaradityar made it known that he wished that the Chozha dynasty would be fostered by his brother Arinjayan and the latter's descendants. And so it was that the Chozha throne became the seat of the youngest prince and his progeny, having skipped the lineages of Rajadityan and Kandaradityar.

Parakesari Arinjayan did not live long after Kandaradityar. He followed his older brother to Kailash within a year.

The emperor's aides, subordinate kings and courtiers crowned Prince Sundara Chozhar king, satisfied that the empire would prosper under him. Rajakesari Sundara Chozhar did full justice to the position fortune had bestowed upon him. He led the army on a series of conquests, winning back Pandiya Naadu and Thondai Mandalam. He drove the Rashtrakuta forces away from the banks of the Thenpennai river.

Sundara Chozhar's sons, Aditya Karikalan and Arulmozhi Varman, proved to be peerless warriors who might well surpass their father. They marched to the battlefield at a tender age, leading the vanguard. They were invaluable lieutenants to their father. Everywhere they went, the goddess of victory Vijayalakshmi smiled upon the Chozhas.

3

'THIEVES! THIEVES!'

Our hero Vandiyadevan amused himself studying the illustrated histories of the Chozha emperors, from Vijayalaya Chozhar to Parantakar II, Sundara Chozhar. Aha! What incredible men they had been, without exception! How courageous they had proven themselves in battle! Each had treated his living breath as a trifle and never hesitated to put his life at stake for the expansion of the empire. They had achieved unparalleled greatness for themselves and their kingdom, and each of their biographies outdid the stories of mythological heroes and their deeds, the ancient epics of the land. Chozha Naadu was blessed to have been ruled by such a dynasty. The territories over which they ruled today were blessed too.

Vandiyadevan noticed another crucial aspect in the paintings that depicted the life stories of the Chozha emperors. For every Chozha emperor, there was a Pazhuvoor king playing his right hand, standing by to carry out the tasks that could only be entrusted to an exemplary lieutenant. In every scene of battle, this Pazhuvoor king could be spotted plunging bravely into the fray.

It was a Pazhuvettaraiyar who first laid siege to the Thanjai fort and captured it from Muththarayar. When an aged Vijayalaya Chozhan, who had lost the use of both legs, made his way to the battle arena in Tiruppurambiyam, it was another Pazhuvettaraiyar who offered him his shoulders and served as his mount. It was yet another Pazhuvettaraiyar who crowned Aditya Chozhan king and oversaw the pattabhishekam performed at the coronation ceremony. When Aditya Chozhan lunged for Aparajita Varman's elephant and killed the rider, it was a Pazhuvettaraiyar who bent over to make a springboard of his back and shoulders for the king to gain momentum for the leap. In the various wars led by Parantaka Chakravarti, it was the Pazhuvettaraiyars who were at the vanguard, holding the tiger flag aloft. As a wounded Rajadityan fell to the ground at battle, it was a Pazhuvettaraiyar who held his head and eased the prince on to his lap, to give him the news that the Rashtrakuta armies had fled the field. It was the Pazhuvettaraiyars, too, who were right by the side of Arinjayar and Sundara Chozhar as they went about their heroic deeds in war.

As he studied the artwork, Vandiyadevan was lost for words. It was no surprise that the Pazhuvettaraiyar brothers wielded such influence in Chozha Naadu today. Nor was it surprising that Sundara Chozhar sought their opinions on everything.

It was clear, though, that he'd landed himself in a terribly complicated situation. Chinna Pazhuvettaraiyar had quite obviously begun to nurse some sort of suspicion regarding his intentions. Whatever those suspicions were, they would be confirmed once his elder brother entered the city. The story of his manipulations with the signet ring would come out. And then he would be done for.

Vandiyadevan had heard tell of the dungeons in Pazhuvettaraiyar's palace. They might throw him in there. Once someone was imprisoned in those dungeons, it was unlikely he would ever come out alive. If he happened to, he would be a living corpse, bereft of all reason and sanity, and reduced to skin and bones.

Aha! How was he to get himself out of this peril? He would have to find a way to leave the fort before Periyavar arrived. Our hero had even lost the desire to meet the Pazhuvoor Ilaiya Rani once more. All he wanted was to escape with his life before he was sucked into the dungeon. Although he had lost the scroll, he could still meet Kundavai Piraatti in person and give her Aditya Karikalar's message. She might choose to believe him, or not. But how was he to get out of the Thanjai fort now?

Another question rose in Vandiyadevan's head at this juncture—what had happened to the clothes he had been wearing? It struck him that his royal welcome and his being given this gift of new clothes had all been part of a ruse to examine his clothes. The scroll intended for Kundavai Devi must have fallen into the hands of the Thalapathi. No, there was no doubt. This was exactly what had happened. Now, he realised why Chinna Pazhuvettaraiyar had held his hand in such an iron grip that he hadn't been able to sidle away along with the poets. And why three men had been stationed to guard him. Aha! A ploy! He needed a ploy. Yes, he had one in mind! Yes, it was time to put it into action! Veeravel! Vetrivel!

Vandiyadevan looked out of one of the windows of the Chitra Mandapam. Chinna Pazhuvettaraiyar, surrounded by his entourage, was riding his horse towards the mandapam. Aha! This was the right moment. He couldn't afford to delay this by even a second!

The three bodyguards who had been busying themselves with chokkattan at the threshold folded up their game and stood up. They had heard the sounds that heralded the arrival of their lord and master.

Vandiyadevan approached them and said, 'Brothers! Where are the clothes I was wearing?'

'What do you want with those filthy clothes now? We have given you new silk garments in accordance with Ejamaan's orders,' one of them said.

'I don't need new clothes. My old clothes were good enough. Bring them to me right away!'

'They've been sent to the dhobi. We'll bring them to you once they're ready.'

'No, no! I won't hear of it! You're thieves! I had hidden my money in my old clothes. You have taken them to steal my money. Bring them to me now! Or else...'

'Or else what will you do, boy? You'll lop off our heads and send them off to Thanjavur, will you? But this *is* Thanjavur. Keep that in mind.'

'Ade! Are you going to bring my clothes back right away? Or not?' Vandiyadevan said to the man who had spoken.

'I can only bring them to you if they're still around. We've thrown those soiled things to the crocodiles. How can I fetch them from the crocodile's stomach?'

'You thieving scoundrels! Do you think this is a joke? Here, I'm going to tell your Ejamaan, just you wait and watch!' said Vandiyadevan, and made for the entrance.

One of the three stepped in his way to stop him. Vandiyadevan punched his nose hard. That was all it took. The man collapsed to the floor in a faint. Blood began to drip from his nose.

Another approached Vandiyadevan as if he planned to wrestle him, extending both his arms before him. Vandiyadevan gripped both those extended arms, stuck one of his legs between those of his opponent and gave his arms a mighty twist. That put paid to him. He sank to the floor with an 'Ammadi!'

As the third made for him, Vandiyadevan aimed a kick at his knee. He fell down, wailing.

All three rose again to surround Vandiyadevan, but they were more prudent this time, keeping a safe distance even as they made the right noises.

By this time, the horse had reached the door of the palace. Vandiyadevan threw all his power into his voice and hollered, 'Thieves! Thieves!' and leapt upon them. The three men tried to overpower him, but he screamed, 'Thieving scoundrels! Thieving scoundrels!'

Chinna Pazhuvettaraiyar strode into the hall, demanding, 'What is this commotion about?'

4

PUT TO THE TEST

The moment he saw Chinna Pazhuvettaraiyar, Vandiyadevan stopped fighting the guards and began to walk towards the commander. The three men rushed to contain him. They held on to his limbs, but Vandiyadevan ignored them. Their grip didn't hinder him from walking the few steps to cover the distance between himself and Chinna Pazhuvettaraiyar.

'Thalapathi! You've arrived at just the right time. These thieves have not just stolen my belongings, but tried to kill me just now! Is this how one treats a guest? Is that the culture of Thanjavur? I am not simply your guest, but the emperor's too. You heard for yourself what the queen said. I am a messenger who comes bearing a scroll from the crown prince himself. If I'm subjected to such torment, what would they not do to someone else! I can't believe you have thieves in your employ. In our Thondai Mandalam, we impale thieves, no questions asked!'

Vandiyadevan's outpouring fell upon Chinna Pazhuvettaraiyar in a torrent. The Thalapathi had barely recovered from his shock at watching the young man overthrow three of his elite guards at once. He was even more tempted to induct him into his personal army. So, he said in a conciliatory tone, 'Hold on, thambi, have some patience! I don't think these men would have stolen your money or possessions. Here, let me interrogate them.'

'That is my very request. Interrogate them, and then grant me justice! Please make arrangements for my clothes and belongings to be returned to me,' said Vandiyadevan.

'Ade! Leave that boy alone and come here now. What did I ask you all to do, and what have you gone and done? Who asked you to lay a hand on him?' asked the Thalapathi angrily.

'Ejamaane! We did just as you instructed. We gave him an oil massage and bath, and dressed him in new clothes and ornaments. We offered him a feast, and then brought him to the Chitra Mandapam. He was looking at the portraits here for some time. Suddenly, he asked us for his old clothes. And then he began to attack us right away!' one of them said.

'Did all you three louts get beaten up by this stripling of a boy?' said Chinna Pazhuvettaraiyar, glaring gimlets at them.

'Ejamaan! We didn't unleash any force on him because he was a royal guest. Give us leave now, and we'll see to him!'

'Enough of your chest-thumping. Stop this drivel. Thambi! What do you say?'

'I say give them leave, and give me leave too. It has been a while since I went to war and had a good fight with an enemy. My shoulders are itching for battle. Let me teach them a lesson in hospitality towards royal guests!' our hero said.

Chinna Pazhuvettaraiyar smiled and said, 'Thambi! Please wait for battle with Chozha Naadu's enemies to scratch those itching shoulders of yours. As you know, the emperor is ill, and we have orders to ban all fights and unpleasantness inside the palace premises.

'In that case, ask them to bring me my clothes and belongings right away.'

'Dei, what have you done with them?' demanded Chinna Pazhuvettaraiyar, turning to the guards.

'Ejamaan! We have followed your orders and stowed them away safely.'

'Thalapathi! See how they lie! Just now, they said the clothes had been sent to the dhobi. Now, they say they have "stowed them away". Next, they'll claim *you're* the thief,' Vandiyadevan said.

The commander looked at the guards and said, 'Fools! I only asked that this boy be given new clothes. What did I ever say about his old clothes?' He then turned to Vandiyadevan and said, 'These morons are blathering on, thambi. Let it go. Why are you so worried about your old clothes? Had you kept something of importance in there?'

'Yes, I had some gold coins for my expenses on the journey ...,' Vandiyadevan began.

Chinna Pazhuvettaraiyar interrupted with, 'Don't you worry about that. I'll give you how much ever money you want for your expenses.'

'Thalapathi! I am the messenger of Prince Aditya Karikalan. It is not in my nature to hold out my hands for money from anyone else ...'

'In that case, I'll ensure that your clothes and the money you had kept in them are returned to you. There was nothing else hidden away in your clothes, was there?'

Vandiyadevan thought for a moment. Chinna Pazhuvettaraiyar noted his hesitation.

'There is another thing of great importance in my clothes. I trust that your men would not have meddled with it. If they have so much as laid a finger on it, I'll make mincemeat of them!'

'Aha! How you rage! If you don't watch out, you just might forget where you are and whom you're addressing. I'll let it go because you're just a boy. What is this thing of such great importance?'

'Thalapathi! I cannot speak of it. It's confidential.'

'The prince is the Mahatanda Nayagar of the Northern front. His authority only holds north of the Paalaar river. Here, it is the emperor's authority that counts.'

'Thalapathi! It is the emperor's authority that holds sway everywhere that the tiger flag flies. Who ever questioned that?'

'Which is why I say nothing can be kept secret from me within this fort. It is the well-being of the emperor I have in mind when I speak these words.'

'Thalapathi! The Chozha empire owes you and Periya Pazhuvettaraiyar an immense debt of gratitude for the fact that you have protected the emperor with your life and soul. I heard his words of praise to you today. The emperor said it is for fear of you that Yama does not dare step into the Thanjai fort. What profound words those are!'

'Yes, thambi. If we hadn't brought the emperor from Pazhaiyarai to Thanjai and beefed up his protection, who knows what might have come to pass? The plans of the conspirators from Pandiya Naadu might have borne fruit!'

'Ah! You too say the same thing. So, then what I heard must be true!'

'What have you heard?'

'That there is one conspiracy against the emperor, and another against his sons.'

Chinna Pazhuvettaraiyar bit his lip. It hit him that he had just been had. He had taken this chap for an innocent boy, and ended up tying himself in knots while trying to catch the latter out. Now, he was in the unenviable position of having to fend off the boy's barbs and offer explanations to counter his accusations. He wanted to end the conversation before it got worse.

'Why worry your head about such things? We're

here to unravel any conspiracy that may be brewing, and protect the Chozha royal dynasty. What do you demand of me now? You want your old clothes back. That's all, isn't it?'

'I want my old clothes, yes, and also the things that were inside.'

'You still haven't told me what those things were.'

'If I have no choice but to tell you, I will. But the responsibility for my breaking confidentiality lies with you. The prince gave me another olai, along with the one intended for the emperor.'

'Another olai? For whom? You never spoke of it!'

'I didn't because it was confidential. I speak of it now because you have forced me to. The prince had sent an olai to be delivered to Ilaiya Piraatti Kundavai Devi in Pazhaiyarai.'

'Oho! That would mean you won't be able to take the epistle the emperor is set to give you tomorrow to Kanchi right away. What urgent situation has arisen that warrants the prince's sending an olai to Ilaiya Piraatti, I wonder?'

'Thalapathi! It is not my wont to read letters addressed to other people. I have no objection to your reading this scroll, as you did the one addressed to the emperor. The responsibility for that, as I said, lies with you. All I want is my gold and scroll returned to me, rather than lost to theft.'

'Have no fear on that account. I will bring your belongings myself,' Chinna Pazhuvettaraiyar said, and made for the door. Vandiyadevan followed right behind him. Noticing this, the commander of the fort threw a glance at his retinue, prompting half a dozen bodyguards to block Vandiyadevan's way to the doorstep. Vandiyadevan decided there was little point in starting another fight, and stood back.

Not much time passed before Chinna Pazhuvettaraiyar returned. Behind him, bearing a tray as if it held invaluable treasures, came a servant tasked with restoring Vandiyadevan's dirty clothes to him.

'Thambi! Here are your clothes. They're safe. Search them carefully so you're satisfied nothing is missing,' said the Thalapathi.

Vandiyadevan did as he asked. There were more gold coins than there had been when the clothes had been taken from him. The olai for Kundavai Devi was there too. How had the gold multiplied? And how had the scroll that had gone missing even before the clothes were taken off his person returned as if by magic? It must have undergone Chinna Pazhuvettaraiyar's scrutiny before he had put it back in those clothes. Why had he done this? And why had he left extra gold in those garments? He was a wily one, the commander. Vandiyadevan wondered in which other ways he would be put to the test. He must exercise extreme caution, he thought, or he would fall into a trap.

'Is everything as it should be? Your gold, your belongings?' asked Chinna Pazhuvettaraiyar.

'Let me check,' Vandiyadevan said, and began to

count the gold. He set aside the surplus, and said, 'Thalapathi! I was born into the Vaanar clan. I bear a message from Aditya Karikalar. I don't desire what does not belong to me.'

'Your honesty is laudable. But you may keep these for your expenses enroute. When do you wish to leave? Today? Or would you like to stay the night, rest awhile, meet Periyavar while you're at it and then leave?' asked the Thalapathi.

'I will certainly not leave before I have a darshan of Periya Pazhuvettaraiyar, so I'm inclined to stay the night. But please tell your men not to lay a hand on my things,' said Vandiyadevan, pocketing the excess gold.

'I'm glad to hear you'll stay. You will have no cause for complaint from here on out. Do feel free to ask for anything you want at any time.'

'Thalapathi! I would like to look around this Thanjai Nagar. I do have your leave to do so, don't I?'

'You can certainly look around. Here, these two men will accompany you and show you around the fort. All I ask is that you don't leave the fort. The gates will be shut in the evening, and you won't be able to return if you're wandering about outside. You're free to go wherever you like inside the fort,' Chinna Pazhuvettaraiyar said. He then signalled to two men, and spoke to them softly. Vandiyadevan could guess what his instructions must be.

5

A WOMAN ON A TREE

Flanked by the two bodyguards the commander had assigned him, Vandiyadevan set off to explore the Thanjai fort. It was fairly obvious to him that the men had been appointed solely to ensure that he did not escape. He had little doubt that the guards at the gates would have also been given orders not to let him out. But he would absolutely have to leave the fort before dusk. It would be quite impossible to escape once Periya Pazhuvettaraiyar arrived. It would be hard enough to stay alive.

Even as Vandiyadevan loitered about the fort, checking out its various corners, his mind was searching for possible escape routes. First, he must shake off these two bodyguards. Then, he must run from the fort. How could he pull that off? He didn't know.

It wouldn't be much trouble to get away from the guards. He could throw both over his shoulders in a moment, and run while they were still dazed.

But where would he go? Everyone knew that the Pazhuvettaraiyar brothers had built the fort like a vault. It was said that even air couldn't seep in through cracks without their knowledge and permission. This very morning, the emperor himself had said Yama couldn't enter the fort. How did one escape from such a fortress?

If he so much as nudged them, the two bodyguards would raise hell, and he would be surrounded. The next step was the dungeon, or death. There was little point in attacking them. He would have to use brains over brawn. However formidable a fortress it was, it must have a secret subterranean passage. How could he find out where this passage was? Who would know? And if someone knew, would he or she tell him?

As he was walking, his head crowded with ideas and prospective outcomes, he remembered the Ilaiya Rani of Pazhuvoor. Aha! If anyone inside this fort would help him, it was she. But he couldn't quite be sure of that either. He could try using Azhvarkadiyaan's name once more. To work all this magic, he would have to find out which of these palaces was Periya Pazhuvettaraiyar's. And once he did, he must meet the Rani without these two louts' knowledge, or they would run right to Chinna Pazhuvettaraiyar and tell him. Who knew which hells would break loose then? And what if he successfully shook them off and met the Ilaiya Rani at Pazhuvettaraiyar's palace, only for its lord to return while he was still inside? He would have voluntarily thrust his head into the lion's den.

Even as Vandiyadevan's mind was busy working out possibilities, his eyes and mouth were running their own parallel tracks. His mouth kept up a steady stream of questions to the bodyguards—'What is this?', 'What is that?', 'Whose palace is that?', 'Whose mansion is this?', 'What is this structure?', 'Which gopuram is that?'—while his ears remained alert for 'That is Periya Pazhuvettaraiyar's palace' or 'This is the Pazhuvoor Ilaiya Rani's palace'. His eyes observed everything, and situated him precisely within the fort. He noticed that along with the busy thoroughfares, there were several little alleys and side streets. Gardens with tall trees and lush bushes abounded in the fort city. It wouldn't be hard to slip into one of those streets and make his way to one of those gardens. He could even fly under the radar for a day or two. But he must ensure no one was looking when he disappeared, and that no one would come looking for him either. If Chinna Pazhuvettaraiyar sent his numerous soldiers on a manhunt, there was no way he could stay hidden.

The other option was to seek refuge in someone's house. Who within the fort would grant him such refuge? Perhaps the Pazhuvoor Rani. He would have to summon all his powers of imagination and make up a believable story to tell and sell. But first, he would have to slip away from these two …

Aha! What was that noise? Why such commotion? Oh! Such a huge crowd had gathered! What were they going to watch?

Dear God, I know you're by my side, Vandiyadevan thought, as they arrived at a corner and saw a procession passing with drums and cymbals and wind instruments raising such a noise as to split the skies. *Here's a way out. Here's a solution!*

It was the Velakkaara army. They had had their daily darshan of the Maharaja and were making their way out of the fort. What if he slipped into this procession? Aha! What better option could have offered itself up?

The two bodyguards wouldn't let him get away quite so easily, surely? They would plunge into the procession with him. And surely, the guards at the fort gates wouldn't be so blind as to fail to spot him among the Velakkaaras and stop him? But he had to give this a shot. It was a godsend. If he did not use this opportunity, there could be no bigger fool in the world than he.

As usual, he turned to the bodyguards and asked, 'What procession is this?'

'The Velakkaara army,' said one.

Vandiyadevan began to ask him details. Once he learnt their history, he said he would give anything to join such a courageous lot and wished to see them up close. He moved towards the procession even as he spoke. Not long after, he said, 'I want to see the people playing the thaarai[1] and thappattai[2] up front', and promptly blended into the Velakkaara army procession.

He moved cleverly so his position within the squad kept changing. And all the while, he chanted louder and more energetically than anyone else. Some of the Velakkaara soldiers stared at him curiously. Some wondered who this madman was. Others figured he had had too much to drink. But no one stopped him or shoved him aside.

The two bodyguards didn't dare step into the procession. They figured Vandiyadevan would have to eventually step out anyway, and they could get hold of him then. They stayed by the edge of the road even as they kept pace with the procession.

At this time, a woman who was coming down the road from the opposite direction, bearing vats of curd, stepped into an alley to make way for the soldiers.

One of them looked at her and said, 'Amma! I'm thirsty. Will you give me some curd?'

The woman replied with an audacious, 'The curd is over. I can give you two slaps if you'd like.'

Another soldier who heard this said, 'Oho! Why not? Give us that at the very least!' and approached her.

The woman took to her feet in a fright. The man ran after her. Two others broke off to help him in his pursuit. With all three raising shouts, no one else understood quite what had happened. They did realise some sort of game was under way, though.

Vandiyadevan had watched it all. He made a split-second decision. As we know already, it was not in our hero's nature to hesitate to put thought into action. So, he yelled, 'Run! Run! Catch! Catch!' and took off in pursuit of the curd-seller.

She ran for a while, and then turned into an alley. When her pursuers followed, they could find no trace of her. She had disappeared into thin air! The soldiers didn't make much of this. They turned back to join the procession again. Vandiyadevan alone stayed behind. He ran further down the alley, and then turned into a smaller one, and then yet another. It was only after he had taken a few turns that he slowed to a walk.

We're aware, of course, that the Velakkaara army leaves the fort at dusk. The little streets into which Vandiyadevan had snuck were already dark. Some alleys cowered under looming walls, and others hid under the canopies formed by imposing trees. Vandiyadevan did not stop anywhere. Unmindful of the direction he was taking, he plodded on. At some point or the other, he would encounter the outer wall of the fort. He would think about the next step once he got there. After all, he had all night.

It wasn't long before he could barely see ahead. One of the alleys brought him to a dead end, right up against a high wall. In the dark of the night, he bumped into it before he noticed its existence. He could only see that it was a wall. Its exact height and depth were impossible to determine at this time. It could be the wall of the fortress itself. He might as well camp here for the night, he thought. Once the moon rose, he could find his bearings. Until then, he wasn't likely to come across a better spot than this.

By this time, Chinna Pazhuvettaraiyar's men would have run back to report that their charge had gone missing. The commander would have sent his men in pursuit in all four directions. He would have suspected that Vandiyadevan had contrived to exit the fort with the Velakkaara army. A furious search would be conducted both within and without the fortress.

Let them search, Vandiyadevan thought to himself. *If I don't trick them all and get out of here, I'm no scion of the Vaanar clan, and my name is not Vandiyadevan!*

But the moonrise would make it easier for Chinna Pazhuvettaraiyar's men to find him. They might even land up right at this spot; well, let them come. All he had to do was jump into a thicket, and then who could possibly find him?

Vandiyadevan made these plans as he leaned against the wall. He was a young, healthy man, and he had spent the entire day walking about, and so sleep came up to embrace him even as he sat. The breeze stirring through the leaves and branches of the trees teased them into a lullaby, and Vandiyadevan found his eyes closing as if he was intoxicated. He dozed off.

When he woke, the moon had begun its downward journey. The moonlight slipped through the trees to give him some idea of where he was.

Vandiyadevan reminded himself of his present situation. He couldn't believe he had fallen asleep against the wall. Even less could he believe that he was wide awake now. What had woken him? Surely he had heard a voice? Had it been a human voice? Or an animal voice? Or the cry of a nocturnal bird? Had it even been a voice?

Vandiyadevan looked about himself. He could see creepers on the wall. Ah! This could not be the outer wall; it was not quite high enough. But perhaps it was a wall belonging to one of the palaces inside the fortress? Or even of the garden of one such palace?

He got to his feet, looking up at the wall. For a moment, he froze. His breath caught. His insides rose right up to his chest and suffocated him. He had had such a fright he could barely think. What was that creature up on the tree by the wall?! He had heard stories and legends about the betaal that lived on trees. They all came to mind now.

But did the betaal speak? In a human voice? And a woman's voice too? This betaal seemed to be speaking in a female, human voice. What did it have to say?

'What is this, aiya? You dozed off against the wall, did you? How many times I had to call out!'

Ah! This was no betaal. It was a woman. A human one. She was seated on one of the branches of a tree. Was this a dream? Or was it actually happening?

'Look at that, you're still half-asleep! Here, I'm lowering a ladder for you. Climb carefully. Don't go and lose your footing now!'

Even as she spoke, the woman reached for a light,

bamboo ladder and leaned it against his side of the wall.

Vandiyadevan had no clue what this was about. But how could he miss a lucky opportunity that had sought him out?

Well, what would happen would happen. And he would deal with the consequences later. For now, he should simply climb the ladder and get out of the alley. He could ask questions after he had reached a safe spot.

Once he was three quarters of the way up, the woman called out again. 'Have you no sense of time? How could you make such a delayed appearance? Ilaiya Raniammal is waiting for you there, and you go and fall asleep against a wall!' she said.

Vandiyadevan nearly fell off the ladder in his shock. Fortunately, he managed to grab at a stone that jutted out of the wall and find a handhold.

The woman had to be referring to the Pazhuvoor Ilaiya Rani, surely? How had she known where to find him? Was it some sort of mayamantra? And why was she so keen to see him? Perhaps ... perhaps ... had he climbed a ladder that had been lowered for someone else? Whatever it was, he wasn't going to back out now. He would find out what this was about soon enough.

Once he had got to the top of the wall, the woman reached for his hand and helped him up. The moon shone on her face. By this time, Vandiyadevan had lost all capacity to feel surprise, which was why he managed to retain his balance even after he'd recognised her for the curd-seller whom the Velakkaara soldiers had given chase. Whatever further surprise or surprises awaited him that night would be lost on him; he was quite saturated with surprise already.

'Umm! Why are you sitting on the wall and gaping at me? Get the ladder back inside and jump down, quick!' the woman said, and began to make her way down the tree.

Vandiyadevan did as she said. He realised he had stepped into a spacious garden. Some distance away, he could see the domes, sculptures and trellised balconies of a palace, as if through a dream.

He cleared his throat, readying himself to ask whose palace it was.

The woman hissed, 'Ssh!' and put a finger to her lips to ask him to keep his peace. She then turned to lead the way. Vandiyadevan followed her in silence.

6

THE LATA MANDAPAM

As the woman wove her way through a narrow path among the dense trees, Vandiyadevan did his best to keep up with her. It was rather hard to negotiate the path in the dark of the night, avoiding the trunks and branches. He nearly walked right into a tree and stepped back in the nick of time, dazed.

The woman turned back and demanded, 'Why have you stopped? Have you forgotten the way? You claim you can see in the dark, don't you?'

Vandiyadevan responded by placing a finger on his lips and saying, 'Sssh!' as she had done earlier.

Just then, they heard a noise from beyond the boundary wall. It sounded like footsteps. The two resumed their walk through the path. After they had gone some distance, Vandiyadevan allowed himself a little laugh.

The woman turned again and asked, 'What did you see just now that made you laugh?'

'I didn't see, I heard.'

'Meaning ...?'

'Didn't you hear the footsteps of my pursuers? The fact that they have been taken in made me laugh.'

She looked at him with some trepidation and asked, 'Someone is pursuing you? What? Why?'

'If that wasn't the case, why would I have stumbled my way through this pitch dark, run into the boundary wall and sat down right there?'

The breeze blowing through the garden shifted the boughs so a ray of moonlight shone on Vandiyadevan's face.

The woman looked at him in surprise and perhaps with a trace of fear.

'What are you looking at?' he asked.

'I'm looking to see if you are ... you.'

'If I weren't I, who else would I be?'

'Last time you stopped by, you had a thick moustache?'

'What a question! Won't a man who is compelled to enter homes by jumping over boundary walls need to switch disguises every now and again?'

'You look younger now than you did last time.'

'Inspiration tends to make one youthful.'

'And what have you found that has inspired you so much?'

'When one has the grace of your Maharani, could one lack for inspiration?'

'There's no need for sarcasm. Our Ejamaani may

be the Ilaiya Rani now, but she will certainly be the Maharani one day.'

'That's exactly what I'm saying.'

'You won't stop with that, will you? You'll claim it was your tantric and mantric powers that made her the Maharani! And then you might ask for half the kingdom too!'

Vandiyadevan had got the answers he had sought. He remained silent for the rest of the walk. Not a word escaped his lips, although a multitude of thoughts crowded his head.

Whom was he going to meet? It might be the Pazhuvoor Ilaiya Rani, but it could also be Madurantaka Devar's wife, the daughter of Chinna Pazhuvettaraiyar. The woman who was leading him to the Ilaiya Rani believed he was the mantravadi. How was he to conduct himself when he was presented to the Ilaiya Rani, whoever she was?

My heart, don't lose your courage! Vandiyadevan told himself. *For as long as one is brave, one is assured of victory. I won't run out of ideas when the time comes. I'll find a way. None of the perilous situations in which I have found myself has defeated me yet. Could I possibly be defeated now, and that too by a woman?*

They were nearing an imposing palace. But the woman did not lead him to the main entrance. She did not head towards the back either. Instead, they approached the lata mandapam that extended into the garden from the side of the palace. When they went closer, Vandiyadevan saw that the lata mandapam served as a connecting passage between two enormous palaces. There was a striking difference between the two buildings. The one to the right glowed from the light of hundreds of lamps. Sounds of laughter and movement danced in waves from behind its walls. The palace on the left, however, was entirely cloaked in darkness. Not one lamp had been lit. In the moonlight, its stark walls seemed to rise right up to the sky. But it appeared to be inhabited only by silence and blackness.

The woman who had escorted Vandiyadevan from the boundary wall turned once they reached the lata mandapam, signalled to him to remain where he was and went inside. He did as she asked. It was then that he noticed the fragrance of the flowers in the lata mandapam. Appappa! What a heady perfume this was! It worked its way up one's nostrils like woodsmoke and toyed with one's head.

He heard two voices inside—that of the woman who had led him there, and then another, particularly sweet one.

'Ask him to come in at once! Why even ask? You know I've been waiting all this while!'

The notes of her voice were so intoxicating as to make one lose consciousness. It was indeed the Pazhuvoor Ilaiya Rani's voice. There was no doubting it now. The next moment he would be right before her. How would he handle this situation? And what would she make of the fact that her visitor was not the mantravadi she was expecting, but the man who had run his horse into her palanquin? Would she be surprised? Angry? Perhaps pleased? Or would she remain impassive, hiding the emotions she felt so well that he wouldn't be able to figure out what she was thinking?

The woman stepped out and signalled to him to enter.

Vandiyadevan went over to her, and then looked inside the lata mandapam. The sight before his eyes would be forever etched in his mind.

A lighted wick placed in a golden lamp made the room shine bright as its rays bounced off the gilded walls. Some sort of exquisite scented oil must have been used for the lamp, for a lovely fragrance emanated from the wick. Leaning gracefully against the arm of a flower bed filled with exotic blossoms was a woman.

She was indeed the Pazhuvoor Ilaiya Rani. When he had seen her in the palanquin by day, she had struck him as a beauty. By night, in the light of the golden lamp, it was as if beauty had taken the form of a goddess and come down to earth. The smell of the flowers, the perfume from the lamp and the perfection of the Pazhuvoor Ilaiya Rani's form had a narcotic effect on Vandiyadevan.

Vandiyadeva! Watch out! Just once, you allowed yourself to get drunk. You realised your brain had slowed, and your ideas were getting muddled. You resolved then that you would never, ever allow yourself to drink again. Don't allow this intoxication, so much more potent than alcohol, to rob you of your senses! our hero told himself.

The Pazhuvoor Ilaiya Rani Nandini parted her lips in slight surprise, revealing the hint of a row of perfect teeth, the moment she saw Vandiyadevan. It suited our man that she had lost her powers of speech.

With a little laugh, he said, 'Ammani! Your maid had a sudden doubt—was I really the mantravadi or not? And do you know how she asked me this? "Are you … you?" she said.' And he laughed again.

Nandini smiled. Lightning flashed before Vandiyadevan's eyes. The next moment, honey dripped into his ears as he heard her voice again.

'These doubts tend to occur to her every now and again! Vasuki! Why are you standing here like you're rooted to the ground? Go to your spot! If you hear footsteps, bang hard on the door,' Nandini said.

'Right away, amma!' Vasuki said, and went down the corridor that led to the brightly-lit palace on the right. Vandiyadevan could make out the vague outline of a threshold some distance away. This was where Vasuki settled down.

Nandini lowered her voice and said, 'Does she really suspect you're not a mantravadi? What an idiot! Most people who claim to be mantravadis are frauds. You're the real mantravadi! What mayamantram did you use to get here at this hour?'

'Ammani! I didn't use any mayamantram. I simply

scaled the ladder that had been placed against the wall,' Vandiyadevan said.

'That much is obvious, but what mayamantram did you use to fool that girl?'

'All I had to do was smile at her in the moonlight. That did it! If she hadn't fallen for that, my plan was to use the ring you had given me.'

'You've kept that ring safely, haven't you? Why didn't you use it to come to the front entrance in broad daylight? Why turn up like a thief in the night?'

'Ammani! Your brother-in-law Chinna Pazhuvettaraiyar's men are all thieves. First, they took my clothes and belongings and tried to make away with them. Then, they followed me without letting me out of their sight for even a moment. It took the life out of me to shake them off. I finally got away from them, and used side-streets and alleys to make my escape, when I ran into your boundary wall. I was figuring out what to do, but then I saw the ladder leaning against the wall, and figured you had made arrangements to rescue this miserable creature. I now realise I was mistaken. Do forgive me.'

'But I have nothing to forgive.'

'How do you say that, ammani?'

'You were not entirely mistaken. Do you know why I had wanted to see the mantravadi?'

'I don't know, ammani. I'm neither a sorcerer nor a clairvoyant.'

'I haven't been able to get you out of my mind

since I saw you last morning. I wanted to know why you hadn't come to see me yet. It was to divine this that I sent for the mantravadi.'

'That is some surprise.'

'What is?'

'What you said just now. I haven't been able to get you out of my mind since I saw you, either.'

'Do you believe in connections from a previous birth?'

'As in?'

'If two people are bound by friendship or blood in one birth, it is said a similar bond will follow in the next one too.'

'I didn't believe in such things until yesterday. But the events of yesterday have made me a believer.'

Although Vandiyadevan's words might appear to be a lie, he was thinking of the woman he had seen at the astrologer's house in Kudandai when he spoke those words. But Nandini, who had no knowledge of what else the day had brought Vandiyadevan, assumed he was referring to *her*.

'But that was not why you came to see me. You said something about Azhvarkadiyaar Nambi having sent a message ...'

'Yes, ammani, it was to convey that message that I first sought to meet you. But once I caught sight of your face for the first time, I forgot everything else.'

'Where did you meet Azhvarkadiyaar? What message has he sent?'

'I met Azhvarkadiyaar Nambi near Veeranarayanapuram. He was attempting to prove Lord Vishnu's might with the help of his staff. Right then, Periya Pazhuvettaraiyar's entourage began its procession. Your palanquin followed his elephant. Perhaps you wanted to see what the commotion was, but your lovely hand made its way through the screen to part the curtains. Having realised you were the occupant of the palanquin, Azhvarkadiyaar wanted to send you a message. Since I was going to stay at the Kadambur palace that night, he made me his messenger. But I could not find an opportunity to meet you in Kadambur. It was only on the road to Thanjavur that I was able to make your acquaintance, and that too because your palanquin ran into my horse!'

Nandini's face was angled away from him as Vandiyadevan spoke. He couldn't read her expressions. But as he finished his speech with the story of the palanquin and the horse, she turned towards him and flashed him a lovely smile. 'Yes; the palanquin I ride is always up to some mischief!' she said.

7

THE MANTRAVADI

The roar of perigai drums echoed from afar.

The 'bomm-bomm' of ekkaalam trumpets rent the air.

Human voices screamed victory cries.

They could hear the grand gates of the fort being thrown open and then drawn closed, followed by the sounds of the hooves of horses and the stamping of elephants.

Vandiyadevan could see that Nandini was distracted by the noise.

The woman who had been posted on guard duty jumped up in panic, moved towards them and said, 'Amma! It appears Ejamaan has come.'

'I know,' said Nandini. 'You go back to your place.'

She then turned to Vandiyadevan and said, 'The Dhanadhikari has entered the fort. He will enquire after the emperor's health, meet the Thalapathi of the fort and then come here. You must leave before he reaches the palace. What did Azhvarkadiyaar say?'

'Ammani! That Veera Vaishnava icon claimed you were his sister. Is that true?' Vandiyadevan asked.

'Why do you find that hard to believe?'

'It isn't easy to believe a parrot and an ape were born of the same womb, is it?'

Nandini laughed and said, 'What he said is true, in a sense. We grew up in the same house, the same household. He loved me as a sister. Poor man, I have betrayed him.'

'Well, that's all right, then. I can tell you what he wanted me to say. His message is that Krishna Bhagavan is waiting for you. And I believe all of the Veera Vaishnava bhaktas, crores upon crores of them, are aching for the sight of your marrying Lord Krishna.'

Nandini sighed. 'Aha! This longing of his hasn't abated yet, I see. If you see him again, please tell him this from me—ask him to forget I ever existed. Tell him I am absolutely unqualified to attain the reward that Andal[1] was given.'

'I don't agree, amma!'

'With what?'

'I don't agree that you cannot attain the reward that Andal was given. Andal had to pray and sing and sob and make garlands to get Krishna to marry her. But you will have no need to go to such trouble. All Krishna has to do is lay eyes upon you, and he will ditch Rukmini, Satyabhama, Radha and all the gopis, and set you on the throne where they used to sit.'

'Aiya! You're adept at mugastuti[2]. I don't like that.'

'Ammani! What is mugastuti?'

'To praise someone to one's mugam, one's face.'

'In that case, I ask that you turn your back to me.'

'Whatever for?'

'So that I can praise you to your back instead of your face. That is not wrong, is it?'

'You're quite the sophist.'

'Now it is you who is indulging in mugastuti, isn't it?'

'Then why don't you turn your back to me?'

'Maharani, be it on the battlefield or be it to a beauty, I will never turn my back. You are at liberty to endow your mugastuti on me.'

Nandini broke into a peal of laughter. 'You are indeed a mantravadi. There's no doubt that you possess extraordinary skills of sorcery. I don't remember when I last laughed out loud like this,' she said.

'But, ammani! It is awfully dangerous to let you laugh! They say, "Tadakaththil taamarai siriththu magizhndhadhu; thenvandu mayangi vizhundhadhu"—The lotus beamed with a joyful smile in the pond; the honeybee, intoxicated, fell into a faint.'

'So, you're not just a mantravadi, but a kavi too.'

'I'm not fooled by flattery, and I'm not fazed by insults.'

'Who insulted you?'

'You called me a "kavi"[3] just now, didn't you?'

'What do you mean?'

'When I was a little boy, some people used to call me "kurangu moonji", monkey face. It is after many, many years and from your coral lips that I am destined to hear that epithet now.'

'Did someone call you, of all people, "monkey face"? Who are those geniuses?'

'None of them is alive now.'

'Well, that's not what I meant. I meant you appear to be someone who sings kavita, who composes poems.'

'I do compose poems every now and again, but I reserve that for my foes. Those who will not die by my sword may die by my word.'

'Aiya, king of poets and the bravest of lions, you haven't yet done me the honour of revealing your name.'

'My given name is Vandiyadevan, and my titular name is Vallavarayan.'

'A royal clan, then?'

'I am of the ancient Vaanar clan, which had a grand name in times gone by.'

'And what is your domain now?'

'The sky above my head and the ground beneath my feet. Now, I am the undisputed lord of the entire universe.'

Nandini looked Vandiyadevan up and down.

'It wouldn't be impossible for you to have your inheritance, your kingdom, restored to you. It's been known to happen.'

'How is that possible? Can a tiger's prey be restored from its stomach? Can an empire that has been swallowed by the Chozhas be restored to an heir?'

'I can make it happen.'

'Ammani! No, please don't! I have never greatly desired to rule a kingdom. Even if I had nursed such lofty ambitions, they would have vanished after meeting Sundara Chozha Chakravarti. It struck me that to be an emperor who is entirely dependent on everyone else is far worse a fate than to be a free man who has no idea where his next meal will come from.'

'I'm of the same opinion,' Nandini said. Then, as if she had suddenly remembered something, she asked, 'Why are Chinna Pazhuvettaraiyar's men looking for you?'

'Like your maid, he has his suspicions about me too.'

'What suspicions?'

'How I got my hands on the signet ring with the palm tree emblem.'

A shadow flitted across Nandini's face. Vandiyadevan thought he could discern a hint of fear.

'Where is the ring?' she asked, in a shaky voice.

'Here it is, ammani! Would I let it go so easily?' he asked, and showed her the ring.

'How did he know you had the ring?' Nandini asked.

'I've always wanted to meet Sundara Chozha Chakravarti. I used the signet ring to realise this dream. The fort commander asked me how I got my hands on the ring.'

'And what did you say?' asked Nandini. There was a tremor in her voice.

'I did not use your name, ammani. I said Periya Pazhuvettaraiyar had given it to me, at the Kadambur palace.'

Nandini heaved a sigh of relief, and her face and voice relaxed as she asked, 'Did he believe you?'

'Not quite, I think. That's why he's got his men following me around, no? He must have wanted to present me to Periyavar and figure out the truth once he's back.'

Nandini smiled and said, 'You need have no fear of Periya Pazhuvettaraiyar. I'll make sure he doesn't gobble you whole.'

'Ammani! The entire world is aware of the sway you have over the Dhanadhikari. But I have some urgent work outside, and I need to leave right away. That is why I beg you for help.'

'What is this urgent work?'

'All sorts of things. For instance, I have to meet Azhvarkadiyaar and tell him your response. What should I say to him?'

'Ask him to forget that he ever had a sister called "Nandini".'

'I could tell him, but it won't happen.'

'What won't happen?'

'His forgetting you. If I, who have chanced upon you a couple of times, find it impossible to forget you, how can someone who has spent his entire life with you hope to do so?'

A look of triumph crossed Nandini's face. Her sharp eyes turned to Vandiyadevan, and she fixed him with a piercing stare that appeared to see into his very heart.

'Why were you so keen to meet the chakravarti?' she asked.

'Why must it surprise you that I should want to meet that sundara purusha whose praises the world sings? It is typical of kings to want their courage and machismo to win praise, for their realm and wealth to grow. This is the sort of eulogy they wish to hear, the prayers they want from their people. But what do our holy men wish upon our emperor?

'*Sundara Chozhar vanmayum vanappum*
Thinmayum ulagir sirandhu vaazhgenave

'They pray for the longevity of his looks rather than his rule. I have always wanted to meet this Manmadha[4] of our times, the Kalyug.'

'Yes, the emperor takes great pride in his appearance. And his selva[5] kumari is even more conceited.'

'His kumari? Of whom do you speak?'

'That vain, spoilt creature who lives in Pazhaiyarai,

that Ilaiya Piraatti Kundavai Devi ... she's the one of whom I speak.'

Vandiyadeva! You're a lucky man. The chance you were looking for has fallen into your lap! Make good use of it, Vandiyadevan said to himself.

Nandini, who had been reclining gracefully against the backrest of her seat, suddenly sat up straight.

'Aiya! I have something to ask. Will you accept?' she asked.

'Ask away, ammani!'

'Let us come to an agreement, you and I. You will help me, and I will help you. What do you say?'

'Ammani! You are the queen of the most powerful man in the Chozha empire, the Dhanadhikari. Everything you wish for can be made to happen in the manner that you wish it to, thanks to him. I have absolutely no influence with anyone. How could I possibly be of use to you, how could I possibly *help* you?' Vandiyadevan asked.

Nandini trained her eyes on him and studied him in silence, wondering whether he was speaking from the heart. Vandiyadevan withstood the stare, unfazed.

'I need a trustworthy man to carry out certain confidential tasks. If I get you a job in this palace, will you consent?' she asked.

'I have already committed to just such a role in the service of another great lady. If she decides not to employ me after all, I will come back to you.'

'Who is this great lady, who dares compete with me?'

'The very lady of whom you spoke with such affection a while ago, Ilaiya Piraatti Kundavai Devi.'

'Lies! Lies! Impossible! There is no way this could have happened! You're simply mocking me!'

'Maharani! This scroll has been subjected to the perusal of many eyes. So the world won't come to an end if you look at it too,' Vandiyadevan said, and held out the olai Aditya Karikalar had addressed to Kundavai.

Nandini held the scroll up to the light and read it. It was as if a flash of lightning darted from her eyes as she looked up. Vandiyadevan was suddenly reminded of a poisonous snake's forked tongue. He trembled involuntarily.

Nandini looked at him regally, and asked, 'Aiya! You do intend to get out of this fort alive, don't you?'

'Yes, amma! That is why I sought you out. I need your help.'

'I can offer you only conditional help.'

'Do tell me the conditions.'

'Whatever reply Kundavai writes to this, you must bring me that scroll and show it to me. Will you?'

'That is a dangerous proposition.'

'You thumped your chest a while ago, and claimed you never turn your back on danger, didn't you?'

'Well, if one is taking on great danger, there must be a proportionate reward, don't you think?'

'Reward? It's a reward you seek, is it? You will win a reward such as you cannot have dreamt of.

The sort of reward for which the all-powerful Periya Pazhuvettaraiyar has been praying for years!' Nandini said, and then approached him.

The full force of her beauty hit him like a weapon. Our poor man's head swam.

Oh, my heart, stay steadfast, be brave. Don't lose your mind, Vandiyadevan said to himself.

Right then, as if to save him, an owl hooted with particular insistence. Once. Twice. Thrice.

Vandiyadevan's hair stood on end.

Nandini glanced in the direction of the sound and said, 'So the real mantravadi has arrived.' She then turned to Vandiyadevan. 'I have no need for his counsel now. But I must give him a brief audience for the trouble he has taken to come here. He might come in handy to get you out of the fort, too. Go there, and keep yourself hidden in the dark while I finish with him,' Nandini said, gesturing in the direction right opposite the one in which her maid had gone earlier.

8

'DO YOU REMEMBER ...?'

Nandini went to the garden entrance of the lata mandapam and clapped thrice.

We can't say whether her face had clouded over from fear, or from the dark shadows cast by the trees.

For some distance, ancient trees with enormous trunks, and creepers winding their ways up those gnarled trunks, made gaunt shapes in the fading light. Beyond, there was only the inky black of night.

Clawing through this inky black and tearing the creepers apart, the mantravadi made his appearance from behind a tree.

Nandini returned to her flower bed. Her lovely features wore a sense of calm now.

The mantravadi entered the lata mandapam. The light of the golden lamp fell on his face.

This is a familiar face! Who is he? Oh, yes! He is one of the men from the group that held a secret conference at the Tiruppurambiyam pallipadai. He is the one who emptied his bag of gold coins into a heap on the forest floor. He is the man who instructed the others to 'kill Azhvarkadiyaan the moment you see him, at the very place you spot him'—Ravidasan.

Even as he arrived, his face simmered with rage. When he saw Nandini reclining against the floral bed, the very embodiment of peace and contentment, his cat eyes glared gimlets at her. The very air around him turned hot and dry from the fires of fury that blazed from within his powerful frame.

Seating himself on the wooden bench before Nandini's bed, he began to chant, 'Hoom! Hreem! Hraam! Bhagavati! Shakti! Chandikeshwari!'

'Enough! Stop it! That damned servant woman has gone and fallen asleep on the doorstep. Tell me what you came here to say, quickly! *He* has entered the fort,' Nandini said.

'Adi paadagi! You traitor!' Ravidasan hissed, in a voice that resonated with all the venom of a cobra poised to strike.

'Whom are you talking about?' Nandini asked calmly.

'I'm talking about none other than Nandini the Ingrate; none other than the Ilaiya Rani of Pazhuvoor! None other than you!' said Ravidasan, pointing his index finger dramatically at her.

Nandini made no reply.

'Woman! It appears you have forgotten certain incidents that ought to have been etched into your memory. Let me remind you of them,' said Ravidasan.

'Why dig up the past now?' said Nandini.

'Why now, you ask? I'll tell you. Let me remind you, and then I'll tell you,' Ravidasan said.

Nandini sighed as if she knew there was little point in trying to stop him, and then turned away.

'Rani! Listen! One fine day, three years ago, in the middle of the night, a funeral pyre blazed by the banks of the Vaigai river. This was no send-off with the final rites officiated by a priest according to the shastras. The pyre had been built from dry branches and twigs and leaves foraged from the forest floor. A corpse that had been hidden behind the trees was then brought and laid on the wood before the pyre was lit. The dry branches and twigs and leaves crackled and the flames rose high into the air. Some people spotted you skulking in the dark and brought you there. Your hands and legs were bound. Your mouth was stuffed with cloth. The hair that is so beautifully arranged in a bun and decorated with flowers now hung loose that day, dragging raggedly against the forest floor. Those people wanted to burn you alive in the pyre.

'"Let the fire burn some more," one of them said.

'Those men threw you to the ground and then swore a terrible oath. You were listening. They had gagged you, but hadn't bothered blindfolding you or covering your ears. And so, you kept those eyes and ears open. Having taken their oaths, they came towards you. You, who had stayed silent until then, tried desperately to make some sort of sign with your bound hands. You opened your eyes wide, knitted your eyebrows together and made all sorts of tormented faces.

'One of your captors said, "She wants to say something!"

'Another said, "Must be the same old story. Throw her into the pyre!"

'Yet another said, "No, no! Let's hear what it is she wants to say before we toss her in. Get the cloth out of her mouth!"

'Since he was their leader, they took the cloth out of your mouth. Do you remember what you said then, woman?' Ravidasan asked, and then paused.

Nandini neither replied nor turned to face him. The revulsion and terror in her heart were writ large on her countenance, as was the resolve of a truly terrible divine pact. Each of her black eyes played host to a single teardrop that trembled at its corner.

'Woman! You refuse to speak! All right! Don't. Let me remind you of that too. You said you, too, like all those men, had sworn to exact revenge. You swore that you had more reason to take that oath than any of them. You said you would use your beauty and intelligence entirely in the service of that oath. You promised to help them to the best of your ability. You averred that you had already decided to take your own life once that oath was fulfilled. None of the others believed you. But I did. I believed you, and I stopped them from throwing you into the fire. I saved your life. Do you remember all this?' Ravidasan asked, and fell silent.

Nandini inclined her body so she was facing him and said, 'You ask if I remember this. All of this is written in indelible letters, forged as if by fire, branded into my heart.'

'Later, we were walking by the shores of the Kaveri, along the forest path. Suddenly, we heard the approach of horsemen. We decided to separate and hide in the forest, each in a different spot. But you alone went against that decision and stood your ground, in broad daylight. Those men took you captive. Their leader Pazhuvettaraiyan was intoxicated by your loveliness, and fell into your honey trap. You married him. The rest of the group told me I had been had. I did not give up on you. I contrived to catch you alone. I wanted to put a dagger through your treacherous heart and kill you. But you begged me to spare your life yet again. You said you had orchestrated all this so we could fulfil our vow. You swore you would help us from the inside, even while living in this palace. Is all this true or not?' Ravidasan demanded.

'All this is true. Who has claimed otherwise? Why are you recounting the story over and over again? Tell me what you're here for!' Nandini said.

'No, woman! You don't remember. You've forgotten everything. You've plunged yourself into the luxury of the Pazhuvoor palace, and have forgotten your oath! You feast on meals that celebrate the six culinary flavours, ornament yourself in exquisite jewellery, drape yourself in fine cloth, sleep on silks and flower beds, and travel in an ivory palanquin! You are the queen of Pazhuvoor! Why would old memories carry any meaning?'

'Chhi! Who wants these beds and silks and clothes and jewellery? Do you think I'm slave to these material things? Not at all!'

'Or perhaps you have fallen for the handsome face of the young man who crossed your path? An old oath could have been subsumed in the fervour of new romance, couldn't it?'

For a fraction of a second, Nandini was startled. She made an immediate recovery and said at once, 'Lies! All lies!'

'If it is all lies, why didn't you send your servant girl to the usual place although I'd sent word ahead that I'd be coming here today?'

'I did send her. But someone else got in using the ladder meant for you. That fool of a girl mistook him for you, and ushered him in. How is that my fault?'

'What does it matter whose fault it was? My very life was in danger. The fort guards who were looking for that youth were about to catch me. I jumped into the pond in the woods by this palace, and stayed underwater until I was all but out of breath. I surfaced only after those men had left. That is why I'm even alive. I was dripping wet ...'

'You deserve it. Think of this as your having washed off the sin of suspecting me of treason.'

'Woman! Swear to this! Are you not besotted with that young man's looks?'

'Chhi! What kind of talk is this! Does anyone talk of the good looks of men? It is only in this shameless Chozha Naadu that they celebrate the king's handsomeness. Male beauty must be measured by the battle scars on a man's body, shouldn't it?'

'Well said. Assuming you speak the truth, why did that young man come here?'

'I told you earlier, Vasuki mistook him for you and brought him here.'

'Why did you give him the signet ring that you've refused to give even me?'

'To bring him here so I could speak to him. Now that I've done that, I'm going to take the ring back from him and ...'

'Why did you bring him here? What were you yapping about with him all this while?'

'I was *yapping* with him keeping a crucial prospective advantage in mind. He will cause things to turn in our favour.'

'Adi paadagi! You've shown your pennbudhi[1] in the end, the stupidity of the woman you are! You've gone and revealed our secret to a stranger whom ...'

'Why are you panicking? There's no reason for you to rant and rave. I haven't revealed a thing to him. On the contrary, I extracted a secret from him. And I inferred a great deal.'

'What did you *infer*?'

'He's taking a scroll from Kanchi to Pazhaiyarai. He's taking it to the tigress in Pazhaiyarai. He showed it to me. I was just telling him he would have to show me the reply she wrote, when you landed up.'

'The scroll be damned, and the stylus be damned. Of what use is all that to us?'

'Your brain has reached its saturation point. We have sworn to wipe out the tiger clan. But the lot of you think only of the male tigers. You forget that the dynasty can grow from the tigress, too. And that's not all. Who do you think pulls the strings in this Chozha empire? The old man who has lost all his strength, lost even the ability to move and lies in his sick bed? The princes in Kanchi and Lanka?'

'No! The man who has had the good fortune of winning you for his queen, the Dhanadhikari Pazhuvettaraiyar. The whole world knows it!'

'That's wrong too. The world believes that to be the case. The old man, too, has been fooled into thinking it is so. And you have been fooled as well. In reality, it is the tigress in Pazhaiyarai who is running the show. That arrogant woman sits in her palace and pulls the strings. She believes she can control all the puppets. I'm going to put her in her place. And I'm going to use this young man to do that ...'

Ravidasan's face showed signs of surprise and respect. 'Some skill, you have. I must admit that. But how do I know any of this is true? How do I trust you?'

'I'll hand that young man over to you. You take him through the subterranean passage out of the fort. Blindfold him when you take him. Then lie in wait near Pazhaiyarai. Bring him back here with the scroll on which Kundavai writes her reply. If he tries to escape, or tries to trick you, do away with him at once.'

'No, no! You and he can go to hell. Chinna Pazhuvettaraiyar's men are scouring the fort for him now. If I went anywhere with him, I'd be putting myself at risk. No. Just tell me what I came to hear.'

'You haven't told me what that is yet ...'

'Preparations have been made for men to go to Kanchi and Lanka. The ones who are going to Lanka have a tough task ahead of them. They'll have to conduct themselves with great expediency ...'

'What do you want me to do about that? You want more gold? Is there no limit to the lust for gold of you lot?'

'The gold is not for our personal use. It is to finish the task we have undertaken. Why else have we allowed you to sit here? The men who are going to Lanka will have no use for the gold coins of Chozha Naadu. It is Lankan gold coins that we need ...'

'Why take so long to say something so simple? I'd kept it all ready even before you asked,' Nandini said, and bent under the cot. She reached for a bag, and handed it over to Ravidasan. 'Here's a bagful of Lankan gold. Take it and leave! *He* will be here any moment!' she said.

As Ravidasan took the bag and made to leave, she said, 'Hold on! At least, show that young man out of the fort. Let him go his own way after. I have no wish to show him the secret passage.'

She rose and peered at the palace, cloaked in dusk.

She couldn't see a thing. She made a sign with her fingers. She clapped softly. It was of no use.

She and Ravidasan walked some distance through the passage that led from the imposing mansion to the exit. They went nearly up to the threshold.

But there was no sign of Vandiyadevan. In all four directions, near and far, there was simply no sign of him.

9

THE LIONS CLASHED

The residents of Thanjavur had singled the Pazhuvoor brothers out for their deepest respect, and never missed an opportunity to show it. It was the Pazhuvettaraiyars who had rejuvenated that ancient city, and brought it lustre and influence in the kingdom.

A procession of elephants, horses and camels will always draw a crowd. But when Periya Pazhuvettaraiyar started off on a journey, or returned from one, people thronged both sides of the main street to gawk at his entourage. They would shout cries of victory and wish him well. They would rain flowers and pori grains down upon the procession.

Typically, when Periya Pazhuvettaraiyar returned to the city, his brother would stand at the entrance of the fort to receive him. When the brothers embraced, it was as if the Nilgiri and Podhigai mountains had uprooted themselves, walked over to each other and grown arms to throw around the shoulders of the other.

When the brothers mounted horses or elephants and rode side by side, it was as if one needed ten thousand eyes to take in the sight. Some said they were like Hiranyaksha and Hiranyakashipu.[1] Others compared them to the Sundopa Sundar brothers.[2] Still others said they were as loyal to each other as Rama and Bharata and as great a complement to each other on the battlefield as Arjuna and Bhima.

But that day, when Periya Pazhuvettaraiyar entered the Thanjai fort with the usual fanfare, the streets were not bursting with onlookers as they would otherwise be. The festive atmosphere was absent. Chinna Pazhuvettaraiyar was not in his place outside the fort either.

The Dhanadhikari made straight for his brother's palace. He figured something crucial must have held up the commander. Perhaps the emperor's health had taken a turn for the worse, or ... or ... perhaps it was indeed all over? He pared down his parade to the bare minimum circuit, and headed for Chinna Pazhuvettaraiyar's palace.

When his brother arrived to receive him, Periya Pazhuvettaraiyar could make out that he was troubled. Something about his features suggested he was anxious, even panicky. After a quick embrace, they went to the private chambers where high-level councils were held.

The moment they were alone, Periya Pazhuvettaraiyar asked, 'Thambi! Kalantaka! You don't seem to be your usual self. What has happened? Is the emperor well?'

Kalantaka Kandar, whom we know as 'Chinna Pazhuvettaraiyar', said, 'The emperor is as he always is. There is no improvement or setback in his condition.'

'Then why do you look so forlorn? You weren't at the entrance of the fort to receive me. The town seems tense, the celebrations muted?'

'Anna! There has been a minor incident. It isn't anything significant. I'll tell you about it later. How did your mission go?'

'It was a complete and total victory. Everyone who was invited was present at Kadambur. They agreed unanimously that your son-in-law, Madurantakan, was the rightful heir to the throne. They greeted him with cries of victory, and said they were willing to go to battle if we couldn't come to an amicable settlement with the royal family. Kollimazhavan and Vanangaamudi Munaiarayar themselves fell in with our plans, so what obstacle could possibly present itself? Sambuvarayar has offered us his fort, army, wealth and all else that he owns for the war effort. His son Kandamaaran is just as keen. We needn't worry about Nadunaadu and Tirumunaippaadi Naadu. Chozha Naadu, of course, is all ours. Tirukkovaloor Malayaman, Pallavan Parthibendran and Kodumbalur Velaan are the only ones who might demur. Of them, Kodumbalur Velaan is in Lanka. What can the other two achieve by themselves? All that's left for us to do is present the case to the emperor and have our will done.'

'Well, it's all very well that the leaders are on our side. But what about the people? What if they object?' Chinna Pazhuvettaraiyar Kalantaka Kandar asked.

'Aha! Who cares about the people's opinion? Is it in consultation with the subjects that kingdoms go about their business? If the people dare to object, we'll ensure that they never poke their noses into such matters again. But I don't think there will be any need for such measures. If it is the emperor's will, they will abide by it. Besides, Arulmozhi Varman is fortunately in Lanka. If he were the heir in question, or even present in the kingdom, the people's blind love for him might prove a problem. Aditya Karikalan isn't too popular. It will be easy for Madurantakan to win their affections. He's already known for his Shiva bhakti and his noble nature. Besides, he is even more fair of face than the sons of Sundara Chozhar. They say "Agaththin azhagu mudaththil theriyum"—the face is the index of the mind. So, these fools will believe his mind is just as beautiful as his face, and throw their support behind him. Anyhow, why do you worry when I'm around? Surely, you trust me to handle these things?'

'But what about the Velakkaara Army? How do we handle them?'

'The Velakkaara Army men have sworn to protect Sundara Chozhar with their lives, but not his sons. Even if they presume to interfere, you have your own personal army, don't you? It won't take much more than a naazhigai[3] to throw the entire lot in the dungeon, will it?'

'Anna! But our biggest challenge will be the opposition from Pazhaiyarai. Who knows what sort of conspiracy the matriarch and the maiden might come up with? We must turn our attention to that ...'

'Thambi! Kalantaka! You're telling me my biggest challenge will come from two females, of all things! I have a talisman that will put paid to their mantra-tantra, don't worry.'

'The emperor has ordered that we send out invitations asking his sons to come to Thanjai.'

'Aditya Karikalan won't come. Arulmozhi Varman might decide to honour his father's request. We'll just have to stave him off. It is only after Madurantakan is given the title of crown prince, seated on the throne and given all the authority of the rightful heir that we can allow either of the princes to step into the city. Leave this to me. You spoke earlier of a minor incident. What was that about?'

'A young man arrived from Kanchi. He was carrying one olai for the emperor and one for Kundavai ...'

'What did you do with him? Divested him of the olais and threw him into the dungeon, I presume?'

'No, Anna! He said he met you in Kadambur, and that you had asked him to deliver the scrolls to the emperor personally. Is that the truth?'

'Aha! No! Brazen lies! There was a young man who, uninvited, entered the Kadambur palace saying he was a friend of Kandamaaran's. But he never mentioned these missives to me. His very face made me suspicious! Have you gone and let him fool you?'

'Yes, Anna! I have been fooled. Because he used your name.'

'You idiot! What did you do after? Did you allow him to deliver the olai to the emperor? Did you not even read it for yourself?'

'I did read it. There was nothing of import in there. An invitation to the golden palace at Kanchi. That young man handed over the olai and was whispering something about "Abaayam" to the emperor ...'

'Did you suspect his intentions at least at that point and imprison him?'

'I did suspect his intentions, but I did not imprison him.'

'Then?'

'He said he wanted to tour the city. I sent him with an escort of two bodyguards. He gave them the slip and disappeared. I was busy making arrangements to hunt him down. That was why I didn't even come to receive you at the entrance of the fort. I have sent out a warning to the people of the city, and ...'

'Ada chhi! You call yourself a man? You've gone and got fooled by a prepubescent boy! I'm the moron here, for having given you the name "Kalantaka Kandan"—the warrior who conquers time and death. I'm the moron for having appointed you commander of the fort. I deserve this and more for my pains! Aren't you embarrassed, for having been taken in by a stranger using my name?'

'It wasn't just your name. He showed me your signet ring too. Did you not give it to him?'

'No, never! Am I a fool like you, to be taken in that way?'

'He did have the signet ring. He showed it to me. He showed it to the guards at the entrance of the fort too, and that was how he was allowed in. If it wasn't you who gave it to him, there is only one other person who might have.'

'Of whom do you speak?'

'Can you not guess? It is the Ilaiya Rani of whom ...'

'Chhi! Watch your tongue! Or I'll have to cut it out.'

'Cut my tongue out if you will. Lop my head off, too, if you will. But I will not stop speaking until I have told you what's been on my mind for the longest time. You've taken a cobra for a pet because you were enraptured by its beauty. It *will* bite one day. It will ruin us all. Please, don't let this happen! Chase her away, and move on!'

'Kalantaka Kanda! I, too, am going to tell you something that's been on my mind for the longest time. You're free to speak your mind about any other issue. If it is your opinion that I am in the wrong about anything at all, you have every right to tell me. But one word against the woman I have married and made my queen, and I will strangle you with the very hands that raised you; I will pierce your heart with the very dagger I taught you how to hold. Watch out.'

The angry exchange between the brothers resounded outside the chambers like the roars of two lions about to fight each other. Their words were subdued by the thick walls of the inner chambers, but the snarls made their way outside. Everyone who heard the thunderous voices wondered what catastrophe had struck, and trembled in terror.

10

NANDINI IN A SULK

When Periya Pazhuvettaraiyar returned to his palace at last, it was well past midnight, and the third jaamam had begun. His mind was in turmoil. The night wind that raked up the dust on the street and swirled around him, soiling his clothes and person, seemed less turbulent than the storm that raged in his heart, filling his mind with filth.

He felt remorse and guilt at having spoken as harshly as he had to his beloved brother. He knew Kalantaka's affection for him knew no bounds. It was that fraternal love that had prompted his brother's words. Yet, why did he have to drag Nandini into this mess for no reason? Why had he accused her as he had? Perhaps it was human nature. When one was in error, it was but natural to shift the blame on to someone else. One might expect that of ordinary men. But was it right for Kalantaka to stoop to that level?

Kalantaka had allowed that scoundrel to escape

from right under his nose. And he had brought in a woman, and that too his madani—his older brother's wife, whom he should love and respect as he would his mother—in trying to downplay his own role in the messenger's getaway. Was it befitting of his reputation? What did it say of his courage, of his masculinity?

Well, Kalantaka *had* asked forgiveness for his words, hadn't he?

I must let it go, Periya Pazhuvettaraiyar thought to himself. *There is no point in thinking about this.*

Yet, could it be possible that there was an iota of truth in what Kalantaka had said? Perhaps Periya Pazhuvettaraiyar had gone soft in his dotage, and become besotted with beauty? She was a woman he had come across in the woods. And he had stood up for her and raged against the brother who was born of the same womb as he, the brother who had been by his side through a hundred battles, the brother who had put his own life at stake numerous times to safeguard Periya Pazhuvettaraiyar's.

What had she done to merit such a defence? He had no idea who she was, or where she came from, or which clan she had been born into. At times, her words and demeanour did rouse his suspicions. Chhi, chhi! His brother's words had stirred such ugly thoughts in his head too. This was entirely unfair! She loved him with all her heart and soul. She treated him with utmost devotion, and delighted at his every success. At times, she would share her opinions with him and run ideas by him. She had desired him when he was well past his prime, when he was over sixty years of age. Didn't that say enough about her fealty?

She was so lovely as to incite the jealousy of the celestial apsaras. If only a swayamvaram were organised for her, Indra himself would come down from the heavens to win her hand. There couldn't be a king in this world who wouldn't want her for his wife. Ah! If Sundara Chozhan had only seen her, he would have wed her himself. How foolish it was to mistrust a woman like her! It was said that old men who married beautiful maidens ruined their own lives with baseless suspicions. He had witnessed several instances of this himself. And yet, could he allow himself to make the same mistake and become the laughing stock of the town?

Even so, perhaps he would do well to have it out with her. There were unanswered questions that must be resolved. She asked for his signet ring every now and again. Why did she need it? What did she do with it? She went off to the lata mandapam by herself every now and again. Why? He had heard that she received some sort of mantravadi at the mandapam every now and again, and she had admitted to it herself. But she hadn't given him a justification for the mantravadi's visits. Whom was she trying to jinx? What did she need to know from the mantravadi? For what was she using his services?

Worst of all, she had made him a 'kalyanam

panniyum brahmachari'—a celibate married man. How long would this go on? Every time he approached her, she staved him off by claiming she was on a viradam or nonbu of some sort. But she would not give him details. What viradam, what nonbu, what penance, what prayer? It reminded him of folk tales where scheming women found ways to wrap their husbands around their little fingers without ever making a compromise themselves. No, he would no longer give her place to do as she pleased. Tonight, he would speak to her. He would demand, and get, the answers due to him!

When Pazhuvettaraiyar arrived at the threshold of his palace, his consorts and guards and servants and maids were in full attendance. But the woman his eyes searched for was missing. The Ilaiya Rani was conspicuous by her absence. He asked after her, only to be told she was still in the lata mandapam. What could be keeping her there after midnight? Was she trying to insult him? He felt a surge of anger towards her. It was in this mood that he crossed over to the kodi mandapam.

Just as he reached the kodi mandapam, he saw Nandini and her companion approach from the opposite side. The moment she laid eyes on him, she stopped and turned away to look into the darkness of the garden, refusing to meet his eyes. Her companion stood some distance away.

Even when Periya Pazhuvettaraiyar had walked

right up to her, Nandini did not turn to look at him. He had been all set to take her to task. And now he was tasked with having to mollify her.

'Nandini! My kanmani! Why are you angry? Why won't you even look at me?' he asked, placing an iron-like hand as gently as he could on her delicate shoulder.

Nandini, for her part, reached up with a hand softer than a petal and pushed his vajrayudha of an arm away from herself. Ammamma! Could such a silken touch pack so much power?

'My very life breath! It is my good fortune to receive a touch from your lovely hands, even if it is only to push me away! From Tirukonamalai in Lanka to the Vindhya hills, no soldier has been able to achieve what you have, and I consider it a blessing to be at the receiving end from your hands. But you must tell me why you're angry. My ears ache to hear your honey-like voice!' the hero of a thousand battles said in a beseeching tone.

'How long has it been since you left me all by myself? Has it not been four whole days?' said Nandini, her voice trembling. Those tones melted a heart that had been unmoved by raised swords and spears. Periya Pazhuvettaraiyar might as well have been a wax candle left out in the summer heat.

'Is that why you're so angry? Can't you bear a separation of four days? What will you do if I have to go to war? You won't see me for months!' he said.

'Did you imagine that I would allow a separation of months from you? Throw that thought right out of your mind. If you have to go to battle, I will accompany you to war like your shadow ...'

'What a thought! If I took you to the battlefield, would I be able to bring myself to fight? Kanmani! This chest and these shoulders have borne the brunt of cruel arrowheads and sharp spears. People and poets alike sing praises of the sixty-four scars I bear. But if your flower-soft skin should be pierced by so much as a thorn, my heart would break. That little thorn would do what generations of swords and spears have failed to do. How could I possibly take you to war with me? It hurts me to watch you stand on the hard floor. Come this way, come sit on your bed. Let me see your lovely face. Do you think these four days have been hard on you alone? Every moment away from you feels like an epoch to me. Let me drink in the face I have missed for so very long!'

With those words, he took Nandini's hand and led her to the bed of flowers.

Nandini wiped her eyes, and lifted them to meet her husband's.

The Dhanadhikari finally saw her pearl-like teeth through a tiny smile. In the glow of the golden lamp, it made for a sight that stole his breath away. One could give up all three worlds just for a hint of his wife's smile. But he did not have three worlds to give. He could give up his all, his body and soul and wealth for her. And yet, she never asked him for a thing. As that bravest of warriors reflected on this, all thought of taking her to task and confronting her with unanswered questions fled from his mind. He would do her bidding. He would wipe the dust at her feet. Why, he *was* the dust at her feet. Any sort of addiction is dangerous. But nothing makes one lose one's mind as easily as intoxication with a beauty.

'You were away for four whole days. That was bad enough. But why didn't you come see me the moment you returned? Your brother is dearer to you than I, isn't he?' Nandini said. She then pouted and gave him a sideways glance that toyed with his heart.

'It wasn't like that, kanmani! I longed to come straight here, with all the force of an arrow that has just been shot from a bow. But I had to ensure that idiot boy Madurantakan arrived safely through the subterranean passage. That was why I was held up at my brother's palace ...'

'Aiya! I am invested in your every task. It is my desire to see all your efforts bear fruit. And yet ... it troubles me when I think of your taking a man along in the palanquin meant for me. Everyone believes you take me with you wherever you go ...'

'Do you think this state of affairs makes me happy? Not one bit! But we've taken on a mammoth task. I'm forced to put up with all this so that we may realise that dream. Besides, have you forgotten that it was your idea in the first place? That it was you who suggested the palanquin would be the ideal guise for me to take Madurantakan around? It was you, in fact, who said he should use the subterranean passage to get in and out of the fortress so that no one would know!'

'I simply did my duty. It is a wife's duty to help her husband fulfil his ambitions, isn't it? The idea popped into my head, and I told you. But for that to have this impact on you and …'

'Was that all you did? This Madurantakan used to smear his body with vibhuti and cover his neck with rudraksha garlands and chant "Nama Shivaya" all day long. His world was the temple. He was his mother's son. He had no interest in ruling the kingdom. We tried everything, but nothing would induce him to lay claim to the throne. All you did was talk to him a couple of times, and he turned into someone else entirely. Now, he hankers after power so much that, in his head, his kingdom stretches from Lanka to the Himalayas, from the earth to the skies. He is in an even greater hurry than we are. He is itching to sit on the throne. Nandini! In the case of this boy, you've worked some sort of mayamantram … Which brings me to this … when you yourself are capable of such magic, what need have you of this mantravadi? People talk. They say such things. The fact that he visits you in the lata mandapam …'

'My lord! It is your duty to cut out the tongues of the people who say such things, and shred them to pieces. That will teach them! I have already told you why I receive the mantravadi. If you have forgotten, I will remind you now. It is to counter the poison of that snake in Pazhaiyarai. You and yours are men who pride yourselves on your masculinity. You believe in confrontations on the battlefield. You dismiss women. You show your contempt for us with bravado. "After all, a woman! What can she do?" you ask. You think it is beneath you to do battle with women. But one woman can do more damage than a hundred men. It takes one to know one. You can't even begin to comprehend the machinations of Kundavai's mind. I can. You might have forgotten the humiliation she visited upon us, but I never will. She looked at me in the presence of hundreds of other women, and said, "It's all very well for that man on his deathbed to lose his mind with lust. But what were *you* thinking, di? Why did you go and marry that old man?" Can I forget those words? "You sparkle like a celestial mohini. Any prince would marry you and make you his royal consort. Why did you have to go and choose that ancient buffalo for a husband?" she asked. Can I forget *those* words?'

With that, Nandini began to sob. The tears flowing from her eyes poured in streams down her cheeks and soaked her breasts.

11

THE WORLD WAS SPINNING!

Pazhuvettaraiyar was aware that his choosing to get married in his twilight years had provoked many a snide comment. He had heard, too, that Kundavai Piraatti was among those who had spoken disparagingly of his union with Nandini. But no one had told him her exact words until now. When he heard Nandini relay them, it was as if his fury was being fanned by the bellows of a furnace. His breath came in angry spurts, 'gup-gup'. Nandini's tears were as ghee that fuelled the fire raging in his heart.

'My darling! Did that heartless wretch dare use those words? Did she call me an "ancient buffalo"? Well, let that be. I will … I will … see what I do to her! I will be the buffalo that stamps on an alli stalk with its feet, I will crush her like that alli stalk and throw her aside. Just you watch! I will … I will …,' Pazhuvettaraiyar found himself stammering in a frenzied rage. It would be quite impossible to describe the horrific contortions of his face.

Nandini tried to pacify him. She laid a flower-soft hand on his iron fist, and laced her fingers through his.

'Naadha! I always knew you wouldn't be able to bear to hear of the humiliation to which I was subjected. But must a lion who can break the skull of an elephant in musth and drink its blood stoop to pounce on a measly cat? Kundavai is just a mewling cat. But she is a mantrakari. It is her maya and mantra that have enabled her to manipulate everyone. They are but putty in her hands. The kingdom itself is putty in her hands. The only way one can beat her at her game is to find mantras that will counter her spells. If this is not to your taste, all you have to do is tell me, and I will leave the palace right away ...,' Nandini said, before breaking into sobs again.

Pazhuvettaraiyar's blinding wrath gave way to blinding lust.

'No! No! You can call a thousand mantravadis if you wish. But do not speak of leaving the palace! You are all there is to my life. Why, you *are* my very life! What can a body do once life has deserted it? This separation you have enforced is killing me as it stands. You who know all these mantras, why don't you teach me one?'

'Naadha! What use do you have for mantras, you whose hands wield the sword and spear? Leave the maya-mantra to the helpless woman that I am. What do you need mayam or mantram for?' Nandini said.

'My darling! My body trembles with desire when

you open your coral lips and call me “Naadha”. The sight of your face drives me senseless. It is true that my hands wield the sword and spear. I use those weapons against my enemies in the battlefield. But what purpose will they serve me in the kodi mandapam? I have no arrows to counter those of Manmadha, do I? It is you who possess those arrows. You ask me what use I have for mantras. I ask you for a mantra that will put out the fire that torments my body and soul. Tell me a mantra that will stave off my desire. Or, do me the honour of allowing me to caress your lovely skin. Let me quench my thirst. Find a way to save my life! Kanmani! It has been two-and-a-half years since we married each other according to the shastras, as the world watched. And in spite of this, we are yet to live as man and wife. You speak of viradams and nonbus, and keep me away. You are torturing the very man to whom you gave your hand in marriage. Let our life together begin, or end mine by poisoning me with your very hands!'

Nandini shut her ears tight and gasped. 'Aiyayo! Do not speak such cruel words! If you say such a thing again, I will do as you say and bring poison to end this life. But it will be I who drinks it. I will die and you'll be free of the torture to which I subject you. You can live in peace.'

'No, no! I will never repeat what I said to you. Forgive me! Could I possibly live in peace if you were to poison yourself? I, who am already half-mad, will go completely mad!'

'Naadha! Why must you go mad? The very day we married each other, our two bodies began to share a single life. Our two souls merged into one, our two hearts merged into one. Every beat of your heart echoes in mine. Every thought that crosses your mind is mirrored in mine. A twitch of your eyebrows brings tears to my eyes. A twitch of your moustache hurts my insides. When our lives have been knitted into a single fabric, why must you even think of this lowly body? This body is made of mud. One fine day, it will turn to ash and dust and blend into the mud of this earth!'

'Stop this, stop this! These terrible words hurt my ears!' Pazhuvettaraiyar hollered. Refusing to let her interrupt, he plunged on, 'You call this a body made of mud? Lies! Lies! Let your sweet lips that smell of honey never speak such lies again! You say your body is made of mud? Never! There are numerous women in this world. Perhaps Brahma fashioned their bodies from mud, perhaps he sculpted them from stone. He might have mixed ashes and dust into them for all I know. But do you know how he crafted your lovely form? He collected the flowers that had fallen from the mandara trees of Devalokam. He then came down to Tamizhagam and collected the petals of the pink lotuses blooming in our temple ponds. He went back to Devalokam and soaked them in the golden goblet where the amritam, the nectar of the devas, is stored. He let the petals marinate until the nectar and flowers had turned into a paste. He mixed rays of moonlight into the paste. He then called the musicians of Tamizhagam and asked them to play the yazh. He let the waves of music from the yazh waft into the paste. And it was from this paste that he rolled out your skin.'

'Naadha! You speak as if you were right by Brahma's side when he did all this! Am I the only one who fits this description? Your antapuram is home to so many women, of whom most are from royal clans. You have led long nuptial lives with each of them. It has been but two-and-a-half years since you set eyes upon me, and yet ...,' Nandini began, but Pazhuvettaraiyar cut her short.

Perhaps the only way he could release the dam of emotion threatening to burst within was through words, in the absence of any other outlet. Perhaps a torrent of poetic speech would put out the wildfire of desire that singed his body and soul.

'Nandini! You speak of the women in my antapuram. It was to foster the ancient lineage of Pazhuvoor that I married those women. Some of those damned women turned out to be sterile. Some others brought forth daughter after daughter. I made my peace with it. This was all God had destined for me, I thought. I pushed all thought of women out of my mind. I immersed myself in governance. There was no space for any preoccupation but the expansion of the Chozha kingdom.

'It was under these circumstances that the final

stand with the Pandiyas played out. Although there were many commanders, far younger than I, entirely capable of managing the war effort, I was not able to hold myself back from entering the fray. And if I hadn't entered, we would not have seen such a resounding victory either. Having decimated the Pandiya army and flown the flag of Chozha Naadu in Madurai, I went to Kongu Naadu. I was returning from there, walking by the banks of the Kaveri. It was in a thicket along the way that I saw you.

'At first, I could not believe my eyes. It must be an illusion, I thought. I blinked once. When I opened my eyes, you were still there. You must be a vanadevadai, a wood nymph, I thought. You would disappear the moment I approached. But you did not disappear. Perhaps you were like the celestial maidens of the puranas, an apsara or Gandharva beauty sent from Devalokam to the earth because of a punishing curse. You would not speak our language, I thought. "Woman! Who are you?" I asked. You replied in Tamil, and said, "I'm an orphan. I seek refuge from you. Save me!"

'As I brought you home in the palanquin, thoughts I had never before encountered assailed my consciousness. I had seen you before, somewhere, sometime. But I racked my brain, and couldn't remember where or when or how. Then, the scales fell from my eyes. I could see the truth. It wasn't in this birth that I had met you. Our connection is far deeper than that. Birth after birth, we were bound together. The memories of those lives we had lived came back to me all at once. You were once born as Ahalya, and I was Devendran, the lord of the devas, Indra. I forsook my heavenly kingdom, risked the curse of the rishi and came down to earth to be with you.

'In another life, I was King Shantanu. I was on a hunt by the banks of the Ganga when I saw you. You were the very river in human form. I fell in love with you.

'In yet another life, I was born as Kovalan in Poompattinam. You were Kannagi. I had abandoned you because of an evil spell that made me lose my mind. But then, I came to my senses and sought you out again. I took you with me to Madurai. I then went to sell your anklet so we could start our life anew. But misfortune and malice saw me lose my life. I was sentenced by the Pandiya king.

'It was to avenge that death that I took this birth, and it was after I had taken my revenge on the Pandiya clan that I saw you in this lifetime. You are the very Kannagi who was born all those centuries ago!'

As Pazhuvettaraiyar spoke of his reminiscences of past lives, Nandini avoided his gaze and looked elsewhere. The emotions that played across her face were lost on him. If only he could have caught them, it is unlikely he would have gone on as he did.

When he stopped for breath, Nandini turned to him and said, 'Naadha! The couples of whom you speak are not quite appropriate. Those stories were rather ominous. Perhaps you should say you were Manmadha and I, Rathi!' She flashed him a smile that lit up her entire face.

Pazhuvettaraiyar's own face was infused with pride and joy. However indifferent a man was to his own appearance, could he but delight in being called Manmadha by his beloved? Yet, he contrived to sound modest and said, 'Kanmani! You are certainly Rathi. But surely it is inappropriate to call me of all people "Manmadha"! You prove that love is blind.'

'Naadha! To my eyes, you are indeed a Manmadha. What is male beauty but courage? There is no warrior as brave as you in all of this land. The other aspect that lends beauty to men is compassion towards the weak and helpless and innocent. Am I not proof that you show such compassion? You took a poor orphan, of whose ancestry and origin you had no idea, into your home and heart. You've poured your love on me, encouraged my every effort. I won't keep a man such as you waiting long for what you ask. My viradam and nonbu will soon be over ...'

'Kanmani! Tell me for which cause you have undertaken this viradam and nonbu. I will ensure it comes to pass as soon as I can,' said the king of Pazhuvoor.

'The descendants of Sundara Chozhar, who believes there is no Manmadha but he, must never sit on the throne of the Chozha empire. And that conceited Kundavai must be cut down to size.'

'Nandini! Those two things have all but been accomplished already. Neither Adityan nor Arulmozhi Varman will be crowned king. All those who wield power in the kingdom have thrown their support behind Madurantakan.'

'*All* of them? Is this really the case?' asked Nandini, enunciating every word.

'All but two or three. Kodumbaluran, Malayaman and Parthibendran won't enter an alliance with us. But there is no need to worry about them.'

'Even so, we must exercise caution until the deed is done.'

'Of course. I *am* being cautious. Any slip is because of the foolishness of others. Just today, there was one such slip. A young man from Kanchi pulled a fast one on Kalantakan, met the emperor and gave him an olai ...'

'Aha! You heap praise on your brother. How many times I've told you that he is reckless!'

'Well, he has behaved like an imbecile in this case. He claims the young man showed him the signet ring of this palace.'

'Well, someone who has been conned will come up with some excuse or the other. Has no effort been made to capture this young man?'

'Is it likely that no efforts are being made? Our men are scouring the fort and the town. He will be caught somehow or the other. Our mission hasn't been endangered in any way. Once the emperor dies, it will be Madurantakan who ascends the throne ...'

'Naadha! It is now time for me to reveal what my viradam is …'

'My love! I have been asking you this very question.'

'Madurantakan—that nincompoop, that fool on whose face the very sight of a woman will put a smile—ascending the throne is not enough for me …'

'What, then? Tell me what you would like, and I'll make sure it happens!'

'My lord, when I was a little girl, a famous astrologer took a look at my horoscope. He said I would go through terrible calamities until I turned eighteen …'

'What else did he say?'

'That my life would change direction once I turned eighteen. That I would attain a position I could never have dreamt of, one where I would wield unparalleled power …'

'That has come to pass! Tell me who this astrologer is, and I will do a kanakabhishekam for him, and shower him with gold.'

'Naadha!'

'Kanne!'

'The astrologer said something else too. May I tell you what that was?'

'Of course! You absolutely must!'

'He said the man who marries me will ascend the throne of a great empire, and have the rulers of fifty-six kingdoms accept his suzerainty and pay tribute to him. Will you ensure that this comes to pass?'

When these words fell on Pazhuvettaraiyar's ears, Nandini and her floral bed began to spin before him. The lata mandapam was spinning. The pillars of the mandapam were spinning. The trees in the garden, shadowy in the dark, were spinning. The higher branches, outlined against the moonlight, were spinning. The stars in the sky were spinning. The palaces on either side were spinning. The very world was spinning.

12

THE DARK PALACE

Let us now turn our attention to Vandiyadevan, and see what has happened to him since he went missing. We last saw him find a hiding spot by the dark palace. He tried his best to eavesdrop on Nandini and the mantravadi. But it was of no use. He couldn't make out a word. And he couldn't drum up much enthusiasm to listen in either.

It struck him that all through his interaction with Nandini, his senses had dullened. It was as if he was under the influence of a narcotic. It was best to escape without meeting her again. She might be even more dangerous than the Pazhuvettaraiyar brothers. He was in full possession of himself around them; his shoulders were strong, his instincts sharp. He could reach for his dagger in an instant. He had the luxury of choosing either brain or brawn to beat them.

But this Mohini drew a veil over his intelligence. His limbs went weak, and he didn't think his fingers could summon the strength to hold the dagger if the need arose. Who knew what calamity might visit him if he were to meet her again? To top it all off, she had a mantravadi with her too. Who knew what spell the two of them might cast on him?

What was her quarrel with Kundavai Piraatti, he wondered. Her hatred for the princess flew like sparks from her eyes. For all he knew, Nandini might change her mind and hand him over to Pazhuvettaraiyar. Women were famed for their fickle natures and impulsive decisions, weren't they? So, he must ensure he made his escape without setting eyes on her again.

But how was he to do this? He would have to go back into the garden and find a way out. He would have to climb the wall. But what if the guards who were on the lookout for him were lying in wait? Was there no other option?

Vandiyadeva! Luck has come to your aid every time you were in a fix. Think! Think! Put your brains to use. Put your eyes to use. Look around yourself. There's that dark palace! Why does it remain unlit? What could be hidden away inside? If I were to sneak in from here, where will I end up? What could it open on to? Should I give this a shot? Should I perhaps just explore? I might find something useful. Even if it is of no help now, it might come in handy sometime in future, our man thought to himself.

How could he enter the palace, though? An enormous door with a gigantic lock barred his way. Appappa! How sturdy it was! The surface was rock hard … Ah! What was this? There appeared to be a little door hidden away in the larger one. Just a touch … oh! It opens! Well, here was the luck that had kept him going all this while. All that was left to do was to enter the palace, then.

The little door had been so cleverly crafted that one could not see its outlines against the larger door. Vandiyadevan pushed against it, and entered the dark palace. The first thought in his mind was that not even Nandini should find out he had discovered the door. He pulled the smaller door shut behind himself. It was as if the darkness intensified manifold the moment he closed it. He had made out the shadowy shapes of several large pillars in the few seconds the door had been open. Now, he could see nothing at all. The darkness was so complete, one could not even imagine such nothingness. Chhi, chhi! This was quite natural. Anyone who moved from a well-lit place to a dark one would feel this way. All he had to do was to give it a while. The cloying darkness would lighten once his eyes were accustomed to it. He would soon be able to see the outlines of objects, and eventually their shapes too.

He knew this from experience. And yet, why did the darkness make him so uneasy? There was no point in standing still. He would do well to walk around and find his bearings. He could feel his way forward. He had made out a pillar in the moonlight when he had first entered. It could not have vanished.

Vandiyadevan stuck his hands out before him like a blind man and took a few steps forward. Soon enough, he felt the pillar against one hand. Ah! What a huge pillar it was, crafted from granite. He wound his way around the pillar and went forward. Not long after, he came across another pillar. He could only feel these shapes, not see them. Had he suddenly gone blind? No! That was madness. How could an eye lose sight for no reason at all? He went further ahead. His hands did not feel any pillars after this. But he had a sense that he was sinking into a pit.

Ah! Here was a step! Thank heavens, he had managed to keep his balance. How much longer and how much further could he walk in the pitch dark? He felt a sudden, inexplicable terror. He did not have the fortitude to push on, he thought. He would turn back. He would open the door, and go right back to the lata mandapam. It would be a better idea to meet Nandini and do as she told him to than to wander around in this treacherous darkness. He would make whatever promise she demanded, and then think about how he could get out of the deal later.

Vandiyadevan turned to go back to the lata mandapam. But was he going in the same direction from which he had come? Who could tell? He walked on, but he did not find anything familiar. Where had those granite pillars disappeared? What if he could not find the hidden door? Was he doomed to spend the entire night going round and round in the blackness of the palace? Good god! What had he got himself into?

Aha! What was that sound? 'Sada-sada.' Where had it come from? It must be bats, flapping their wings. It was but natural for bats to congregate in such darkness. No! This was not the sound of batwings. He could hear footsteps. Human footsteps! Surely, they were human? Or … could it be that …? Vandiyadevan's throat went dry. His tongue was stuck to the roof of his mouth.

Suddenly, he felt a body bump into his face.

Vandiyadevan summoned all his strength and threw a mighty punch. His hand hurt like it had been shattered. He felt the body with his other hand, and realised he had not just bumped into a pillar in the dark, but also punched it. If not for the searing pain in his hand, the 'vin-vin' of jangling nerves, he would have laughed at his own foolishness. He did feel less apprehensive, though. One couldn't quite say his fears had entirely disappeared, because when he strained his ears, he could still hear footsteps. Now they sounded like they were going away, and now they sounded like they were approaching him. Vandiyadevan stayed where he was, but his eyes followed the direction of the sound and stared desperately into the dark.

Ah! Light! There! Somehow, there was light! It was becoming gradually brighter. Why, it was coming towards him! He could smell smoke. Someone was carrying a flare. Perhaps it was Nandini, come to seek him out? That would be a good thing. But what if it was someone else?

The most prudent course of action would be to

wait and watch. There was no shortage of places where he could hide in here. From the glow of the torch in the distance, it was evident that he was in an expansive hall, punctuated by enormous pillars, upon which the faces and forms of terrible demons had been carved. A stairway approached from below, took a turn on this floor and then went further up. The flare seemed to be making its way up from below.

That would rule out Nandini.

Thoughts of the dungeon came to him now. Was it under this palace that the famed torture chambers were hidden away? Was someone approaching from there? Vandiyadevan had heard so much about the horrors of the dungeon that his body began to tremble. Sweat poured out of his every follicle, down to his feet. He quickly sought out the shelter of a pillar. Our Vandiyadevan did not lack for courage, but even his limbs went numb at the idea of being carted off to the dungeon. He found himself shivering.

Three forms emerged from the stairway. They were all humans. One was holding the flare. Another was holding a spear. Between them was a third man who wasn't carrying a thing.

When the light fell upon their faces, Vandiyadevan's breath stopped. He all but jumped out of his skin. He could barely contain his shock. The party was led by none other than his dear friend Kandamaaran! The person in the middle created a strange illusion for a moment in Vandiyadevan's mind. It seemed to him that it was the Pazhuvoor Ilaiya Rani. But the very next instant, the illusion disappeared. He realised it was a man. Then, he realised it was Madurantaka Devar, of whom he had caught a glimpse at Kadambur Sambuvarayar's palace. The third man, who held the flare, was a stranger. Perhaps he was a bodyguard or some sort of palace employee.

Vandiyadevan's mind was racing. It didn't take him long to figure out why they had chosen to come up through the subterranean stairway. The Ilaiya Rani had arrived in the palanquin the previous evening. Periya Pazhuvettaraiyar had reached the Thanjai fort sometime ago. They had both used the main entrance of the fort, and their processions had been greeted by the townspeople. But no one must know that Madurantaka Devar was going in and out of the palace. That was why they were using the secret passage. Perhaps this was the grand mystery that the perennial night of this palace was hiding.

Kandamaaran must have met Periya Pazhuvettaraiyar at some point, somewhere, after seeing Vandiyadevan off at the banks of the Kollidam, and been recruited to carry out this confidential mission. He was to escort Madurantaka Devar to safety through this passage.

Aha! Vandiyadevan remembered now. 'I have some work in Thanjavur. I might end up coming there myself,' Kandamaaran had said, hadn't he?

What if he stepped out of his hiding place and went up to Kandamaaran all of a sudden? What would his friend do? The moment this thought occurred to him, Vandiyadevan brushed it aside. If he were to show his face to Kandamaaran now, the latter would have to kill him in order to fulfil the promise he had made. Or, Vandiyadevan would have to kill his friend. It made no sense to put himself and his friend in such a quandary.

By this time, the three men had gone further up the stairs, and the light was disappearing with them. Vandiyadevan wondered whether he should follow them, and dismissed that idea as well. He was certain they were going to Chinna Pazhuvettaraiyar's palace. To follow them would be to stick his head back in the lion's den from which he had escaped by the skin of his teeth. It made little sense to go back to the lata mandapam too. In all likelihood, Periya Pazhuvettaraiyar would be there.

What option did he have, then? Why, what if he climbed down the stairway and saw where it led? With this thought, our young hero began his journey down the stairs.

13

THE CRYPT

Vandiyadevan lowered his feet carefully as he walked down the dark subterranean passage, just about managing not to fall. The steps led downwards for a while, before the ground turned level. After a while, another set of stairs began, which led to a lower landing. Vandiyadevan stretched out both arms, but could not feel a wall. The passage was a rather broad one for a secret tunnel, he thought.

He had not gone much further down the landing before the stairs began to lead upwards. They seemed to curve a bit too. Appappa! Heaven alone knew for how long he would have to stumble and fumble in the pitch dark.

Aha! What was this! The darkness was lifting slowly. He could make out a very, very dim light ahead. Where was it coming from? Could it be a skylight that let in the moon's rays? Or a small window somewhere in the walls? Perhaps there was a hidden lamp ...?

No! No! What on earth was this? Surely the sight before his eyes had to be an illusion? Or had he lost his mind? Was his brain conjuring images from nothing?

He was in an enormous hall. It had been fashioned by excavating into the rock. A crypt. No wonder the ceiling was so very low that he would bang his head against it if he were to stand erect. The dim light he had spotted was not coming from outside, neither from a skylight nor from a window. It seemed to glow from various spots in the crypt, from little heaps that were spread out through the hall.

Ah! What precious items these were that had somehow trapped the moon within themselves! In one corner were bejewelled crowns, embedded with pearls and rubies and diamonds. In another corner were thick gold necklaces, navaratna chains, pearl chokers ... and what was that in the cauldron with a gaping mouth? Good god! It was filled with white pearls that looked like punnai buds!

In a mud pot were gold coins that radiated a halo-like glow. And in a heap by the side were bars of gold. So, this was the treasury of the Thanjai palace, hidden away in a crypt! It should come as no surprise that this dark palace adjoined the Dhanadhikari's own, and that it housed a vault of gems. Ammamma! Bhagyalakshmi, the Goddess of Wealth, and Adirshta Devathai, the Goddess of Fortune, must have conspired to bring him here. He had stumbled upon a dizzying, stunning secret through no effort of his own.

How could he put it to use, though? Well, he would think about that later. He was loath to leave this place. He could spend a lifetime in this crypt, running his hands through the various wonders it housed. His body would know no hunger and no thirst. Sleep wouldn't dare approach him. Here was the bounty of an entire century of Chozha victories. Here was the evidence of the bravery of army upon army that had marched into alien lands and conquered them all. This must be the storied navanidhi[1]. Not even Kubera could compete with this, surely? What reason could one possibly have to leave such a room?

Vandiyadevan walked round and round the crypt, stopping at a different pile each time. He lifted the bejewelled crowns lying unceremoniously in a corner. He ran his fingers through the ruby necklaces in another corner. He plunged an arm into the cauldron filled with pearls. He tossed around the gold coins inside the pot.

His eyes fell upon something large and shiny sprawled on the floor. He couldn't make out what it was. He went closer, and then bent down to examine it. Aiyo! For God's sake! It was a skeleton! A skeleton that had once supported flesh and blood and skin and hair and a nose and a face and eyes and ears, a whole human being!

Ah! The skeleton was moving! It had come to life and was getting to its feet! The rattling noise it made sounded like the clink of gold coins. The skeleton appeared to want to say something to him!

Every little hair on Vandiyadevan's body stood on end. He wondered if he had gone completely insane.

Chhi chhi! It wasn't the skeleton that was getting to its feet! It was a bandicoot that had made its home inside the skeleton! The rodent was running across *his* feet now. Yes. Phew. The skeleton was still sprawled on the floor. But it had certainly said something to him.

'Run away from here! Don't linger! I used to be a living being, just like you. I was trapped here. I lived here, and I died here. And I'm now a heap of bones. Run away, run now!'

It had screamed out a warning. He would live if he escaped right now. Or he would end up like the man that the skeleton had once been—like the skeleton the man had become.

Vandiyadevan decided he would leave. But how was he to get out? He could no longer see the stairs that had led him here. Everywhere he went in the crypt, the demon of darkness was waiting with its mouth open to swallow him whole. He could barely feel his feet. He seemed to be teetering on the edge of a bottomless hole. How had the stairway he had used to get here disappeared? It had to be somewhere. Vandiyadevan looked. And looked. And looked, and looked, and looked. Nothing.

In a corner, he saw a heap of gold coins. There seemed to be some sort of net over them. He squinted at the net, and realised it was a spiderweb. This triggered a thought in his head.

The wise had said mannaasai, pennaasai, ponnaasai—lust for land, lust for women, lust for gold—were but a spiderweb. The spider had spun its web and was lying in wait. A fly would land on it from somewhere, and find itself stuck. The spider would then pull the fly towards itself and eat it alive. Those three kinds of lust had the same effect—a man could lose his way and fall into the web that would lead him to his death. There was no way out once he had fallen.

Mannaasai, pennaasai, ponnaasai ... he had experienced all three kinds of desire that very day. Nandini, the Ilaiya Rani of Pazhuvoor, had tried to entrap him in her web. She had roused his lust for land, telling him he could regain his ancestral kingdom. Her beauty had robbed him of his powers of speech, thought and deed. And finally, the demon of greed was trying to ensnare him in this very crypt! He had escaped the first two, and must now run from the third.

Why get involved in such things? What need had he for a kingdom? For wealth? For women? His palace was the very earth, with the sky for a ceiling.

He thought of the ancient Tamil proverb 'Yaadum oore, yaavarum kelir'—Everywhere was home, everyone was family. Every town and village was one's own. Every human being was a relative of one's own. He would just wander from place to place. He would find joy in the first floods of rivers, the first blossoms of trees, the colours on birds, the trains on peacocks, the peaks of hills, the pinnacles of humanity, the blue of the sea, the waves of the ocean, the sky and the stars and the clouds. He would eat wherever food was served; he would sleep wherever rest was offered. Aha! That was the life, wasn't it? Why forsake such an easy existence for one burdened with secrets and intrigue and desire and danger? All he had to do now was find a way out of this crypt. Then, a way out of the dark palace and the Thanjavur fort. And then, make sure he never walked into such a mess again ...

Aha! He could hear a door open and close ... footsteps were coming his way again! The wonders of the night would never cease. Neither would its terrors. This time, the footsteps sounded far away. They seemed to be coming from both sides too. Vandiyadevan strained his ears and listened carefully. He stared into the darkness, willing his eyes to tear away the night and its sightlessness. Soon enough, he saw the wondrous sight he had been expecting.

It appeared to him to be happening somewhere else, on a stage in the distance, while he sat among the audience, in the very last row of a vast theatre.

A flare materialised from one wing of the stage. Another pushed aside the curtain of the opposite wing, and appeared from that side. The two flares moved towards each other. Two tall, dark forms were silhouetted against the first flare. Against the second flare were outlined two other forms—one had a tall and powerful frame, while his companion was slim and delicate. Both sets of bodies were approaching each other.

Vandiyadevan stared so hard his eyes smarted before he realised who the four people were. The tall, dark forms on the left belonged to the men who had escorted Madurantaka Devar through the subterranean passage a short while ago—Kandamaaran and a guard. From the right, Pazhuvettaraiyar was walking forward with Nandini by his side.

What would happen when the two flares met? Would it be something explosive? Or would they let each other pass with no fuss? Vandiyadevan could barely breathe from the excitement of his anticipation.

The two couples met. It was evident they had startled each other. They all nearly stumbled in surprise. But nothing untoward occurred. Pazhuvettaraiyar addressed Kandamaaran. He appeared to be asking a question. Kandamaaran seemed to reply. Vandiyadevan could not hear either the question or the answer. Then, Pazhuvettaraiyar pointed towards the stairs. Kandamaaran bowed deeply to pay his respects, and then made for the steps. Pazhuvettaraiyar made a sign to the man who was holding the flare, behind Kandamaaran's back. The man made no reply, but touched his mouth with his hand in a show of obsequiousness, bent low, straightened up and then hastened after Kandamaaran. Pazhuvettaraiyar and the Ilaiya Rani went off in the opposite direction.

This sequence of events had occurred as if in

shadow play or puppetry, and was over in a matter of moments. Vandiyadevan observed that the site of their meeting was right by the stairs that led down to the secret tunnel. Aha! It was a good thing he had wandered into the crypt. If he had been caught between the two couples, who knew what would have become of him?

Well, he should turn his thoughts to escape. Clearly, Kandamaaran was leaving the same way he had ushered Madurantaka Devar into the palace. That must be the very path from which he himself had strayed into the vault. If he followed Kandamaaran now, he would find himself outside the palace. He would then find an escape route to leave the city. If he had no other choice, he could recruit Kandamaaran to his cause. If his friend didn't come around ... well, he would just have to deal with him and the guard, render them useless and make his way out. So, that was decided then—he would follow Kandamaaran.

At first, the light from the flare seemed to be headed his way. Vandiyadevan caught his breath. Then, the light moved away. He had used the opportunity to study his surroundings and find his bearings. He could now see the stairway through which he had arrived. He went down the first set of stairs, and then back up. He made sure he kept the flare within his sight, without going close enough to attract attention. He was careful to walk silently. It would have been quite impossible to find his way through that winding, twisting, curling, spiralling path in the dark. Long live Kandamaaran! How would he ever repay this involuntary service his friend had done him?

Vandiyadevan could not have expected that a chance would offer itself up quite so soon …

The subterranean passage came to an abrupt end against a forbidding wall. No one would have guessed that the wall might house a door or other opening. But there must be one! A secret tunnel must have an exit, surely?

The man carrying the flare shifted it from his right hand to his left. He felt in the wall for something with his right hand, and then made as if he was moving a lever. A slim crack appeared in the wall. It then broadened until a man could pass through. The torch-bearer pointed towards the exit. Kandamaaran said something to him, and then put a foot through the opening. His other foot was still in the tunnel, and his back was fully turned.

Aha! What was happening? What was the other man doing? He was reaching for the dagger at his waist! Good god! He had plunged it into Kandamaaran's back! The nasty creature! The coward had just stabbed someone in the back!

Vandiyadevan ran forward and took a great leap. The man turned at the sound of his footsteps, and saw Vandiyadevan's furious face in the light of the flare.

14

'IS THIS YOUR IDEA OF FRIENDSHIP?'

As he leapt into the air, Vandiyadevan's immediate instinct was to save Kandamaaran, any which way. But he would have to set the treacherous guard right before he did anything else, or he would meet the same fate as his friend. He landed with one arm around the man's neck in a chokehold, and the other reaching for the flare. He pushed the flare out of the guard's hand so it fell to the floor. The impact caused the smoke to rise, and the flame to subside.

Twisting the guard's neck, Vandiyadevan used all his force to push him to the ground. The man's head hit the wall hard as he fell. Vandiyadevan picked up the flare and went close to examine him. The guard lay like a corpse. Yet, not wanting to leave it to chance, Vandiyadevan used his angavastram to bind his hands.

This entire sequence of events took our hero seconds to orchestrate. Then, he ran towards Kandamaaran, half of whose body lay inside the secret tunnel and half outside. The dagger was buried in his back, and his own spear lay nearby. Vandiyadevan moved outside the passage and dragged his friend's limp body out. He took the spear too. Right away, the door began to close on its own. The wall absorbed its secret into itself and stood stolidly in the darkness.

Vandiyadevan realised from the wind that blew in forceful gusts that he had managed to get out of the fortress after all. The canopies of the trees and the ramparts of the fortress all but blocked out the moon, which cast such dim light he could barely see before him. Vandiyadevan hauled Kandamaaran on to his shoulders, and carried his spear. He took a cautious step forward. He felt the ground give way beneath him, and had a sudden sensation of freefall. He stuck the spear into the earth and held on with all his strength, just about managing to regain his balance.

He peered down. In the shade of the trees and in the shadow of the outer wall, he could just about make out a river in spate. He could see the foam and froth that indicated just how rapid the current was. Thank heavens! Karanam thappinaal maranam—one false step, one missed chance, and death was certain. God had saved him.

That evil guard ... but what was the point of cursing him? He was simply obeying his master's orders. The plan must have been to kill Kandamaaran and toss his body into the river. If Vandiyadevan had indeed slipped, the two of them would have met the very fate that had been intended for his friend. Even on the off chance that Vandiyadevan had contrived to swim to safety, he could not possibly have saved Kandamaaran.

Vandiyadevan knew that the Vadavaaru River passed close to the Thanjai fort at one point. This must be that very river. Although the Vadavaaru wasn't particularly full at that time of the year, it was probably at its deepest here. Vandiyadevan tested this by lowering the spear into the water. Even when the spear was all but submerged, he couldn't feel the river bed. Aha! What truly terrible men these were. Well, he had no time to dwell on such things. He had to ensure that both he and Kandamaaran got away from here.

He walked along the riverbank, making sure he did not slip. He carried his friend over one shoulder and the spear in one hand. Kandamaaran grunted and mumbled every now and again, which Vandiyadevan found reassuring. He was alive. That was enough for now. In some time, the wall of the fortress turned away from the river. He could see a dense forest ahead. There were thorns on the ground, which made it hard to walk.

Aha! What was this now? A tree had fallen across the river. It must have been a tall one, uprooted by the force of the water. It stretched up to the halfway point between the two banks. Vandiyadevan stepped on it. The wind and water made the fallen tree sway in place. Its branches and leaves bobbed up and down in the river. The going would have been hard enough with this, but the wind, too, was blowing impossibly hard. It was by sheer force of will that Vandiyadevan reached the other end of the tree. He lowered his spear into the water. Thankfully, this was a shallow patch. He got down into the water carefully and walked forward, negotiating the uneven river bed, the gushing waters and the tearing wind. He could feel his body trembling all the way. Kandamaaran almost slipped off his shoulder several times. When Vandiyadevan got to the other bank, his clothes were drenched up to the waist and carrying his ajanubahu[1] of a friend had exhausted him.

The moment he saw a tree whose foliage would give them some respite from the wind, he set his friend down gently upon the forest floor. He wanted to rest for a while. And also see whether his friend was still alive. What was the point of lugging a corpse through this treacherous path? He might as well do as the guard had planned, and toss Kandamaaran into the current. No! No! His friend was breathing, albeit heavily.

What should he do next? Pull the dagger out of Kandamaaran's back? But that would cause his blood to gush out, and the loss of blood could even kill him. The wound must be tended to and dressed immediately. But it was impossible to do this all by himself. Whom could he recruit to his aid?

He thought of Senthan Amudan. His house and its

garden were by the banks of the Vadavaaru. If his sense of direction was right, the house must be nearby. If he could only get Kandamaaran to Amudan's home, his friend would survive. Yes. He would give this a shot, Vandiyadevan decided.

As he made to lift Kandamaaran, Vandiyadevan was stunned and delighted to see that the latter's eyes were open.

'Kandamaara! Do you recognise me?' he asked.

'Yes, I do. Of course, I do. You are Vallavarayan Vandiyadevan. How could I not recognise such a dear friend? A friend so dear he has just stabbed me in the back?' Kandamaaran said.

Those last words hit Vandiyadevan like a whip.

'Aiyo! Was it I who stabbed you in the back …?' he began, but then a thought struck him and he fell silent.

'No, you didn't stab me. Your knife stroked my back. Ada paavi! It was for your sake that I was rushing back through the secret passage. I was running to find you before Pazhuvettaraiyar's men did. I was trying to make sure that no one harmed you before I got to you. I promised I would find you and recruit you into Chinna Pazhuvettaraiyar's elite army. And how you have betrayed a friend who had your best interests at heart! Is this your idea of friendship? How many times we have sworn to each other that we would always be there for one another, we would always help each other! You've thrown it all away now. I was going to warn you about a great change that is in the offing for Chozha Naadu. Adada! Whom can one trust in this world?' Kandamaaran said, before closing his eyes again. The length and fervour of his speech had drained his strength and robbed him of his consciousness again.

'Couldn't you find anyone more worthy of your trust than the Pazhuvettaraiyar brothers?' Vandiyadevan muttered.

Tears pricked his eyes. Perhaps it was best he hadn't said what he had been about to say. He hoisted Kandamaaran on to his shoulder and resumed his journey.

He could smell a particular fragrance—the scent of flowers that bloomed at night teased his nostrils. Yes, he hadn't been wrong in thinking he was in the vicinity of Senthan Amudan's house. He followed his nose and came to the garden soon enough, but ...

What a sight it was! The garden bore no resemblance to the one he had seen the day before. It was quite like the Ashoka Vanam after Hanuman had wreaked havoc in it, the Madhu Vanam after the Vanaras were done with it.[2] Aha! Pazhuvettaraiyar's men must have come here looking for him, and left the garden in this state. Adada! How much effort Amudan and his mother must have put into tending this nandavanam! And the monsters had laid waste to it all!

Then his thoughts turned to the precarious position in which he himself was. What if there were spies, or even soldiers, lying in wait for him somewhere nearby?

Well, he would just have to deal with them as he had with the guard. Thankfully, his horse was still tied to the tree. How had they spared the horse? Perhaps to serve as bait for Vandiyadevan?

What option did he have? He would have to leave Kandamaaran with the good people of this house, and set off on the horse. He could not afford to let the poor animal slow down until he had got to the safety of Pazhaiyarai.

He trod as softly as he could until he reached the thinnai[3] of the house, where Senthan Amudan was sleeping. Vandiyadevan rapped him on the shoulder to wake him. Amudan woke with a start, and Vandiyadevan clapped a hand over his mouth so he wouldn't scream. Then, he whispered, 'Thambi! You're the only one who can help me now. I've got into a terrible mess. This is my closest friend, the son of Kadambur Sambuvarayar, Kandamaaran. Someone had plunged a dagger into his back. I saw him on my way, and carried him here.'

'Cowardly wretches! They stabbed him in the back! True warriors, I see,' Amudan said. After a pause, he added, 'I'll do my best to look after him. Groups of soldiers have been coming in a steady stream since early evening to look for you. They've destroyed the entire garden. But that doesn't matter, as long as you make your escape. Thankfully, they haven't taken your horse. Go, get on the horse right now and leave!'

'That is the plan. But we must do something to save him.'

'You don't worry your head about that. My mother will know what to do. She's quite the expert at treating such wounds,' Amudan said.

With that, he got to his feet and tapped twice on the door of the cottage. The door opened right away, and his mother appeared at the threshold.

The two of them carried Kandamaaran inside, and laid him gently on the bed. In the light of the night lamp, Senthan Amudan spoke in sign language to his mother, who seemed to understand everything he was conveying. She stared hard at Kandamaaran, and then examined the wound. She went into another room, from where she fetched several herbs and a soft cloth. She looked at the two young men standing before her.

Senthan Amudan held Kandamaaran in a tight grip. Vandiyadevan threw all his strength into pulling out the dagger that had been sticking out of his friend's back all this while. Blood gushed out in a torrent. Kandamaaran screamed from pain even in his unconscious state. Vandiyadevan clapped a hand over his friend's mouth, and Amudan pressed a firm hand against the wound to staunch the flow of blood. His mother placed the herbs against the wound, and bound it with the cloth. Kandamaaran grunted and then began to mumble.

They could hear running feet in the distance.

'Go! Go! Quick!' Amudan said.

Vandiyadevan took the blood-soaked dagger and spear in his hands, and then stopped midway to the door.

'Thambi! Do you have faith in me?' he asked Amudan.

'I have faith in God. I am fond of you. Why do you ask?'

'I need a favour. I'm not sure of the way out from here. I need to get to Pazhaiyarai as fast as I can. I have an important message to deliver to Kundavai Piraatti. Would you accompany me for a while, and show me the road I must take?'

Senthan Amudan turned to his mother and made a series of gestures. She didn't seem surprised. She signalled for him to leave and return, and made signs to indicate that she would look after the wounded man.

Amudan and Vandiyadevan got out of the cottage and mounted the horse, Amudan sitting behind the seasoned rider. Vandiyadevan first got his horse to pad along without making a sound. Once they had ridden for a while, he gave the animal a sharp slap on the side. The horse reared and flew forward.

At that very moment, half a dozen soldiers landed up at the door of the cottage, and began to bang on it.

Amudan's mother opened the door and stood at the threshold.

'We heard a commotion here. What was that?' demanded one of the soldiers.

Amudan's mother babbled unintelligibly.

'What's the point in speaking to this deaf-mute? Let's go inside and search!' another said.

'But she's blocking the way!'

'Where did that flower-seller boy go?'

'Push the oomai[4] aside and go inside!'

Amudan's mother tried to say something in her garbled language. She shouted at them. One of the men made to shove her aside, but she used all her force to push him away and slam the door shut on his face. However, the soldiers pressed against the door, and she wasn't able to draw the bolt. Shouting even louder, she moved aside all of a sudden and let the door fly open.

Three soldiers tumbled to the floor as the door gave way. The others stepped on their fallen comrades to get inside the house.

'He's here!' one of the men yelled.

'Oh, so he's got caught, has he?' another said.

'He might run away! Get him and bind him with chains!' yet another said.

The oomai howled.

'There's a river of blood here!' one of the soldiers gasped.

The oomai held up the lamp and pointed it at the man who was lying on the bed. 'Baeh, baeh, baeh!' she said.

'Ade! This seems to be someone else!'

'Baeh! Baeh!'

'Is he the same man who came here yesterday?'

'Baeh! Baeh!'

'Where is your son?'

'Baeh! Baeh!'

'Oomai piname![5] Shut up now! Ade! Look carefully. Does anyone know what he looks like?'

'This is not he!'

'No, it is!'

'No, not at all!'

'Baeh! Baeh!'

'Whatever it is, this man is a stranger. Lift him! Let's take him!'

'Baeh! Baeh! Baeh! Baeh!'

'Saniyane![6] Keep quiet!'

Four of the men lifted Kandamaaran off the bed.

'Baeh! Baeh! Baeh! Baeh!' Amudan's mother hollered without pause.

'Ade! I can hear something … it sounds like a galloping horse!'

'Half of you carry him, and the rest go and see what is happening outside!'

'No, no! Let all of us run after the horse. This fellow won't go anywhere.'

They dropped Kandamaaran to the ground and ran out of the cottage.

'Baebaeh! Baebaeh! Baebaeh!' Amudan's mother set up a wailing that followed right on their heels.

15

PAZHAIYARAI

Before Vandiyadevan surmounts all manner of difficulties and evades all manner of dangers and arrives at the city of Pazhaiyarai, we invite our readers to come along with us to Pazhaiyarai Padi[1] and grace that beautiful haven.

Let us stop on the southern bank of the Arisilaru and look at the city. Adada! Does the word 'city' do it justice? It is a jewel ornamenting the lovely forehead of Tamizhthaai,[2] a netri chutti studded with emerald, ruby and sapphire stones.

The rivers and streams and ponds and fields are bubbling with the fresh waters of the season. Flowers of various hues bloom in them. The cool shade of the coconut and punnai trees that sing with lushness welcomes us. The decorative kalasams of enormous palaces and mansions whose upper balconies kiss the sky and the golden stupis of temple gopurams dazzle in the sunlight.

Appappa! And how many little towns there are within this grand city known as 'Pazhaiyarai'! Nandipura Vinnagaram, Tiruchatthimutram, Patteesuram, Harichandrapuram, along with their temples, are all accommodated within the capital of the Chozha empire. There are four Shiva temples, one for each direction—Vadathali to the north, Keezhthali to the east, Metrali to the west and Thenthali to the south. There are four army camps where the soldiers reside—Arya Padaiveedu, Puduppadaiveedu, Manappadaiveedu and Bambaippadaiveedu.

And in the centre of all this is the Chozha palace—but is it just one palace? Before Vijayalaya Chozhar's time, it *was* a single palace. But since, new palaces have been built around it so that each prince and princess may have his or her own. Not even a thousand eyes would suffice to take them all in, and not even the creative powers of ten thousand poets would suffice to describe it all.

Sekkizhar Peruman, who was born a couple of centuries after the time in which we find ourselves, sang:

Therin meviya sezhumani veedigal sirandu
Paaril neediya perumaiser padi Pazhaiyarai

With streets of shining, pearl-like stones crowded with chariots
The padi that claims the greatest fame of all on earth is Pazhaiyarai

If this was how he sang of this city two hundred years after its most glorious period, one can imagine how splendid it must have been in Sundara Chozhar's time.

Yet, the first time we visit this grand old town, we are not destined to see it at its very best. We haven't had the fortune of arriving when Sundara Chozha Chakravarti was ruling from the palace of Pazhaiyarai.

After the emperor's ill health took him to Thanjai, the number of important visitors from across the seas—kings of other countries, royal envoys and ministers—has dwindled.

Among the soldiers who once lived in the army camps, half are now in the battlefield at Eezham, cementing the reputation of Tamilians for courage. Most of the others are either stationed in the northern frontier or at Madurai. So, the army camps are now largely populated by women, children and the elderly.

The Velakkaara Army once inhabited Mazhavarpadi, but all its members have left along with their families to protect the king in Thanjai, and therefore that part of the city is a ghost town. We are greeted by closed doors and locked homes.

The ministers, councillors and officials charged with royal duties are in Thanjaipuri with their families too.

Even so, there is no lack of footfall and ebullience in the streets of Pazhaiyarai when we visit. Those who now walk these roads are largely temple architects, sculptors, devotees of Shiva, singers of the Devaram, palace employees, temple priests and tourists who are here for a darshan of the temple idol or to watch the fun at the Tiruvizha.

There is a sense of festivity in the air today. Men and women and children seem to be in a mood for celebration. They are dressed in their very best clothes and are sporting their most precious jewellery. Little groups of people gather at the street corners to watch actors sing and dance. What is going on? Let's look closely. Yes! It appears a lot of people are dressed as Lord Krishna and as the gopis and the cowherds of Brindavan.

Look, there is a Krishna carrying a mountain! And a Devaraja, Lord Indra, worshipping at his feet.

Here, look, another Krishna who is being worshipped by a Brahma wearing a mask with four faces, one for each direction!

Aha! Now, it's all clear. Today is Sri Jayanti, the day Krishna was born. The people of this city are celebrating this day with much pomp and splendour.

We see scenes of Uriyadi Tirunaal[3] playing out as we walk. The merrymakers are splashing turmeric water about.

There is a great crowd assembled at the Nandipura Vinnagara Vishnu temple. Oh, what do we have here?

Kanden kanden kanden
Kannukiniyana kanden!

I saw, I saw, I saw,
I saw sweet sights!

Who is singing these lines? The voice sounds familiar! Ah, it is our old friend Azhvarkadiyaan Nambi himself! There is a cluster of people around him. Some appear to be lost in devotion. Others are giggling, mocking the man. One feels anxious that Nambi's staff might split a skull in two if this goes on much longer.

There is a commotion now, right outside the Vinnagara temple. The chariots and palanquins that were waiting by the corner of the street are being brought to the entrance of the temple. A group of regal women appears at the temple door. They must belong to a noble family, surely?

Yes. Yes! Who should they be but the women of the royal household, Pazhaiyarai palace itself! The queens and princesses are leaving the temple. Heading the procession is Sembiyan Mahadevi, popularly known as 'Periya Piraatti'. Born into the Mazhavarayar clan, she was the queen consort of Kandaradityar, the epitome of Shiva bhakti. Look at the glow on her face, aged as she is and wearing the garb of widowhood! Why, she radiates divinity!

Right behind her is Queen Kalyani, born into the Vaidumbarayar clan, wife of Arinjaya Chozhar. Aha! Can one find words to describe such loveliness? Even in her twilight years, her face sparkles with beauty. How stunning she must have been in her youth, we wonder. It should be no surprise that her son Sundara Chozhar is famed for his good looks.

Next in line is the other wife of Sundara Chozhar, Seraman's daughter Parantakan Devi.

She is followed by … ah, are these the celestial apsaras descended to earth? Kundavai Piraatti, Vanathi and the other young princesses we last met by the banks of the Arisilaru now make their appearance at the temple gate.

Since Vijayalayan's time, the members of the Chozha dynasty have been worshipping Shiva with his consort Durga as their kuladeivam—the deity of the clan. But they had no quarrel with Tirumaal, Lord Vishnu. It appears they have come to worship at the Perumaal temple, since it is the day of Krishna's birth.

Just as Periya Piraatti Sembiyan Mahadevi was getting into her palanquin, Azhvarkadiyaan's voice fell upon her ears. There's a fair chance he had started singing louder at the time to this very end. She asked that he be brought before her.

Azhvarkadiyaar arrived, all deference before Periya Piraatti.

'Tirumalai! It's been a while since I saw you. Were you on a pilgrimage of the sthalams?' she asked.

'Indeed, thaaye, I was. Tirupati, Kanchi, Veeranarayanapuram … I have been to numerous kshetrams and had a darshan of those deities. Everywhere I went, I saw and heard the most wondrous things.'

'Come to the palace tomorrow and tell me all about these wondrous things.'

'No, amma. I'm afraid I have to leave tonight.'

'In that case, come this evening to see me.'

'I will, thaaye. Your wish is my command. It is my good fortune that you grant me an audience.'

Kundavai pointed at Azhvarkadiyaar and said something to her companions, who broke into peals of laughter.

Azhvarkadiyaar turned in that direction, as if to learn what had amused them so much. Kundavai Piraatti's eyes appeared to speak to him. Azhvarkadiyaar nodded and bowed, signalling that he understood her silent message.

Sembiyan Mahadevi's palace was at the very centre of the cluster of palaces that made up the royal compound. In the sabha mandapam was a throne made of gold and studded with navaratna stones, and this was where the matriarch sat. This incredible lady, an heir to Karaikkaal Ammaiyaar and Tilagavatiyaar in her devotion to Lord Shiva, wore a sari of plain white silk, vibhuti on her forehead, a rudraksha mala and no other ornament. She was living proof that one could be the very embodiment of austerity and renunciation, even while surrounded by the greatest of comforts and the grandest of treasures. She needed no crown or jewellery; her regal mien and radiant face evidenced that she had been born into a royal clan and married into another—she was a queen among queens. It should be no surprise that every member of the Chozha royal family, without exception, saw her as his or her very god, and never went against her wishes.

But lately, there had been some turmoil. The respect instilled by the combination of fear and devotion that deities inspire seemed to have evaporated in one case.

The son of this queen among women, Madurantaka Devar, had gone not only against his mother's wishes but also her express orders, and married into the Pazhuvettaraiyar family. Sembiyan Mahadevi had also heard that he had designs on the Chozha throne, and this troubled her greatly.

It was customary for the mutram and sabha mandapam of Sembiyan Mahadevi's palace to teem with sculptors and Devaram singers. Shiva devotees and Tamil poets from faraway lands came in droves, and left with rewards from the matriarch. Temple priests arrived with prasadam from their pujas to Lord Shiva.

Today, we see sculptors and devotees from the towns of Tirumadhukundram (Virudaachalam), Thenkurangaaduthurai, Tirumazhapadi and a few others, assembled to petition that their Shiva temples be rebuilt with stone. They had brought sketches of building plans, and in some cases scale models, to make their cases before the queen.

Having granted the first two requests, Periya Piraatti asked when the representative from Mazhapadi came forward, 'Mazhapadi? Which Mazhapadi is this?'

'The very Mazhapadi where the deity who called out to Sundaramurti Swamigal resides!' said the representative.

'I have never heard this story.'

'When Sundaramurti Swamigal was on a pilgrimage to the various sthalams of Chozha Naadu, it so happened he had to cross a river,' the man began. 'As he got into the river, he heard a voice call, "Sundaram! Have you forgotten me?" Sundaramurti was startled. He recognised the voice of his lord.

'He turned to his disciples and asked, "Is there a Shiva temple in the vicinity?"

'"Yes, indeed, swami! The Shiva temple of Mazhapadi village is nestled among those konnai trees," one of the disciples replied.

'Sundaramurti hurried to the spot. There was a little temple hidden away amidst the foliage of the konnai trees. Sundaramurti looked at the deity. His heart melted. What compassion the lord had shown him, he thought, in calling out to him as he was about to leave without stopping to worship. "Swami! Could I ever forget you? What a terrible question to ask! Whom would I think of if not you?" he wanted to ask. He sang from the very bottom of his heart:

Ponnaar meniyane
Pulitholai araikasaithu
Minnaar senjadaimel
Milir konrai anindavane!
Minne maamaniye
Mazhapadiyul maanikkame!
Anne unnaiyallaal
Ini yaarai ninaikkene?

He of the golden skin
Who wears a tiger's skin at his waist,

He of the lightning-like locks
Ornamented with a garland of konrai flowers,
He who shines like the most precious diamond,
He who glows like a ruby in Mazhapadi,
If not for he who is my mother,[4]
Whom could I think of?

'Thaaye! That temple remains a little one, hidden amidst the konnai trees. We are here to beg that you grant us leave, and the means, to expand this temple.'

'As you wish,' said Sembiyan Mahadevi.

Azhvarkadiyaar and a companion had made their way to the front of the crowd and were observing the proceedings carefully.

16

'THIS IS ALL HER DOING!'

Now, a sculptor descended from the great artists who had carved out the rock sculptures at Mamallapuram[1] stepped forward. He had brought a scale model to demonstrate a new way of assembling temple stones that he had engineered. He presented this to the maharani.

Periya Piraatti looked at it in wonder, and then turned to the man who had accompanied Azhvarkadiyaan and said, 'Bhattare! Do you see how beautiful and intelligent this architectural model is? I find myself thinking all the important Shiva sthalams in Tamizhagam must be rebuilt in this manner!'

'Thaaye! If that is your wish, what obstacle could come in your way? We could rebuild all the Shiva temples whose praise has been sung in the Devaram in this manner. That way, devotees will recognise them as sthalams that find a place in the Devaram the moment they see the architecture,' Eesaanya Shiva Bhattar said.

'Yes, yes! The padis about which Appar and Gnanasambandar and Sundaramurti have composed songs must be treasured and preserved. The sthalams that have been hallowed by their feet and consecrated by their devotional songs must certainly be rebuilt so that the vimana gopurams soar to the skies, just as the sculptor has shown. These are the only two wishes I have. I often worry that they may go unrealised. If only my nayagar, my lord and master, had not gone westwards and made an untimely journey to the holy feet of God, if only he had lived a little longer … all my wishes would have come true …'

'But why do you have any doubts about this, thaaye? The emperor has ordered that everything you wish must be carried out in the exact manner that you wish it, hasn't he? Both his sons are ready to put your plans into action almost before you make them. Everything they do, their first thought is whether it would be in accordance with your wishes. When this is the case …'

'Even so, I find myself rather jaded. I hear all sorts of things. I believe some people are unhappy about the treasury being emptied to carry out the devotional tasks that I commission. They demand why so many temples must be erected for Lord Shiva. It doesn't bother me so much when other people talk, but I believe the prince at Kanchi himself …'

Before Periya Piraatti could complete her sentence, Azhvarkadiyaan took a step forward and said, 'Thaaye! I am among those who ask that question.'

The maharani looked at him in some surprise. Everyone else stared at Azhvarkadiyaan, their expressions indicating their shock at his temerity.

Azhvarkadiyaan went on in a voice that shook with anger, 'Annaye![2] My heart burns. My soul boils with rage. Can such injustice be allowed to prevail? You who are an avataram on earth of Dharma Devathai herself, the very Goddess of Justice, can you allow such a travesty of that justice?'

Eesaanya Shiva Bhattar interceded at this point. 'Maharani,' he said, 'my brother is given to such rants. He acts like a man possessed. Please do us the grace of forgiving him.'

Back in the day, Shaivites and Vaishnavites had not split into different subcastes. Shiva devotees and militant Vaishnavites could crop up in the same family. The same priest could officiate at both Shiva and Vishnu temples. Eesaanya Shiva Bhattar was among those broadminded priests. Tirumalaiappan was his cousin. They shared great mutual affection. Eesaanya Bhattar, as the older of the two, felt obliged to petition the maharani on behalf of his cousin after the latter's outburst.

Periya Piraatti smiled and said, 'Tirumalai! Calm down. What is this grave injustice to which you allude?'

'Amma! How many temples to celebrate Shiva, who roams like a ghost through cremation grounds, wears ash and skulls, eats human flesh and carries a begging bowl? How many maada gopurams, how many stone temples? Is there not *one* temple befitting of the personage of Lord Vishnu, protector of the entire world? If you won't build a new one, can you not sanction reinforcements to the existing ones at the very least?' wailed Tirumalaiappan.

'Amma! The lord who dances so the entire world may rejoice needs a stage and hall and a small sabha and a sabha of gold and a maada gopuram and a palace with high walls. But surely, Tirumaal, who sleeps through the day and night, doesn't need much more than an alcove? A dark place where he won't be disturbed by daylight or lamp light? What use could he possibly have for maada gopurams and stone temples?' Eesaanya Bhattar asked.

'Anna! It is the Perumaal who sleeps through the day and night who saved the very earth. He is the one who pushed Mahabali down to the netherworld!' said Azhvarkadiyaan.

'And this great saviour of the earth wasn't able to find our Shiva Peruman's feet despite digging his way into that very netherworld, was he?' Eesaanya Bhattar said.

'If your Shivan is of such mammoth proportions, what is the point of building temples for him? He would only bang his head against the roof if he tried to enter the temple! The walls would have to be broken to accommodate him!' Azhvarkadiyaan said.

Periya Piraatti laughed and said, 'Enough. Will

the two of you put a stop to this fight? Tirumalai! What is it you want exactly? Who has decreed that no temple must be built to honour Lord Vishnu? Which vinnagaram would you like me to sanction reinforcements for? Why can't you ask politely?'

'Ammani! Your father-in-law, who is famed in all three worlds, was the great Parantaka Chakravarti. I had gone to Veeranarayanapuram, which is named for his epithet. Veeranarayana Perumal stays up day and night, not so much as blinking his eyes, in order to safeguard the Veeranarayana Lake, which is as large as an ocean. The temple dedicated to such a selfless God is in a shambles. The brick walls are falling apart. If they were to give way, the shore of the lake would give way too, and a hundred villages would be submerged. You must have the Veeranarayana Perumaal temple rebuilt in stone,' said Azhvarkadiyaan.

'As you wish. We will certainly undertake this task. But tell me in detail what exactly must be done. Let the others leave,' said the matriarch of the Chozha clan.

Having understood they had been dismissed, everyone including Eesaanya Shiva Bhattar filed out, leaving her alone with Azhvarkadiyaan.

Sembiyan Mahadevi lowered her voice and asked, 'Tirumalai! To which places did you go? What exactly did you see? What have you heard? Tell me every single thing, down to the last detail! I know you have something of great importance to say or you wouldn't have interrupted me, would you?'

'Yes, thaaye, I have a great many things of much importance to tell you. But I would have waited my turn, if only you hadn't mentioned the prince at Kanchi. I had to interrupt. Who knows how many of those who had assembled here are true to you, and how many are spies? Terrible things are going on in this land. One can't predict who will betray whom, or who will prove to be a traitor,' said Tirumalaiappan.

Periya Piraatti let out a heavy sigh. 'Things have come to such a pass that people of the same family, with blood ties and deep bonds, can no longer trust each other. Everyone is suspicious of everyone else. How much faith Aditya Karikalan once had in me! He showered me with a hundred times the love he did his own mother, showed me a hundred times the respect! And now the very same prince doubts my intentions. Tirumalai! If only I had gone with my nayagar! If only I had left this earth when he did! But he had ordered that I must not be allowed to perish with him. He left behind instructions for me, and said I must fulfil the tasks which he had begun. What an unfortunate wretch I am!' she said.

'Amma! Your lord and master was a great soul with the gift of foresight. He ruled this land like King Janaka. Who could have dreamt of such a blessing in Kalyug? It is the good fortune of Chozha Naadu that he ordered that you stay behind. He has left you the responsibility of ensuring that this empire, which has grown and prospered manifold over the last century, is not ruptured by fraternal and familial dispute. It is only you who can prevent this disaster.'

'I don't have the confidence that I can. My own son no longer obeys me. How can I demand that the offspring of other people follow my orders in such a situation? Well ... let's not talk of this now. You mentioned spies ... who could possibly send spies here? Do you think Prince Aditya Karikalan might have? Has his mistrust of me reached such heights that he would go to this extent?' asked the matriarch.

'I heard with my own two ears, thaaye! Or I would never have believed that Prince Aditya Karikalar nursed suspicions against you ...'

'What did you hear, Tirumalai? What did you hear with your own two ears?'

'I heard what they spoke as they sat by one of the stone temples of Mamallapuram ...'

'Whom do you mean by "they"?'

'Prince Aditya Karikalar, Tirukkovalur Malayaman and Pallava Parthibendran. The three of them were speaking. I hid inside the temple in the dark of the night and eavesdropped on them. Malayaman and Parthibendran had worked themselves into a frenzy. They said the two Pazhuvettaraiyars and your son Madurantaka Devar have come up with a conspiracy and all but imprisoned the emperor. Malayaman said this could not have happened without your consent. The others agreed. Parthibendran said they must raise an army and wage war against Thanjavur to free the emperor from the clutches of the Pazhuvettaraiyar brothers. The others agreed with this too. But the crown prince said one last effort must be made to rescue the emperor from Thanjai before resorting to war. They decided to write the chakravarti an olai and send it through a messenger. I found out who that messenger was. He is no ordinary envoy. He is a man of incredible bravery and skill, with a gift for thinking on his feet. He could double as messenger and spy with ease. If I sneak in through the wooden blinds, he gets one up on me by sneaking in through the kolam dots. He tried to extract information from me without revealing a thing himself. The astrologer of Kudandai did his best to make him talk, but that didn't work either. I heard that he eventually went to Thanjavur and handed over the olai to the emperor ...'

'And what happened after? What did the emperor say in reply?'

'Apparently he said he would write a response to the prince the next day. But before then, the Pazhuvettaraiyars began to suspect that the messenger was not what he seemed and had an escort of soldiers accompany him everywhere. I believe he managed to give all their guards the slip and somehow make his escape.'

'Then, he must be a man of incredible skill indeed. There can be no doubt. What did you do after? After leaving Kanchipuram, I mean?'

'I intended to come straight here, stopping only at

Veeranarayanapuram for a darshan of Perumaal. But by His grace, it so happened I learnt a secret of great magnitude ...'

'What is that? Yet another secret?'

'Yes, thaaye! I heard that a grand feast was being organised at the Kadambur Sambuvarayar palace that night. Periya Pazhuvettaraiyar attended this feast. The Ilaiya Rani's palanquin came along with his procession.'

'Tirumalai! This is all her doing! The peril that threatens Chozha Naadu right now is all because of that girl. Were you able to meet her and speak to her?'

'No, I couldn't, amma. I couldn't! It was to fulfil your command that I took that she-snake into my family and raised her as a sister for so very many years! How many years I looked after her! How many places I visited to learn the pasurams and came back and taught her! My heart feels as if it is on fire when I think back to all this. After becoming the queen of Periya Pazhuvettaraiyar, she won't deign to grant me an audience!'

'What is the use of upsetting yourself over that? That is how this world works. What one thinks and hopes will happen, what eventually happens ... the two are never the same ... Well, so then what happened at Kadambur?'

'I thought the occupant of the palanquin was Nandini, and went to Kadambur with the intention of either meeting her or—at the very least—sending her an olai to warn her. I took an enormous risk and climbed the wall of the Kadambur palace. That is where I learnt that astonishing secret, the one of great magnitude that I mentioned ...'

'Tirumalai! You do this all the time. You build the suspense to a crescendo, without revealing what the matter is. Tell me now, that is this astonishing secret of great magnitude?'

'Please forgive me, thaaye. I can barely bring myself to speak of it. It ... the occupant of the palanquin was not the Pazhuvoor Ilaiya Rani. We had all been under the impression that Pazhuvettaraiyar takes his Ilaiya Rani along everywhere he goes ... we have been grossly mistaken on that account.'

'Then who is Pazhuvettaraiyar taking along with him? Does that old man's lust know no bounds?'

'The occupant of the palanquin was not a woman, thaaye!'

'What do you mean? What kind of man would hide and ride in a palanquin?!'

'Please forgive me, amma! But the person hiding in the palanquin was none other than your son, Madurantaka Devar.'

Sembiyan Mahadevi was stunned into silence for some time.

Then, she mumbled to herself, 'Good God! Such enormous punishment for a past crime!'

Azhvarkadiyaan Nambi filled her in on what had occurred at the midnight conference at the Sambuvarayar palace. One cannot find words to describe the pain this caused the matriarch.

'Aiyo! My son! I tried to raise you as a devotee of Shiva, a Shiva gnana selvan! Is this my reward? Must it be you who brings such infamy to the Chozha dynasty? Must it be you who wreaks such destruction on the Chozha empire?' she lamented.

After some time, she turned to Azhvarkadiyaan and said, 'Tirumalai! Come see me again before you leave. I'll speak to Kundavai in the meantime and see what we can do to avert this terrible danger.'

'Thaaye! It would be prudent not to discuss this even with the princess.'

'Why? Do you suspect her too?'

'Isn't it but natural that I should? Isn't she the beloved sister of Aditya Karikalan?'

'So ...? Tirumalai! You could tell me the sun rises in the west and sets in the east, and I might believe you. You could insist that your Tirumaal is a greater god than Shiva Peruman, and I might yet believe you. But if you were to accuse Kundavai of wrongdoing, I would never believe you. The day she was born, the royal midwife brought me the baby and placed her in my two arms. Since that day, I have raised her. I have raised her with more love and care than the son I birthed. She sees me as her own mother and father put together, and has never shown me anything but the greatest love and respect ...'

'Amma! Let me ask you this one thing—did Kundavai Devi tell you that she has been to meet the astrologer of Kudandai?'

'No. What of it?'

'Did she tell you that she met a young man from the Vaanar clan at the astrologer's house, and again later by the banks of the Arisilaru?'

'No. What line of questioning is this? What do you intend to prove?'

'Only that the princess is keeping a secret from you. The young man to whom I referred just now is in fact the messenger Aditya Karikalar has sent. It wouldn't be wrong to call him a spy.'

'Tirumalai! All this doesn't matter to me. If Kundavai is keeping something from me, there must be a good reason for it. I would rather die than nurse suspicions against her,' said the queen consort of Shiva Gnana Kandaradityar.

'Aiyayo! May such a thing never come to pass! May your faith be founded. The princess has sent for me. I will convey that you wish to see her,' said Tirumalai.

17

THE DELINQUENT SPY

Two thousand years ago, the Chozha king Karikaal Peruvalaththaan had the banks raised on both sides of the Kaveri. For centuries after him, the banks were maintained well. They kept the waters of the river in check. Eventually, the power of the Chozhas waned. The Pandiyas, Pallavas, Kalappaalars and Vaanars grew in strength. Around this time, with her guardian gone, the Kaveri began to breach her banks. A grand breach could even cause the course of the river to change, so that Pazhangaveri[1] became Pudukaveri[2]. When such a drastic change occurred, the river bed would either be emptied of water and turn into fertile agricultural land, or stagnate with residual waters and give way to a lake on which the waters danced like the waves of the ocean.

Towards the south of the Chozha palace, bordering Pazhaiyarai, was one such lake. The Chozha rulers had dug the bed and widened its breadth, so that the natural lake became an artificial creation, always full. This served as a protective barrier for the palace, particularly for the antapurams where the royal women lived. It was no mean feat to enter these waters. Only visitors with close ties to the royal family were permitted on the ferry.

The lovely private gardens of the palace antapurams flourished around the lake. The women of these antapurams could roam the gardens at any time of day or night, with no fear for their safety. They would gather together and laugh without inhibition, they would turn into dancing peacocks and singing koels. Sometimes, they would swim in the lake, or go boating.

It was a Chozha custom for every ascendant to the throne to build a new palace for himself when he came to power. His predecessor's palace would be left to the late king's wives and other offspring.

Within the Pazhaiyarai palace complex, the most impressive, beautiful and regal of the dwellings—after Sembiyan Mahadevi's, of course—was Kundavai Piraatti's. It had been, after all, the residence of Sundara Chozhar for as long as he had ruled from Pazhaiyarai. Once he shifted base to Thanjai, Kundavai became the mistress of his Pazhaiyarai home.

The back garden of this palace was a haven. It housed banyan trees whose upper reaches kissed the skies, and tiny flowering plants too. Creepers wound their way around the trees and served to form natural arbours.

Kundavai and her companion princesses would spend most of their evenings in this garden. Sometimes, they would sit in a large group and gossip. At other times, they would split into their little cliques of two or three and share confidences.

Of late, Kundavai and Vanathi had taken to going away by themselves. That day, they were seated on a vine swing fashioned from the banyan tree. The garden echoed with the chirping of birds and the cheerful laughter of young women. But Kundavai and Vanathi played no part in the general mirth. They didn't seem much pleased by the happiness of the others, either. Were they deep in conversation, then? No, not really.

A woman started singing from one of the arbours. It was Sri Jayanti, and so she sang a song about Lord Krishna. This was the setting—the notes of a flute floated down of an evening, and distressed a woman who was in love with Krishna, reminding her as it did of him. As she spoke of her sadness, a parrot in a tree offered her solace. This was how the song went:

Woman:

Vedanai seidhidum vennilavil—ingu
Veenan evan kuzhal oodhugiraan?
Naadan illaa indha bedhai thannai
Nalindhidudhal enna punniyamo?

In the moonlight that stirs sadness
Which cruel man sees fit to play this flute?
What pleasure or gain could he feel in
Inflicting sorrow upon this bereaved soul?

Parrot:

Vaanamum veyyamum inburume—aiyan
Vaaimaduthoothum kuzhalisaidhaan
Maane undhanai varuththidumo—indha
Maanilam kaanaa pudumai amma!

The earth, the sky and all creatures within
Find joy in the magic of the music he makes
For these notes to inflict sorrow upon you,
Is a wonder this world has never seen, my doe!

Woman:

Poovaiye! Undhanai potriduven—nalla
Punnaimalar koidhu choottiduven—endhan
Aavi kulaindhidum velaiyile—oru
Aarudhal koora nee vandhaniyo?

My lovely flower bud, I'm grateful to you,
I'll make garlands of punnai flowers for you,
In this terrible time, when my spirits sink,
You've thought to sit by me and sing for me.

Parrot:

Kattazhagi! Un kaadhalinaal—engal
Kannan padunthuyir solla vanden—unnai
Vittu pirindha naal mudhalai—nalla
Vennaiyum vembai kasandadhenban!

My beauty! I've come to tell you our Krishna
Is so tormented by his love for you that
Since the very day he left your side, he says
He tastes in fresh butter the bitterness of neem.

Having listened carefully to the lyrics of the latter half, Kundavai turned to her friend the moment the song ended and said, 'Some god this Sentamizh Naadu[3] has found in Krishna! If a god spends all his time gorging on butter and romping about with women, who's to take care of important matters?'

When Vanathi offered no reply, Kundavai asked, 'To what is this stony silence owed, di? Have the notes of Krishna's flute done a number on you too?'

'Akka! What did you ask?'

'What did I ask! What has made such claims on your attention?'

'Nothing. My attention is entirely on you.'

'Adi kalli![4] Why are you lying to me? Your mind is not here, I know. And, I also know to where it has wandered off. Shall I tell you?'

'If you know, please do.'

'I know all too well. It's gone to the battlefield at Eezham. My naïve little brother is there, isn't he? Your mind is preoccupied with schemes—what magic dust can you sprinkle on him to entice him, it wonders.'

'What you said is half true, Akka! My mind does wander off to Eezham every now and again. But it isn't preoccupied with schemes of enticement or magic dust. It worries over his various tribulations—how much suffering he must undergo on the battlefield! How many wounds must have punctured his divine skin! Where does he sleep? What does he eat? And while he faces paucity of the most basic amenities there, here I am, eating the choicest meals, wearing the prettiest clothes, sleeping on the softest mattresses … It hurts. If only I had wings, I would fly to Lanka this very moment!'

'And what will you do there? Make his life even more stressful?'

'Not on my life. Just as Subhadra did for Arjuna and Satyabhama for Krishna, I will ride his chariot into war. When arrows are aimed at him, I will offer up my chest instead …'

'And you think he will stand by and watch as you offer up your chest to these arrows, do you?'

'If he does not wish me to be his charioteer, I will stay back at the army camp and await his return every evening. I will dress his wounds and make his bed. I will cook for him and serve him his meals. I will play the veena so his pain is lulled, and sing him to sleep …'

'None of this can come to pass. Chozha warriors do not take their women to war.'

'Why is that, Akka?'

'They are not daunted by wounds; they are far more scared of women than weapons, really.'

'Why is that, then? What are women going to do to them?'

'Women won't do anything to *them*. But then if exquisite beauties like you were to descend on the battlefield, isn't it likely for the enemy warriors to become besotted with you and come surrender? How will our Chozha heroes display their heroism under such circumstances? Our Chozha dynasty doesn't want to become famous for winning wars using women.'

'Could such a thing be possible? Are our enemy warriors so very foolish as to become besotted with female beauty in the middle of a war?'

'Why not? Adiye, Vanathi! Remember the young man we ran into at the house of the astrologer, and then again by the banks of the Arisilaru?'

'Yes, I do. What about him, now?'

'The moment he saw us all, you remember how he acted as if he was intoxicated?'

'Yes, I do. But you're wrong when you say, "the moment he saw us all, he acted as if he was intoxicated". It was the moment he saw *you*. He didn't so much as glance at the rest of us, Akka!'

'Vanathi! You're lying! Are you trying to flatter me?'

'Not at all. I have something to ask you. Will you answer me truthfully?'

'Why don't you give it a shot?'

'Why did that young man come to your mind just now?'

'You've become rather cheeky, girl! Why, what is wrong with his coming to mind?'

'Who said it was wrong? Not I! Why, it's quite natural. I, too, have been worried about what became of that young man after.'

'Why should that bother you?'

'Why not, Akka? Once one meets someone, if one remembers him every now and again, isn't it but natural to wonder what became of him?'

'Natural, she says! We shouldn't let our minds get distracted and disturbed like this. I ... Vanathi! Do you hear parai drums? What does that voice say? Let's listen carefully!'

Indeed, the sound of parai drums being beaten came from a far-off street, punctuated by a crier shouting something. When the two women listened carefully, they heard him say:

'A spy from an enemy land entered the Thanjavur fort by presenting an imitation signet ring, discovered royal secrets and ran away! He mortally wounded two men before he made his escape! A young man, powerfully built. He is Indrajit's[5] equal in sorcery and scheming! His name is Vallavarayan Vandiyadevan. Anyone who shelters him will be sentenced to death. Anyone who captures him will be rewarded with a thousand gold coins. The Thalapathi of the Thanjai fort, Pazhuvettaraiyar Kalantaka Kandar, has issued these strict orders!'

The moment the crier finished, the parai beat a 'Tham! Tham! Thadathadatham!'

Kundavai Devi's body trembled.

A maid came running up just then, and said, 'Devi! A Veera Vaishnavar by the name of Azhvarkadiyaar is here to see you. He says it is urgent.'

'I'll be right there,' said Kundavai, and jumped off the vine.

18

THE DISCONTENT OF THE PEOPLE

Once Azhvarkadiyaan had left the sannidhi of the matriarch of the Chozha clan, he'd headed towards the palace of Ilaiya Piraatti. The sights he saw on the streets of Pazhaiyarai filled him with joy. How much energy these people had thrown into celebrating the Tirunaal on which Krishna was born! There was no doubt Vaishnavism would stand tall and spread through Chozha Naadu. There were several reasons Shaivism exercised the greater influence of the two. Over the last century, Chozha emperors had peppered the land with new Shiva temples. The devaram songs of the Moovar[1] had gained fame through recitation in these temples. The chariot festivals of these temples were conducted with pomp and ceremony. And yet, Tirumaal had not been sidelined. The ninth avatar of Vishnu had captured the hearts of the people of this land.

The leelas of the lord in the various places where he had lived—Gokulam, Brindavan, Mathura—had entranced them. Ammamma! How many Bhagavatam troupes were here, enacting those scenes! How many street plays were being staged! And how many innovative costumes and disguises the actors wore to honour the protagonists of these stories! The number of theatre groups arriving in the city had gone up through the day. The crowd had become denser and more impassioned too. Groups were still streaming in from the villages around Pazhaiyarai.

A theatre troupe comprising Vasudeva, Devaki, Krishna, Balarama and Kansa now appeared. Their song and dance and dialogue appeared to outshine those of the other groups, and they were drawing people's attention. Azhvarkadiyaan stopped to watch.

Krishna and Kansa were engaged in an argument. The actor dressed as Krishna was a little boy, who lisped his words as he listed out Kansa's various crimes and then called in his high-pitched voice, 'Come, fight me if you will!'

Kansa retorted in a stentorian voice, 'Ade! Krishna! Your spells and sorcery won't work on me any longer. I'm going to kill you now. I'm going to kill your brother Balarama too. And your father Vasudeva, I'll kill him too. And you see that man standing there, with sandalwood paste smeared in the shape of naamams all over his body? I'm going to kill that Veera Vaishnavan too!'

The moment he said this, the onlookers turned to our man Azhvarkadiyaan and began to laugh. The actors playing Krishna and Balarama turned to look at him too. Many members of the crowd broke away to come near him so they could point and laugh.

Tirumalai Nambi found himself in a fury. He was tempted to run amok through the crowd with the staff in his hand doing all the damage it could. Most importantly, he must use it to break Kansa's skull. But there would be little point in going at his head with the staff. He was wearing a vesham, wooden mask painted with a ferocious moustache and false teeth, and culminating in a crown that covered his own. Overall, it wasn't the best idea to use the staff on this crowd, Tirumalai decided and made his way out of that spot.

The voice of that Kansa—albeit that the actor had made it a point to speak in as deep and thunderous a tone as he could for the character—Azhvarkadiyaan was sure he had heard that voice before. But where? He thought about it as he walked down the street.

Suddenly, a change came over the people. The cheerful crowds were beginning to dissipate. As he went closer to the palace, people seemed more forlorn. What had happened? Why were the groups gathered to watch the festivities disbanding in such a hurry? The notes of musical instruments and the voices of actors were dying down too ...

Instead, small groups of people had gathered at street corners and seemed to be talking animatedly, sharing some sort of secret. As soon as they had traded these secrets, they went on their way, looking around cautiously. Doors had begun to bang shut.

Oh, it was clear now. The parai that had caused Kundavai Piraatti to tremble, and the warning about the spy that the town crier was belting out ... Azhvarkadiyaan heard them now, and realised why the celebrations had been cut short. How effectively this had ruined the mood of the townspeople! Everyone was darting suspicious looks at those walking alone. Some looked askance at Azhvarkadiyaan himself before hurrying away from him.

He could guess what the impromptu gatherings by the street corners were about too. The bits of conversation he overheard served as proof. They were expressing their rage at the dictatorship the Pazhuvettaraiyars had established. It was but natural that the residents of Pazhaiyarai and its surrounding towns would hold a grudge against the powerful brothers.

It was they who had robbed the capital of the emperor of whom the poets sang:

Pazhaiyarai nagar Sundara Chozharai
Yaavaroppar thonnilaththe!

Who in this world could be the equal
Of Sundara Chozhar of Pazhaiyarai Nagar?

Since Sundara Chozhar had been installed in Thanjai, the glory of Pazhaiyarai had been in decline. If only the emperor had been in town on this special day, how much grander the celebrations of Krishna Jayanti would have been! The various theatre troupes that were staging scenes from Krishna's life would have made their way through all the main streets and eventually landed up in the courtyard of the palace. The actors and singers and dancers and musicians and poets would have been richly rewarded by the emperor. Such a massive crowd would have poured into the city as for an observer to think everyone in the entire empire was in Pazhaiyarai today! The stalls and shops would have raked in a hundred times the money they were now, and been a thousand times as busy. When Venugopala Swami's idol was taken out for its procession at night from the Nandipura Vinnagara temple, the streets would have swarmed with men engaged in mock fighting, with silambam sticks and metal weapons. The temple procession would have been accompanied by song and dance and cymbals and drums.

The people of Pazhaiyarai had been deprived of all this because of the Pazhuvettaraiyar brothers. They nursed another, even mightier grouse against the two men. Their beloved Arulmozhi Varmar was in Lanka, waging battle across the seas to ward off the danger posed to Chozha Naadu from that land. Ten thousand soldiers from the city had accompanied him, leaving behind their families. They were in an alien land with a harsh landscape, negotiating brutal forests and treacherous mountains. And they were there to safeguard the honour of Tamizhagam. The prince of Kodumbalur had led the vanguard and taken a spear to his chest for this very reason. Scores of other warriors had fought to the very end like him, and died a heroic death like him, for this very reason. Prince Arulmozhi Devar had promised not to return until he could fly the tiger flag from the palace of Eezham and ensure that the souls of the departed were at rest.

Meanwhile, what were the Pazhuvettaraiyar brothers doing? They were trying to stinge over provisions—food and clothing and weapons—meant for our war heroes! What a travesty of governance this was! The granaries of the Thanjavur fortress were bursting with grains from the year's harvest. For whose plates were those grains destined, if not those of our men in need? The gold and jewellery, bounty from a hundred years of battle, were lying in the treasury. For whose use were those destined, if not that of our men in need? Of what use was anything that could alleviate the suffering of our men in Eezham if it wasn't going to be used for the purpose? What did the Pazhuvettaraiyars intend to do with it all anyway? Carry it to Yamaloka with them?

Tirumalai Nambi was aware of the rumblings of discontent among the people of Chozha Naadu. It was only natural for that discontent to reach its peak in Pazhaiyarai, where the wives and children and parents of the ten thousand men who had gone to war lived.

Under the circumstances, the people of Pazhaiyarai

were seething at the untimely announcement about the delinquent spy and the dire warning issued by the town crier. It became yet another excuse to vent their rage at the Pazhuvettaraiyars. 'Spy!' they said. What nonsense! Which kingdom could have sent a spy to Thanjavur! The tiger flag flew over the entire swathe of land from Kumarimunai to Vadapennai. Which enemy king was powerful enough or foolhardy enough to send a spy to Chozha Naadu? The Pazhuvettaraiyars labelled anyone whom they wanted out of the way a 'spy', so that they could throw him in their dungeons or kill him outright, without following due procedure and consulting the town panchayats. Everyone knew this, and yet everyone was afraid to get involved. It was likely that the so-called spy was innocent, but who could take on the Pazhuvettaraiyars? They were practically ruling the land. Who could call them out on this injustice? It was best to stay out of it all. But how unscrupulous they were!

Azhvarkadiyaan used his keen hearing and his sharp insight to learn that this was what the people of Pazhaiyarai were mumbling to each other as they met by the roadside. All the way to Kundavai Devi's palace, he wondered in what catastrophe this discontent among the people would culminate.

Ilaiya Piraatti had always liked speaking to Azhvarkadiyaan about current affairs across the various kingdoms. He always had news for her, since it was his wont to traverse the lands visiting Vishnu temples.

She was keen to hear everything he had to say. She was just as keen to hear the Azhvar pasurams[2] he had searched out and learnt on these journeys. Tirumalai Nambi could rest assured that he would receive a warm welcome from her. Her face would glow as she asked after him and his loved ones, and then she would engage him in conversation about the religious concepts in those pasurams.

However, it struck Azhvarkadiyaan that the princess' countenance and demeanour were both lacklustre that day. She seemed distracted. When she spoke, she was uncharacteristically flustered, her sentences disjointed.

'Tirumalai! What is the matter? What brings you here?' she asked.

'Nothing is the matter as such, thaaye. I thought you had asked me to come here as usual, so we could talk about the goings-on. It appears I was mistaken. Please forgive me for the intrusion. I will take my leave.'

'No. No! Stay a while. I *did* ask you to come by …'

'Thaaye! It slipped my mind. I had been to pay my respects to Periya Piraatti. She said she wanted to have a word with you on some matter of importance. She has asked me to convey that she would like to see you …'

'Of course. I had been planning to go there anyway. All right … tell me, where have you been on this tour?'

'From Kumari[3] in the south to Venkatam[4] in the North.'

'And what are people speaking of in these places?'

'They speak of the greatness of the Chozha dynasty. They say it won't be long before the empire stretches to the shores of the Ganga, and why, even the Himodgiri, the Himalayas ...'

'What else?'

'They speak highly of the heroism and valour of the Pazhuvettaraiyars. They say the reason the Chozha empire is in such a position of security is entirely due to the Pazhuvoor lords ...'

'Enough about that. What else?'

'They speak with fondness of both your brothers. Particularly of Prince Arulmozhi Varmar. How does one describe the love and affection they have for him?'

'That comes as no surprise. Tell me, is there talk of anything else?'

'They want to know why the beloved daughter of the empire has not married yet. Many of them asked me personally.'

'And what did you reply?'

'I said a prince worthy of our Ilaiya Piraatti is yet to be born ...'

'What next! Such a man is yet to be born, you say! Well, if that is the case, by the time he is of marriageable age, I'll be an old hag. Anyway, that's enough about me, Tirumalai. Is there talk of something else?'

'Whyever not? People are rather stunned by the fact that our Devar,[5] who was all prepared to enter the life of an ascetic Shiva devotee, has suddenly decided to go and marry ...'

'And your darling sister ... the one whom you said would be an icon of devotion and go the way of Andal ... how is she now?'

'What could she lack for, thaaye! She rules the roost in Pazhuvettaraiyar's palace, as his wife and queen.'

'In Pazhuvettaraiyar's palace alone? Why, I've heard that she rules the roost across the entire Chozha empire.'

'There are those who say that too, thaaye. But let's not go into that. Why talk of her on this auspicious day? When you mentioned Andal, something came to my mind. I had gone to Sriviliputhur.[6] I learnt some of Bhattar Piraan Vishnu Siddhar's poems. Listen to this, amma! It is about the day Krishna was born:

Vanna maadangalsoozh Tirukottiyur
Kannan Kesavan nambi pirandinil
Ennei sunnam edhir edhir thoovi
Kannan mutram kalandanar aayitre!

Oduvaar vizhuvaar ugandaalippaar
Naaduvaar nampiraan engutraan enbaar
Paaduvargalum palparai kotta ninru
Aaduvaargalum aayitru aaipaadiye!

In Tirukottiyur, ensconced in colourful maadams[7],
On the day of the birth of Lord Krishna—Kannan, Kesavan
The courtyard of the temple is strewn with oil and chunna

As devotees celebrate the honour bestowed upon them,
this holy birth.

They run, they fall, they sing, they shout in joy.
They search him out, ask where their lord has gone.
As they crowd the streets, singing and dancing,
Ayarpadi[8] *has been recreated here.*

'Thaaye, today this may be said of our Pazhaiyarai too. It is as if Ayarpadi has been recreated here. The people are celebrating Sri Jayanti with so much joy!'

'Yes, yes, that's as may be. But some time ago, there was an announcement in another vein altogether. What is that all about, Tirumalai?'

Tirumalai had been anticipating this question. 'Some spy, they say. He escaped, they say. They have announced a bounty on his head. They will reward anyone who captures him. Why would I pay any attention to this, thaaye? What would I know of such matters?'

'What would *you* know, you ask? You have no clue at all who this spy might be? No suspicions?'

'There is someone I suspect. But it would be dangerous to speak of this out loud. People were staring at me even as I made my way here. What if someone drags me to the dungeon ...?'

'Who has the courage to catch hold of you and drag you anywhere! If you want to tell me what's on your mind, please do. You don't suspect that *I* will drag you to the dungeon, do you?'

'Krishna, Krishna! What are you saying! I have no such suspicion. I saw a strapping young man in Veeranarayanapuram. He said he was going to Thanjavur, but would not say why. He had a barrage of questions for me …'

'How did he look?' asked Kundavai anxiously.

'He had a regal bearing. Appeared to be from a noble family. A handsome young man, well-built. He seemed highly motivated to make something of himself. And also struck me as having something of a temper.'

'You said he had a barrage of questions for you … What did he ask?'

'He asked about the condition of the emperor's health. He also asked about the succession to the crown. He wanted to know about the prince who is leading the war effort in Lanka. I heard that he later asked the same questions of the astrologer of Kudandai.'

'Aha! He had come to the astrologer's house, had he?'

'Oh, yes, I remember now. I believe he barged in on you at the astrologer's house … thankfully, it appears he did not recognise you.'

'Oh … so it is as I thought …'

'What did you think, thaaye?'

'That this angry young man was asking for trouble … that he would soon find himself in a dangerous situation …'

'It is indeed as you thought. I suspect he is the spy. He must be the one on whose head the Pazhuvettaraiyars have placed a bounty.'

'Tirumalai! Will you do me a favour?'

'Your wish is my command, thaaye!'

'If you happen to meet this young man sometime …'

'Shall I hand him in and claim my reward?'

'No, no! Don't! Bring him straight to me. I have some important business with him.'

Azhvarkadiyaan made a show of staring in great surprise at Kundavai Piraatti. Then, he said, 'There will be no need of that, thaaye. I won't have to go in search of him and bring him here. He will come in search of you himself.'

19

EESANYA SHIVA BHATTAR

Having met the princess, Azhvarkadiyaan went to visit his cousin Eesanya Shiva Bhattar. The latter's house was a stone's throw from the Vada Metrali Shiva temple, not more than half a kaadham from the palace. This short trip offered, nevertheless, a view of the immense dimensions of the erstwhile capital and its various attractions.

Azhvarkadiyaan noticed that the Krishna Jayanti celebrations had wound down. When he passed through the residential sections of the city, he observed groups of women speaking angrily amongst themselves at street corners. All of them had seen a husband or a son off to the Eezham war, each wearing a smile on her face as she threw a garland of vanji flowers around his neck. Every home in the padaiveedus could claim a martyr in the family, from the many wars waged by the Chozhas over the years. It was these women who were now expressing their discontent. Again,

Tirumalai wondered in what calamity all this would culminate.

Night had fallen by the time he reached the Vada Metrali temple, which had been immortalised in song by Appar Peruman. Back in his time, Jain devotees had raised manmade hills around the temple, and dug out muzhais—caves—where Digambaras could meditate. As if to commemorate this and remind us of this past, a town called Muzhaiyur still stands near Pazhaiyarai.

When Appar arrived at Pazhaiyarai, having heard of the greatness of this sthalam, he could not find the temple. Being a realised soul with powers of perception superior to those of other humans, he divined that the temple had been buried under the Jain caves. Troubled by this development, he approached the king who governed Chozha Naadu as a representative of the Pallavas and petitioned him to intervene. The king had part of the cave complex demolished. The Shiva temple over which the caves had been built was slowly unearthed. Overjoyed, Appar composed a devotional song.

Eventually, the temple was fortified with stone by the Chozha emperors, and its premises enlarged. But it remained surrounded by the caves, which served as walls on three sides. Unlike most temples, which have four entrances—one in each cardinal direction—this one had a single one. Building other entrances would have entailed the demolition of the entire cave complex.

It would be a short walk to Eesanya Shiva Bhattar's house if Azhvarkadiyaan went through the temple courtyard. The other option was a circuitous route. Azhvarkadiyaan was thus forced to set foot in a Shaivite temple in order to visit his brother without exhausting himself. He noticed a group of devotees standing in the sannidhi. As he went closer, he realised they were members of the theatre troupe he had seen earlier, with its young Krishna and Balarama.

Aha! What has brought them to this temple? he wondered.

Before he could steer his train of thought to its destination, Eesanya Shiva Bhattar hurried out of the temple. He took Azhvarkadiyaan by the hand and all but dragged him back out on to the street.

'Anna! What are you doing?' Azhvarkadiyaan asked.

'I'm about to tell you, Tirumalai! From here on out, our relationship will only exist outside the temple. You're a padidan, a heretic. An apostate who denies the existence of Shiva. Don't you dare step into this temple! Do I make myself clear? I've borne enough from you. I've been tolerant all this while. But the way you spoke before Periya Maharani today was the last straw. You can come home if you like, and fill your fat stomach before you go on your way. But don't ever desecrate this temple with your presence. If you so much as step into this temple again, I'll turn into Chandeshwara Nayanar!'[1]

With that, Eesanya Shiva Bhattar took his cousin by the scruff of his neck and shoved him away before slamming the temple door shut.

'Anna! Anna!' Tirumalai shouted.

Ignoring him, Eesanya Shiva Bhattar drew the bolt from the other side and marched away.

'Oho! So, this is how it's going to be, is it?' Azhvarkadiyaan mumbled to himself.

He stood there for a while. Then, he walked around the temple a few times, caves and all, searching for an entry point. He took care to go towards the left, since going around the temple in the other direction would amount to a pradarshanam, a ritual circle of the temple and therefore worship of the deity. There was no way into the temple except through the entrance his cousin had just shut.

He gave up and took the long route to Eesanya Shiva Bhattar's home. His sister-in-law was fond of him. She enjoyed his witticisms and his stories from the journeys on which he had been. Today, he was in full form. He ate his fill of prasadam from the Shiva temple, and then went out to lie down on the thinnai.

A scene that had unfolded before him on the day he was walking by the Kudamurutti riverbank now came to mind. Having heard the hooves of galloping horses, he had snuck into a bamboo thicket to see what the fuss was about.

The horse that appeared first seemed to be in some sort of frenzy and was completely drenched—from water or sweat, one couldn't quite tell. A young man was seated on the horse, and seemed to be tied to the saddle. He wore an expression of terror, but one could sense a vein of steely determination through his fear. He was being chased by four or five horsemen, armed with spears. It seemed likely he would be caught fairly soon. One of the soldiers raised his spear and aimed it as if to hit the runaway horse, but was stopped by another.

The first rider had to duck under a thick canopy formed by the bamboo stems. As his horse charged under, his hair wound itself around a stray branch. With his hair caught behind him and his torso bound to a flying horse, the young man would have been in a grim situation if not for his pursuers bounding ahead to stop his horse.

The soldiers seemed both stunned and furious when they saw who the rider was. They asked him something, to which he stammered a response.

Azhvarkadiyaan could make out the question, 'Where is he? Where is he?' The soldiers repeated it as they surrounded the young man.

The latter finally said, 'He's been washed away with the current! He fell into the river!' and then broke into sobs.

The soldiers took him and the horse into custody, and left.

Back then, Tirumalaiappan couldn't tell what the incident had been about, but now the pieces seemed to be coming together.

In the middle of all this, the street theatre troupe came to mind. He thought particularly of the body language, appearance and voice of the actor playing Kansa. He thought he could place the voice that had sounded strangely familiar.

Eesanya Shiva Bhattar returned home after officiating in the final puja of the night. He saw Azhvarkadiyaan fast asleep on the thinnai of the house.

'Tirumalai! Tirumalai!' he called angrily.

Tirumalai made as if he was dead to the world.

The Bhattar pushed the door open to enter his home, and then slammed it shut. Tirumalai could make out the sounds of argument from inside. The cousin was involved in an altercation with his wife over Tirumalai's presence.

When he woke in the morning, Eesanya Shiva Bhattar approached Tirumalai and asked, 'When are you leaving on your next jaunt?'

'Once you cool down, Anna,' Tirumalai replied.

'Don't ever call me "Anna" again. From this day forward, I'm not your older brother, and you're not my thambi. You're a blasphemer, an ignoramus, a sandaalan, the lowest of the low ...'

The Bhattar's wife felt sorry for Tirumalai and intervened. 'Why are you cursing him like this? What has he said now that he hasn't been saying all this while? It is you whose devotion to Shiva has become extreme. You're the one who's being intolerant,' she said.

'You know nothing. Do you know how he spoke to Periya Maharani yesterday? "Why build temples for Shiva, who wanders through cremation grounds smearing ash from corpses on his body?" he asked. I felt like someone had poured molten lead into my ears. I heard Maharani couldn't sleep all night because of what he said!'

'He won't say such things again. I'll speak to him, and reason with him. He'll see the error of his ways if one uses the right words and right manner.'

'Right words, right manner, she says. I'm done with all words and all manner of ties with him. Let him go to Rameswaram right away. Let him pray to the same Shiva lingam to which Rama prayed to wash off his sins. Let that be his penance. I won't so much as look at him until he does this,' his cousin fumed.

Tirumalai's lips itched to give it back. But unless he stayed silent, his plans would go awry. He held himself back with a tremendous effort.

The Bhattar's wife took up for Tirumalai again. 'What of it? He'll go to Rameswaram if you ask him to. Let's go with him too. We have remained childless all these years. Perhaps it is because of the sins we've committed in our previous births. We should pray there. Tirumalai, what do you say? Shall we all go to Rameswaram?'

Shiva Bhattar glared at them both, and stormed his way back into the house.

In a while, he returned, seeming more composed.

He sat down and spoke to Tirumalai calmly, 'Thambi, the elders said "Kobam paapam sandaalam"—Anger is the root cause of all evil. And yet, I let myself get carried away. You're not too upset, are you?'

'Not at all,' Azhvarkadiyaan replied.

'In that case, you stay right here. I'll finish the noon prayer and come back home. There are some important matters on which I'd like your opinion. You will stay back, won't you? You won't go away anywhere, will you?' he asked.

'I won't go anywhere, Anna. I have no plans of leaving you yet,' Tirumalai said.

The Bhattar went on his way.

Azhvarkadiyaan muttered to himself, 'So that's how it's going to be, eh?', and then slipped out of the house without so much as telling his sister-in-law he was off. He went around the Vada Metrali temple a couple of times. Every time he heard a sound, he pressed himself against the wall and stayed hidden.

His hopes were not in vain. There was some cautious activity at the entrance of one of the Jain caves. First, Eesanya Shiva Bhattar peered out, looked in all three remaining directions and then stepped out. Behind him was another man. Aha! Who was this? His face was hidden. His physique suggested he might be the man who had worn Kansa's disguise. Who could it be? Azhvarkadiyaan would have to find out. Oho! So this was why his cousin had put on a show of rage and enacted this drama, was it?

The two men who had been in the cave went ahead. Azhvarkadiyaan followed them, darting into hiding spots every now and again.

Soon, they reached the shore of the lake, the very lake that had been expanded to protect the Chozha royal palace, in which the waters rose like waves in the ocean. But this shore was far west of the palace.

Azhvarkadiyaan dove into one of the many dense thickets by the shore, stuck his head between two branches and looked on.

A boat was swaying gently on the waves. It appeared to be a royal boat. The boatman was standing on the shore. On seeing the Bhattar and his companion, the boatman drew his craft towards the shore. The two men got in. As the boatman released the rope and rowed out into the waters, the Bhattar's companion turned towards the shore.

Azhvarkadiyaan could see his face clearly. It didn't come as a surprise. He had been expecting this all along. It was the very same strapping young man he had met at Veeranarayanapuram and Kollidam, and eventually in the coracle. There was no doubt he was the one who had played Kansa too.

Where were they headed now? He would have to find out. Well, rather, he would have to see whether he had guessed correctly.

Among the many mansions on a wide street, belonging to important courtiers of the palace, was a locked one at the very end. It belonged to Sundara

Chozhar's prime minister, Aniruddha Brahmarayar. The minister was away in Madurai, the capital of Pandiya Naadu, putting the new administration in place. His family had preceded him to Thanjavur. And so, his Pazhaiyarai mansion was under lock and key.

Azhvarkadiyaan arrived at this maaligai. The guards bowed reverentially to him. He requested them to open the door, and they obeyed right away. Then, he ordered them to lock him inside, which they did. Azhvarkadiyaan passed all three courtyards of the mansion and arrived at the back garden. A little path wound its way through the trees and shrubs. Azhvarkadiyaan followed this path and took a short cut to Kundavai Devi's royal garden. He secreted himself away in an alcove, and prepared for a long wait.

This would not go in vain.

A scene would play itself before him that begged immortalisation through the quill of a great poet like Kalidasa.

The boat appeared on the shore. Eesanya Shiva Bhattar and Vandiyadevan disembarked, and then mounted the steps to the garden.

Ilaiya Piraatti Kundavai Devi was seated on a marble bench in the garden, some distance from the stairs.

As the men reached the top of the steps, she rose from her seat.

Vandiyadevan looked up at that very moment, into the princess' lovely face.

He stood frozen.

A flowering branch stretched delicately between him and Kundavai Devi, bearing young leaves. A butterfly with vibrantly coloured wings alighted on this branch, and Kundavai was momentarily distracted, inclining her face gently to study the butterfly.

But there was no distracting Vandiyadevan. He couldn't tear his eyes away from Kundavai's face.

The waves rose and fell in the lake.

And then the universe came to a standstill.

Birds stopped singing.

The earth stopped spinning.

Space was frozen.

An age passed, and another, and another.

20

OF WHIRLPOOLS AND WOMEN'S EYES

The Adipurush, the First Man created by God, lived by the side of the mountain. The caves gave him shelter from the rain and wind. The trees gave him fruits to eat. The wild animals trembled at the sight of him. He lived free as a bird and wanted for nothing. Yet, he felt a void within, a lack he could not quite place, a thirst he could not quite define. It plagued him ceaselessly, a troublesome underlayer to everything he did, an ache that begged for reprieve, a magnetic force that drew him towards itself. His heart yearned for a particular kind of fulfilment, some joy he was yet to experience. It invaded his daydreams and nightmares. He searched for it everywhere, to no effect.

His heart hurt. When would he see that unique creation, that fruit of a boundless imagination that had been born just for him, when would he reach the core of that magnetic force that curled itself around him?

When God created Adipurush, he also created Adistree, the First Woman. She lived on the other side of the mountain. She had food to eat and water to drink and a home in the caves. She appeared to lack for nothing. But she was burning within. Her heart was consumed by a fire whose tongues of flame scorched her ceaselessly. A strange power had wrapped itself around her, and was pulling her in some direction. She couldn't tell where it was coming from or where it was taking her.

Between the Adipurush and Adistree towered the higher regions of the mountain, ensuring they did not meet.

But on one hot summer's day, a natural forest fire began to rage. It tore through the vegetation and formed a ring around the mountain. As it raced through the trees and the grass, the Adipurush and Adistree fled to the top of the mountain. It was on the summit that they first laid eyes on each other. Their locked eyes would never unlock. They forgot the forest fire. They forgot what had driven them to the mountain top. They forgot hunger, and they forgot thirst. They knew at that moment that their entire lives had been leading up to this encounter. They realised this was the force that had taken over their bodies, this was the want that had been gnawing at them. They knew, too, that each would fill the void in the other. They were together now, and no power in this world or any other could ever separate them.

As the Lord of Creation Brahma watched this enchanting scene, he sat back, satisfied that his task was now complete.

Our Vallavarayan Vandiyadevan and Ilaiya Piraatti Kundavai Devi now stood as the Adipurush and Adistree had in the beginning of time. They had been born for this moment, for this encounter, their hearts said. But unlike the Adipurush and Adistree, they had led civilised lives, right? And so, they found themselves unable to forget the difference in social status that separated them. They did not give themselves in to emotion, or lose control of their minds and bodies. So, their locked eyes did unlock the very next moment. Each turned to the flowers and trees and butterflies and boats and anything else in the vicinity, just to avoid the other's eyes.

It was only when Eesanya Shiva Bhattar cleared his throat, though, that they remembered they were here on an important mission.

'Is it true that you conveyed to Eesanya Shiva Bhattar that you wished to have a private audience with me?' Ilaiya Piraatti asked, forcing a stern tone into her voice.

The note of authority and severity startled Vandiyadevan.

'Unless I know who you are, how will I answer your question, my lady? I wonder whether perhaps Eesanya Shiva Bhattar has brought me to the wrong place?' he said.

'I wonder, too, whether perhaps that is the case. Whom did you wish to meet?'

'The guiding light of the Chozha clan, the beloved daughter of Emperor Sundara Chozhar, the dear younger sister of Aditya Karikalar, the revered older sister of Arulmozhi Varmar, Ilaiya Piraatti Kundavai Devi is the lady whom I had told Eesanya Shiva Bhattar I wished to meet ...'

Kundavai Piraatti smiled and said, 'It is I who bear, with much difficulty, the weight of all that glory.'

'In which case, that icon of femininity I met at the house of the astrologer of Kudandai and by the Arisilaru riverbank cannot be you, can it?' Vandiyadevan asked.

'Yes, yes! It is I, too, who conducted myself with such disrespect towards you at both those places. You couldn't have expected to run into that uncivilised woman again quite so soon, I'm sure.'

'It isn't quite accurate to say I've run into her *again*, Devi.'

'Why?'

'One can only meet someone again if one has parted from the latter. But you haven't left my mind for a moment ...'

'I didn't quite think wit was the strength of people from Thondai Mandalam.'

'I suppose you think Chozha Naadu has a monopoly on all strengths of the human mind and body.'

'Yes. I must admit I'm guilty of that charge. I suppose you don't like our Chozha Naadu?'

'Why not? I like it well enough. But there are two great perils in this land. The very thought of them terrifies me ...'

'It is true that the swords and spears of our Chozha warriors are perilous weapons. Foreigners would do well to exercise caution when they come here. Particularly when they're working as spies ...'

'Princess! These are not the perils to which I alluded. I, too, carry a sword and spear. I'm well-trained in their use too ...'

'Yes, your aptitude for warfare was made apparent to me that day, on the banks of the Arisilaru. With what force your spear attacked the dead crocodile! All it took was one throw, and all the cotton came spilling out of its body!'

'Ammani! I had no idea that the fearless princesses of Chozha Naadu were mortally afraid of dead crocodiles. Neither was I aware that it was the wont of Chozha warriors to wage war with dead crocodiles. I hurled a spear at the crocodile thinking it was alive. It is neither my fault, nor the fault of my spear that it wasn't.'

'It was the fault of that darned crocodile. It didn't bother to wait until the scion of the superlative Vaanar dynasty saw fit to steer his spear towards it, and died prematurely. That stupid crocodile is entirely deserving of the humiliation of that day. But what, then, were the two perils to which you alluded?'

'The whirlpools that swirl in the waters of Chozha

Naadu after the first flood are perilous. One can never trust those waters. They gave me hell, and all but killed me!'

'How did you get caught in those whirlpools? You strike me as someone who hasn't so much as dipped his feet in water.'

'It isn't quite possible to throw in one's lot with Betaal and then refuse to climb the peepul tree, is it?[1] I threw in my lot with Chozha Naadu, and ended up having to jump into the waters and fight my way out of the vortex of a whirlpool. And that was because of the obstinacy of an idiot boy who was supposed to accompany me to show me the way. Would you believe it, Devi? All this is because that stripling of a boy refused to tell a white lie.'

'You're speaking in riddles. You would do well to speak plainly.'

'I will. I, who arrived as a messenger with the olai from your dear brother, was deemed a spy by the Thalapathi of the Thanjai fort, Chinna Pazhuvettaraiyar, who then put out a call for me to be apprehended and brought before him. I didn't fancy being thrown into prison before my mission was accomplished. So I brought this boy from Thanjai, whose house I'd stayed in, to show me the way out and …'

'In whose house did you stay in Thanjai?'

'The house of a flower seller who lives outside the fort. The lady is an oomai—she's mute.'

'Oho! And her name is …?'

'I don't know the lady's name. But I do know her son's—Senthan Amudan.'

'Ah, it is as I thought. Tell me more.'

'I was riding my horse, along with the boy, headed for Pazhaiyarai. But before we could make a clear getaway, Pazhuvettaraiyar's men were on our trail and fast catching up. As I said, I didn't want to be caught before my mission was accomplished. So as we approached the Kudamurutti River, I told the boy, "I'm going to get down here, thambi! You ride the horse back. They will assume the horseman is me, and give you chase. Once they surround you, they'll realise they've been fooled. If they ask where I am, say I have fallen into the river and drowned." But it seems that boy is descended from Harishchandra[2]. "How can I lie that you have drowned when you haven't?" he asked. So that he wouldn't be compelled to lie, I tied him to the horse and then jumped into the river myself. Ammamma! The whirlpools one finds in the rivers of Chozha Naadu, particularly along the riverbanks! I was sucked into vortex after vortex and it took everything I had to get away. Finally, I latched on to the root of a tree by the riverside and climbed to safety. Devi! Even as I was stuck in one such vortex, nearly suffocating and almost unconscious, what do you think I saw, and what do you imagine I thought?'

'How should I know? Perhaps you were thinking of Gajendra Moksha.'[3]

'No, no; I saw some kayal[4] fish that were caught

just like me, being swirled around the vortex of the whirlpool. And, they reminded me of the eyes of the women of Chozha Naadu. One might even escape from the vortex of a whirlpool. But once one is sucked into the vortex of the eyes of a woman from Chozha Naadu, one has no hope of escape, I thought ...'

'There are those who take pride in accusing women of such things. It is the custom of men to blame their failings on women.'

'And I have faithfully adhered to that custom. How is that wrong?' Vandiyadevan asked.

Suddenly, the melodious notes of a flute wafted down from the palace. This was followed by the 'kin-kinni' of cymbals and the beat of maddalam drums. Then, the lilting voices of young women came in a chorus. They were singing the *aaichiyar kuravai* song from the *Silappadikaram*:

Kanru kunilaa kani udirtha maayavan
Indrunam aanulvarumel avan vaayil
Konrayan theenguzhal kelaamo thozhi!
Kollaiyan saaral kurundositha maayavan
Ellainam aanul varumel avan vaayil
Mullaiyan theenguzhal kelaamo thozhi!

As he who hurled down among wood apples
The demon who came in the disguise of a calf[5]
Descends in our midst today, my friend,
Let us hear the notes of his flute of konrai stems.

As he who stood as a kurundu tree[6]
And sheltered and protected the entire world
Descends in our midst today, my friend,
Let us hear the music from his bamboo stem flute.

Until the song ended, Kundavai and Vandiyadevan stood lost in its words and tune. Then, the cymbals and other instruments took up the beat again, to signal that the dance was about to begin.

'It appears the kuravai koothu is being staged in the palace. I did see a kuravai koothu in the Kadambur palace. But that was of an entirely different genre,' Vandiyadevan said.

'Yes, my friends are learning the kuravai koothu. They will come looking for me soon. Tell me, what is your mission?' Ilaiya Piraatti Kundavai Devi asked.

'Here is my mission. An olai from your brother. I have escaped several perils, guarded it through vortices of whirlpools and women's eyes and brought it to you,' Vandiyadevan said, and brandished the olai.

21

WONDER OF WONDERS

Kundavai Devi took the olai Vandiyadevan was holding out, and read it. Her troubled face, its brows knit from tension, now cleared. She was glowing as she looked up at Vandiyadevan and said, 'You've accomplished your mission, and handed me the olai. What do you intend to do now?'

'My work is done. All I have left to do from here is to return home.'

'Your work is not done. It begins now.'

'I don't understand what you're saying, Devi.'

'The prince has written that you can be trusted with confidential missions, hasn't he? Do you not intend to comply with this undertaking?'

'I did agree to such an undertaking when the prince asked me. But I beg of you not to trust me with such missions.'

'I don't understand your request. Is it among the traditions of the Vaanar clan to agree to an undertaking and then renege on it?'

'It isn't among the traditions of the Vaanar clan to dwell on past glory. Neither is it among our traditions to renege on an undertaking to which one has agreed.'

'Then, why do you hesitate? Is it your hatred of womankind? Or, is it simply that you don't like me?' the princess asked, a smile playing on her lips.

Aha! What a question! Could the ocean not like the moon? If that were the case, why did she reach out with the thousand waves that were her arms and leap high to catch the Purna Chandra, the full moon? Could anyone say the blue sky did not like Bhoomadevi? If that were the case, why did he grow thousands upon thousands of stars to serve as his eyes through the night, just so he could stare at her in their radiance and revel in the sight? Was it possible for a cloud not to like lightning? If that were the case, why did the cloud hold the thunderbolts that strove to tear him apart close to his chest and refuse to let go? Could the bee not like the flower? If that were the case, why did he buzz round and round its petals, finally falling into the lap of the flower from intoxication? Would anyone believe that the moth is not drawn to the flame? If that were the case, why did he give up his own life just to attain the object of his affection? *Devi! Some question you've asked me!* Vandiyadevan wanted to say. *If I did not like you, why would a glance from the corner of your eyes send bolts of lightning through my body? Why would the smile playing at the corner of your lips drive me into delirium?* His heart screamed out the words. But his lips remained motionless.

'Aiya! You have not responded to my question. Perhaps you're thinking, "A brave warrior born into the Vaanar clan cannot stoop to doing the bidding of a *woman*!" When the prince handed you this scroll, did he not tell you what he had written in it?' the princess asked again.

'Devi! I was well aware of the prince's wishes when I left. But I must have begun my journey at an inauspicious hour. I've earned enemies at every stop on my way. I've even made an enemy of my closest friend. There are people baying for my blood in every direction I turn. How can I promise to fulfil any request you might have for me under such circumstances? This is the reason for my hesitation. I can't be the cause for *your* missions to go unaccomplished, for your plans to be ruined.'

'Who are these enemies? Is it all right for me to know?' Kundavai asked anxiously.

'The Pazhuvettaraiyar brothers have set their human hounds loose to hunt me down. My dearest friend, Kandamaaran, believes I plunged a knife in his back in an attempt to kill him. There's a man wearing a Veera Vaishnava guise, who goes by the name Azhvarkadiyaan, and who has been in relentless pursuit of me. The Pazhuvoor Ilaiya Rani Nandini Devi has set a mantravadi on my tracks. I've no idea which of them will get to me when ...'

The encounter he had had with the mantravadi on the night he had managed to escape the river current and swim ashore now came to Vandiyadevan's mind. Since it would be foolish to head for Pazhaiyarai by daylight, he had whiled away the hours in bamboo thickets and plantain groves to stay out of sight. At night, he had walked by the riverbank. Having covered a long distance and exhausted himself, he had come across an old ruin during the third jaamam of the night. It appeared to have been a mandapam of some sort. The moon had shone bright as day on its courtyard, and its rays had lit up some of the inside. He'd crossed over into the recesses of the ruin, found a nook which was sheltered from the light and curled up to sleep. Just as his lids were growing heavy, he had heard the hoot of an owl from close by. It reminded him of the hoot he'd heard at the lata mandapam as he was talking to the Ilaiya Rani of Pazhuvoor. He had sat up with a start. From the darkness of the ruin, two spots of light were staring at him.

Perhaps it would be prudent to leave, he'd thought, and taken a couple of steps. Just then, he had heard footsteps. Someone was stepping into the mandapam from outside. He'd caught hold of a pillar or, rather, the remains of a pillar which had lost most of its bulk to the ravages of time and the weather, and had hidden himself in its shadow. The moon shone on the newcomer.

It was the very mantravadi who had come to meet the Pazhuvoor Rani. The mantravadi was now making straight for the pillar. Vandiyadevan had expected that the man would go past him into the ruin, not realising he was hiding behind the pillar. But the mantravadi, who had padded into the mandapam like a cat until he'd reached the pillar, had let out a bloodcurdling howl as he got close and then wrapped an arm around Vandiyadevan's neck. Choking him, the mantravadi had shouted, 'Take it out! Take out the signet ring and give it to me! If you don't, I'll strangle you to death!'

Vandiyadevan had felt like his neck would break, like his eyes would pop out of their sockets. He was struggling to breathe. But he had steadied his lurching heart and panicking brain and let his body take over. He had held the pillar fast with one arm, lifted a leg and kicked with all his force. The mantravadi yelled in anguish and fell to the floor. At the same time, what was left of the pillar splintered and came crashing down, along with a heap of stones from the roof of the mandapam. A bat flew past, flitting its wings. Vandiyadevan followed the bat out, and set off at a run. He didn't turn back, and didn't stop for breath until he was certain no one was pursuing him.

Even the memory of that night sent a shudder through his body now. Through his terror, he heard Kundavai ask, 'Aiya, how long has it been since you left Kanchi?'

Her voice cleared away the fog of his stupor.

'A week and a day, Devi,' he said.

'It is indeed a wonder of wonders that you have managed to make so many enemies in such a short time. How did you achieve such a unique distinction?'

'That's a long story, Devi.'

'That will not be a problem. You can tell me. It is only after learning the details that I will be able to assign you the task I have for you.'

With this, the princess asked Eesanya Shiva Bhattar to come close and asked softly, 'What kind of person is the boatman?'

'Deaf in both ears. He won't hear even thunder, thaaye.'

'Excellent. Let's get on the boat and go for a ride. I want to listen to the whole story.'

Vandiyadevan was ecstatic. What rare luck this was, to share a boat with the very light of the Chozha dynasty, its goddess in human form? It must have been the prayer and penance of seven whole births that had given him this chance. He would draw out the story for as long as he could once they had got on the boat. He couldn't very well let such a stroke of luck slip out of his grasp, could he?

He was in no hurry, true. But then, from the moment they got on the boat and he began to speak of the incidents at the Kadambur Sambuvarayar palace, Kundavai punctuated every minute with, 'And then? What happened after?', hurrying his narrative along.

As he had sworn to do, Vandiyadevan drew out the story to its last thread. But every reel does come to an end at some point, and he eventually had to arrive at the conclusion. And then, it was time for them to arrive at the shore.

They got off the boat and entered the garden, only to hear the cymbals and musical instruments that signalled that the kuravai koothu was still on. This song from the *Silappadikaaram* was being sung:

Periyavanai maayavanai perulagamellaam
Virikamalavundhiyudai vinnavanai kannum
Tiruvadiyum kaiyum tiruvaayum seyya
Kariyavanai kaanaada kannenna kanne!
Kannimaithu kaanbaar tham kannenna kanne!

He who is so large as for two paces to cover three worlds,[1]
He who works miracles and whose lotus-like navel encompasses those worlds,
He whose divine eyes and holy feet and hands and lips glow red,
He whose body is black as night: Are eyes that do not see him
Fit to be called eyes at all?
Are eyes that blink when they rest upon him
Fit to be called eyes at all?

Madandhaazhu nenjathu Kansanaar vanjam
Kadandaanai nootruvarpaal naatrisaiyum potra
Padarndhaarana muzhanga panchavarku thoothu
Nadandaanai ethaadha naavenna naave!
Narayanavenna naavenna naave!

He who overcame the viciousness and venom
Of Kansa, whose heart is the very seat of ignorance
He who played envoy for the five Pandava brothers[2]

For whom prayers are said by every soul in all four directions:
Is a tongue that won't sing his praise fit to be called a tongue at all?
Is a tongue that won't chant 'Narayana' fit to be called a tongue at all?

Vandiyadevan said, upon hearing this, 'Kansa might be venomous and vicious. But then he did me a great favour yesterday.'

'What is this about? What favour could Kansa have possibly done you?' Ilaiya Piraatti asked.

'It was he who helped me slip into this city,' Vandiyadevan said, and then told her the story.

He had naturally known that Pazhuvettaraiyar's men would have preceded him to Pazhaiyarai. They would be waiting at every entrance gate to the city. The slightest doubt that occurred in any of their minds would see him arrested. How was he to set foot in the city without getting caught?

Nursing these worries, Vandiyadevan had been pacing the riverbank some distance from the city wall, when he'd suddenly spotted a troupe of street theatre actors. He could see Krishna, Balarama and Kansa in the group. Kansa alone wore a wooden mask. An idea had struck Vandiyadevan, and he'd gone up to the group and started a conversation.

During the course of the exchange, he'd casually remarked that the actor playing Kansa wasn't nimble enough on his feet. The actor had taken umbrage and begun to argue with Vandiyadevan. Was our man likely to let go of a fight?

'I can dance far better than you. Want to see?' Vandiyadevan had said, grabbed the mask, worn it and begun to dance.

People who had gathered to watch the argument had egged him on. Some had said he was indeed a better dancer than the actor who was playing Kansa. The actor had stormed off in a huff.

'Let him go. I'll join your group and play Kansa,' Vandiyadevan had told the group, which had been only too happy to oblige.

Once he had finished performing with them through the streets of Pazhaiyarai, where the celebrations were brought to a premature end, he'd done as Aditya Karikalar had told him to and sought out Eesanya Shiva Bhattar at the Vada Metrali temple. The Bhattar had shown him into a cave, bade him stay hidden and then gone to speak in private to Ilaiya Piraatti. He'd returned and told Vandiyadevan that she had agreed to an audience, and then led him to the lake.

Having heard him out, the princess looked at him through eyes brimming with wonder, and said, 'The blessings of the Goddess of Victory Kotravai shine upon the Chozha clan. This is why the Goddess has sent you to me at a time of crisis, to help me out of this.'

'Princess! You are yet to assign me my first task.

You are yet to give me a chance to prove the limits of my capabilities,' Vandiyadevan said.

'You need have no worry on that account. I'm going to assign you a task that is so fraught with danger that all the dangers you have surmounted will seem as nothing.'

Vandiyadevan's heart felt so full it might burst. Joy seeped through his veins. He was ready to cross the seven seas, to take on a thousand lions with his bare hands, to climb to the peak of Mount Meru to pluck the stars out of the sky and bring them to this lady, all to fulfil the duty she was to assign him.

There was a marble arbour in the middle of the garden. Kundavai made her way towards it, followed by the Bhattar and Vandiyadevan. She reached into an alcove within the arbour, from which she retrieved a scroll and a stylus with an ornate gold handle. She wrote on the scroll:

Ponniyin Selva! The moment you see this olai, leave at once and come here. The person who brings the olai will give you the details. You may trust him with all your heart.

She drew a little symbol that resembled an aathi leaf.[3] She extended the scroll towards Vandiyadevan and said, 'You must leave without the slightest delay and take this olai to Eezham. You must deliver this to Prince Arulmozhi Varmar and bring him straight back here with you.'

Waves of delight washed over Vandiyadevan. Of the two wishes he had nursed for the longest time in his heart, one had already been fulfilled. He had had the distinction of meeting the greatest treasure of the Chozha clan, Ilaiya Piraatti Kundavai Devi. And now, thanks to her, his second dream would be realised—he would get to meet Arulmozhi Varmar.

'Devi! You have set me an assignment after my own heart. I will leave right away with the scroll,' Vandiyadevan said, and held out his right hand for the olai.

As Kundavai Devi handed it over, her fingers, soft as kanthal flowers, brushed against Vandiyadevan's hand. His hair stood on end. His heart felt like it would explode. A thousand, no, ten thousand, butterflies fluttered their wings before his eyes. A thousand, ten thousand koels broke into song. Mountains of flowers rained down upon him and bounced off his body.

He looked up and met Kundavai Devi's eyes. His heart ached to tell her things that his mind could not find the words to convey. How could lifeless words find the power to lay bare his soul? It was his eyes that spoke. They came up with poetry that Kalidasa could not have composed. Not even the ancient Tamil poets who had written the *Muththollaayiram*[4] could have come up with the verses that poured out of the whorls of his eyes.

Some distance from the arbour, there was a 'sala-sala' of dried leaves crackling underfoot. Eesanya Bhattar cleared his throat.

Vandiyadevan came back down to earth.

22

THE PARANTAKAR AADURASALAI

The next morning, the Sun God was lighting up the world. As the red rays of the morning sun hit the golden kalasams of the Pazhaiyarai palace, the golden light bounced off them and sparkled. Walking into the city, one would think it was an enchanted town from folklore.

Right before Kundavai Piraatti's palace, an elephant fitted with a howdah and ceremonial jewellery stood waiting. Kundavai and Vanathi appeared at the palace entrance. They proceeded to the steps that had been positioned by the elephant, and mounted them to sit on the howdah.

The elephant headed for the Parantaka Chozha Aadurasalai[1], which was at the very centre of the various army quarters, the earth shaking under his thundering feet. The mahout walked by him, and slowed him down so the women would be more comfortable. The bells of the elephant brought the townspeople to their doors, eager to see what was afoot. Upon realising it was the two princesses out on a ride, they thrilled at the sight, brought their hands together in greeting and bowed low.

The elephant reached the section of town dedicated to the army camps and soldiers' residences. The appearance of these streets was rather different from the rest of town. Plump roosters searched each other out to challenge opponents to a fight. Rams with curled horns surveyed the streets, as if looking for someone to gore, their expressions screaming, 'Who wants to make war?' Hunting dogs had been restrained using either leather leads or metal chains, and harnessed to the pillars of their houses.

Little children were engaged in silambam[2]. As the bamboo sticks clashed against each other, the 'sada sada', 'pada pada' sounds that rose from them carried the echoes of battle.

The outer walls of the houses had been decorated with paintings using saffron sticks and vegetable dyes. They portrayed the leelas of Lord Muruga, the life stories of the Chozha kings and famous incidents from the various wars the gods and kings had waged. Particularly frightening were the depictions of Muruga's destruction of Soorapadman's heads, as each severed one was replaced by another, and of Durga Parameshwari's killing of Mahishasura. On these walls, one could relive scenes from the great wars the Chozha heroes had waged at Thellaru, Thanjai, Kudamookku, Arisilaru, Tiruppurambiyam, Vellur, Takkolam and Sevoor.

The arrival of the elephant triggered a near stampede in these streets. Roosters flapped their wings, 'sada sada', and flew to the roofs, from where they crowed. Children shouted out to each other, and came running with their friends to watch. They quickly knocked on the doors of their own houses to alert the adults inside.

As Kundavai rode down the streets, women and children and the aged assembled at the doors and shouted, 'Long live Ilaiya Piraatti Kundavai Devi!', 'Long live the divine daughter of Sundara Chozhar!' Some followed the elephant, expressing their joy in all the ways they could think of.

Our[3] readers are already aware that this part of town was home to the wives, children and parents of the soldiers who had gone to Lanka. Kundavai Devi had established an aadurasalai for the benefit of these people, using her own income from her landholdings. It was a custom among the Chozhas to honour their ancestors. In Kundavai's lineage, the most celebrated ancestor was Parantaka Chozhar I, her great-grandfather. So, she had named this healing centre 'Parantakar Aadurasalai'. She paid regular visits to the aadurasalai and enquired after the soldiers' families every time, using the opportunity to interact directly with them.

The elephant paused as they neared the aadurasalai. He sat on his giant forelegs and then kneeled so the princesses could get down from their perch. As soon as the mahout led him away, the crowd—particularly the women—descended on the princesses.

'Has the aadurasalai been serving you well? Do the physicians visit you every day and give you the medicines you need?' Kundavai asked.

'Yes, thaaye, yes!' chorused several voices.

'I was being tormented by a racking cough for three months. I took the medicines the physician gave me for a week, and am perfectly fine now,' a woman said.

'Amma! My son fell from a tree and broke his leg. The physician put his leg in a cast and gave him medication for fifteen days. The leg had healed by the time the cast came off. Now, he plays about as before. He's even begun to climb trees again!' another said.

'My mother's eyesight has been on the decline for a while. She came to the aadurasalai for a month, and has been applying the medicines the physicians gave her. She is able to see well again,' a young woman said.

'You see, Vanathi? What ingenious people our Tamizhagam has produced! I wonder how the first physicians figured out which herbs would work on which problems and cure which illnesses,' Kundavai Piraatti marvelled.

'They must have had an extrasensory gift,' Vanathi said, 'A gnana kann, an all-seeing eye.'

'They did come up with all sorts of wonderful treatments. But, unfortunately, they haven't found one that will cure illnesses of the mind such as yours. What can one do?'

'Akka, I don't suffer from any illness of the mind. Would you please do me a favour and stop saying this over and over again? My friends tease me about it constantly, and it's exhausting.'

'You deserve it, di! You've made a mess of my carefree brother's mind, haven't you? Every time he sends someone over from Lanka, he makes it a point to ask after your health,' Ilaiya Piraatti said.

Just then, cries of 'Make way for the physician! Give way to the physician!' were heard.

Bodyguards hustled the crowd to the sides to make a path for the chief physician of the aadurasalai. The elderly man greeted the princesses.

'Vaidiyare![4] You had said there were some special herbs in the forests by Kodikkarai, hadn't you? I sent a young man your way. He can be assigned to fetch them for you. Has he arrived?' Kundavai asked.

'Yes, thaaye! That gem of a boy came with Eesanya Shiva Bhattar. I'll send one of my sons along with him, so he can bring back the herbs from Kodikkarai. I believe your young man has to leave for Lanka. He says he will bring back what I need from there too ...'

'You need herbs from Lanka?' Vanathi asked.

'Yes, thaaye. When Hanuman carried the Sanjivani mountain to Lanka, he flew over the forests by

Kodikkarai. Some of the herbs from the mountain are said to have fallen off and strewn their seeds there. This is why I want those herbs. Now, if just the stray herbs of the Sanjivani are so powerful, imagine what we might be able to procure from the mountain itself! If only I'm able to lay my hands on the herbs I think could be on that mountain, in Lanka, I will be able to cure the emperor ...' said the chief physician.

'May God see that this happens. Where are the two young men now?' Kundavai asked.

'They are inside, amma. They are waiting to take your leave and set off on their journey.'

The chief physician led the princesses inside the aadurasalai. They observed the queues at the thaazhvaarams.[5] The faces of those waiting in the queues lit up as they saw the princess who had established such a wonderful aadurasalai for them, and they greeted her with cries of 'Long live!'

Two men were waiting in the room of the chief physician. Our Vandiyadevan was dressed rather differently, in preparation for his journey to Lanka. Kundavai smiled when she saw him. Vanathi took one look at him, placed him and whispered in Kundavai's ear, 'Akka! This man looks like the one we saw at the astrologer's house!'

'Yes, he does look like that one to me too. He has come to the physician right after meeting the astrologer. Perhaps he has an illness of the mind like yours, who knows?' Kundavai whispered back. She then turned to Vandiyadevan and said, 'Aiya! Are you the one who said he would go all the way to Lanka to fetch the herbs the emperor needs?'

Vandiyadevan's eyes twinkled a message in a secret language that only Kundavai could understand. His mouth, however, said, 'Yes, princess! I'm the one who is going to Lanka. I might even end up meeting the prince there. Would you like me to convey something to him?'

'If you see him, you must certainly convey this message—the Princess of Kodumbalur, Vanathi, has not been keeping well at all. She tends to forget herself and fall into a faint every now and again. If he wants to see the princess before she becomes entirely devoid of her senses, he must leave right away and come here,' Ilaiya Piraatti said.

'I will quote this verbatim, ammani!' Vandiyadevan said, and looked at Vanathi.

The bashfulness triggered by Kundavai's words had infused Vanathi's pretty face with a glow that enhanced her appearance many times over and made her positively lovely. Suppressing the shyness that threatened to overwhelm her, she said, 'Aiya! Please don't say anything of the sort. I beg of you. Please tell him that, thanks to the grace of Ilaiya Piraatti, Kodumbalur Vanathi eats four times a day, and is kept in the greatest of comfort.'

'I will quote this verbatim, ammani!' Vandiyadevan said.

'This is rich! You've told me that you will quote me verbatim, and you've told her that you'll quote her verbatim. Only one of these two messages can speak the truth! How do you intend to …' Kundavai interjected.

'Why is that of consequence, ammani? I will simply quote your statement and her response. Let the prince be the judge of which of them is true,' Vandiyadevan said.

'Very well, but for heaven's sake, don't mix up who said what, and you'll be blessed,' Vanathi said.

Kundavai, not wanting to prolong this exchange, said, 'Vaidiyare! Has the royal scribe[6] sent you the letter that must be given to them?'

'He has, thaaye! I have a letter that says, "*As the bearers of this letter are on a mission to fetch the herbs needed to treat the Chakravarti, all officials along their way are bound to help them in any way they seek.*" Another one was also sent for the attention of the guards of the Kodikkarai lighthouse. I have handed both over to them,' the physician said.

'Right. Then why the delay? Why not leave right away?' Ilaiya Piraatti Kundavai asked.

'Yes, why not leave right away?' Vandiyadevan said.

But it seemed the task of leaving right away was a rather hard one.

The group moved out of the aadurasalai. The elephant sat ready for the princesses to mount. Two stallions steamed and stamped, aching to fly like the wind, as they waited for Vandiyadevan and his companion to get into the saddles.

However, Vandiyadevan was assailed by a battery of doubts every time he turned to go to the horse. Kundavai was prompted to issue warning after warning on various subjects every time she turned to climb on to the howdah. There could be several dangers on the way, and she felt compelled to ensure they knew what to watch out for.

Finally, the princesses mounted the elephant. Vandiyadevan and his companion got on their horses.

But the elephant made no move to leave. Kundavai signalled that those going on a long journey should leave first.

Vandiyadevan turned his horse reluctantly, with no desire to depart. He glanced back one last time at Kundavai Devi, his eyes bright and eager for a sight of that face. Then, as if angry with his horse, he gave the animal a smart whack on the side. The stallion, taking umbrage, took off on all four legs like they were wings. The physician's son had a hard time catching up.

As the elephant began the journey back to the palace, Kundavai sank into her own thoughts. What a bizarre mind and heart she had, she reflected. Why was a heart that had been so unmoved by the greatest of kings and bravest of warriors so affected by this young man who had crossed her path? Why was she so anxious that he must accomplish his mission quickly and make a safe return?

'Akka! What is on your mind?' Vanathi's voice brought Kundavai back to earth.

'Nothing, Vanathi. I was just thinking of the arrogant vibe that young man has. I'm wondering why I chose to send my brother a message through him of all people ...'

'Yes, akka! He seems rather crafty. I'd go so far as to say he's a dangerous thief.'

'What? Why do you say he's a thief?'

'Well, ordinary thieves steal useless things such as gold and silver. But I'm afraid this young man will steal away the very guiding light of the Chozha clan. You won't give space for that, will you?' Vanathi asked.

'Adi, kalli[7]! Do you think I'm cut from the same cloth as you? Nothing of that sort will happen,' Kundavai said.

The elephant hadn't gone far when the princesses saw a large group of women waiting by the side of the road. Asking the mahout to stop, Kundavai Devi called out to them. 'Why are you gathered in a group? Is there something you want to say?' she asked.

One of the women stepped forward and said, 'Thaaye! We haven't had any news of our men who are fighting at the Lankan front. It appears the decree from Thanjavur is that food should not be shipped to them from here? How will starving men wage war, amma?'

'There is no cause for you to worry. The food they need is being sent from the port of Mamallapuram. Do you think your prince will follow whatever the men who run Thanjavur decree? Will he look on uselessly while his men starve?' Ilaiya Piraatti said.

At any other time, Kundavai would have dismounted and spoken to the women, offering them solace and reassurance. But she felt disturbed and restless that day, and longed for solitude.

The elephant headed for the palace.

23

MAMALLAPURAM

We now wish to take our readers to Mamallapuram, with which they are already familiar.

Over three hundred years have passed since Mahendra Pallavar and Mamalla Narasimhar turned this port city into a dreamscape by commissioning the marvellous sculptures they did. The changes that have occurred in the interim are rather disheartening. The glory of the city has faded now.

The palaces and grand residences have fallen to ruin. Crowds no longer throng the streets and port as they once did. Trade is no longer brisk and booming. The enormous warehouses and mountains of goods, newly imported or awaiting export, now only exist in memory.

Once upon a time, the sea had carved out a natural canal by making inroads into the land. This canal was deep enough for large ships to sail right up to the port. Over time, silt has settled into the canal and made it a shallow channel which can only be accessed by small boats. Ships and good carriers are forced to drop anchor further out. Wares that they bring or wait to carry must be loaded on to the smaller craft for transport to and from the land.

It must be said, though, that Mamallapuram has made a few gains through these three centuries. Most striking of these is the stone temple by the shore that immediately captivates our eyes and hearts. Unlike the temples that were carved from the hillside in the time of Mahendran and Mamallan, this temple has been built from blocks of stone that were transported here for the purpose. It stands like a beautiful crown on the head of Samudra Raja, the Ocean King. Adada! How does one find words to describe the expertise with which this temple has been sculpted and structured?

There is another temple, a Vinnagara[1] where the Lord of the Three Worlds Vishnu, known here as Thalasayana Perumal, reclines on his snake-bed. This was commissioned by Parameshwara Pallavan, to whom Shaivism and Vaishnavism were as his two eyes. Tirumangai Azhvar had visited this temple, had a darshan of the Thalasayana Perumal and composed devotional songs that were suffused with emotion. The following pasuram tells us that even in his time, the Pallava empire was flourishing and that Mamallapuram was a port of enormous economic importance:

Pulankol nidhikuvaiyodu
Puzhaikkai makalitrinamum

Nalangol navamani kuvaiyum
Kalangal iyangum mallai
Kadal mallai thalasayanam
Valangol manaththaravarai
Valangol en mada nenje!

In Mallai, where enormous ships
Carrying rare gems of flawless cut
Wait for their turn to approach,
In Mallai, famed for its wealth
Which lies in mounds on its streets,
The Lord lies reclining as
Devotees gather, firm in their faith.
Oh my foolish heart, worship.
Worship these devotees, worship their faith.

In the century following Tirumangai Azhvar's time, the sun began to set on the Pallava empire. Kanchi, which was known as a centre of scholarship, lost its sheen. Mallai, the Mamallapuram known for its waiting ships and wealth in mounds, lost its prosperity from trade.

Yet, the sculptures which had written Tamizhagam into history continued to serve as an indelible source of pride to this land. The scenes that had been carved on rock faces and the chariots and temples that had been hewn from the hills were as resplendent as they had been three hundred years ago. And so, there were more tourists than traders, more people who had come to gawk at these sculptures than bearers and barterers of goods in Sundara Chozhar's time.

Now, a chariot comes flying through these streets. It is drawn by two handsome stallions, and crafted opulently, its roof plated with gold. The richness of the horses' ornaments and grandeur of the chariot, which shines like a second sun in the light of the gloaming, tell us that only royalty could be riding it.

Yes, seated in its cavernous interior are three men with claim to blue blood. One among them is that bravest of warriors, the heir of Sundara Chozhar, Aditya Karikalan. He had gone to war when he was barely past childhood, and notched up a list of achievements with which one would be hard put to compete. In the final showdown against the Pandiyas, he had felled Madurai Veerapandiyan and earned the epithet 'Veerapandiyan Thalai Konda Koparakesari'—The Lion of the Royal Clan Who Beheaded Veerapandiyan.

It was after Veerapandiyan had ascended to the heavens and Pandiya Naadu had been annexed by the Chozhas that Sundara Chozhar took ill. In order to announce that his successor would be Aditya Karikalan, he organised a Yuvarajya Pattabhishekam, declaring his oldest son Crown Prince. With this, Aditya Karikalan was authorised to issue royal decrees and grants on stone tablets signed with his name.

Aditya Karikalan headed for the northern front soon after, to free Thondai Mandalam and Irattai Mandalam from the clutches of Kannara Devan. He chased the armies from Irattai Mandalam to the north of Vada Pennai, and distinguished himself greatly on several battlefields. He was keen to further his gains on the northern front, but this would entail bolstering the army. He stationed himself in Kanchi to facilitate this. The army had no shortage of enlistments, and weapons needed for warfare were being forged, when the Pazhuvettaraiyars threw a spanner in the works. They insisted that efforts on the northern front would have to be halted until the war in Lanka was over.

Other disturbing rumours reached Aditya Karikalan too. He'd learnt that food and other supplies were not being sent from Chozha Naadu to the armies at Eezham. Our braveheart Aditya Karikalan's brave heart was now throbbing with pain.

For about three hundred years before and after our story plays out, heroes of the stature of those about whom we read in our epics were born of the womb of Tamizh Thaai, men who were the equal of Bheema and Arjuna, Bhishma and Drona, Ghatotkacha and Abhimanyu. Their brave deeds would stun those who saw them play out or heard the stories after. Every victory they won on the battlefield further broadened their shoulders, strengthened their arms, bolstered their spirits and whetted their appetites. Elderly men could uproot mountains and hold them above their heads. Children could fly through space and pluck the stars out of the sky.

Two such heroes were Aditya Karikalan's companions on the chariot ride.

One of them was Tirukkovaloor Malayaman. The

Malayamanaadu over which he ruled was known as 'Malaadu' or 'Milaadu' for short. So, he had been given the title 'Milaadudaiyar'. The second wife of Sundara Chozhar, Vaanamahadevi, was his beloved daughter, which made him Aditya Karikalan's grandfather. In age and wisdom, one might compare him to the patriarch of the Kauravas, Bhishma. While Aditya Karikalan was devoted to him, his grandfather's propensity for giving advice tended to test the young man's patience.

The other occupant of the chariot was Parthibendran. He was an offshoot of a branch of the ancient Pallava family tree. He was slightly older than Aditya Karikalan. Having no claim to a royal title, he'd had recourse to only one option in order to leave his mark on history—to prove his valour in war. This was how he had joined Aditya Karikalan. He had served as his lieutenant and right-hand man in the battle that had culminated in the death of Veerapandiyan. The two of them had become intimate friends during this time, and were inseparable now.

As they rode through the streets, the three men were discussing the news that had reached them through the grapevine.

'I can't take the Pazhuvettaraiyars' audacity for a second longer. Every day, they cross a new limit! How dare they deem my messenger a spy? Apparently, they have had a town crier announce that anyone who turns him in will be rewarded with a thousand gold coins! How can I stay silent? The sword in my scabbard is wilting from the humiliation. And you advise me to be patient!' Aditya Karikalan said.

'I did not advise you to be patient. But I told you back then not to send Vandiyadevan on such a crucial mission. I knew that he was too hot-headed for such a delicate task. Flashing swords and flinging spears is one thing, but one needs intelligence and astuteness to play messenger between royals,' Parthibendran said.

The faith the prince showed in Vandiyadevan did not sit well with Parthibendran. It was his wont to take Vandiyadevan down at every opportunity.

'So, you've started off, eh? You can't get through the day without criticising Vandiyadevan, can you? If he isn't intelligent and astute, who is? He accomplished the mission I had assigned him—to hand over the olai to the emperor personally, somehow, somewhere. This has angered the Pazhuvettaraiyars. How is it Vandiyadevan's fault?' Aditya Karikalan demanded.

'I'm sure he didn't stop at what you told him to do. He must have poked his nose in some other business too, I'm certain of it,' Parthibendran said.

'Why don't you keep your peace for a while? Thatha! Why are you silent? What is your opinion? What if we gather a large army and free the emperor from Thanjavur so we can take him to Kanchi? How much longer must we watch the Pazhuvettaraiyars keep the emperor as if in prison? How much more time should we waste from fear of the Pazhuvettaraiyars?' Aditya Karikalan fumed.

Milaadudaiyar Tirukkovaloor Malayaman, a veteran of sixty-six battles, cleared his throat to respond. Just then, the chariot turned a corner and the waves of the ocean were in full view.

'Let us dismount first, thambi! We will talk in the usual place. I'm getting on in years, and I find it rather hard to speak in a running chariot,' Malayaman said.

24

WHEN AN OLD MAN WEDS

The Mamallapuram beach is dotted with rocks of varying sizes. At times, the sea would wash over these rocks, the waves dashing and crashing against their surfaces. At others, the sea would recede, allowing the rocks to dry themselves in the sun. Not even the tiniest stone had been left out by the great sculptors of Mamallapuram, who had carved out scenes that suited every surface that had lent itself to their imagination.

Aditya Karikalan and his companions headed for a nook where two carved boulders stood facing each other, and dismounted. Karikalan and Malayaman sat on a boulder each, as if on a throne, while Parthibendran stood at a polite distance. The waves danced into the nook, sometimes wetting the seated royals up to the knee. As the water bounced off the rocks, the foam fell on their faces like a rain of pearls.

Not far away, the boats were tearing neat lines along the sea as they carried their goods to the fully-rigged frigates that stood waiting to receive them.

'Watching the provisions we had gathered for our march on Irattai Mandalam being shipped off to Lanka makes my blood boil!' said Parthibendran.

'What other option did we have? The most elite of our armed forces are in Lanka. They have notched up victory after victory on the battlefield. They have taken Anuradhapuram, which has seen a millennium of Lankan rule, and raised our flag there. Would you have us starve such stalwarts to death?' Aditya Karikalan asked.

'Who ever said they should be starved to death? Provisions must be sent to them, of course. But let those be sent from the Nagapattinam port of Chozha Naadu, or through Setukarai of Pandiya Naadu. Why must we send them from the parched land of Thondai Mandalam? To say nothing of the fact that this has delayed our northward march!' Parthibendran said.

'My blood boils at the thought too. I don't know what those nasty Pazhuvettaraiyar brothers have in mind! For how much longer can we brook this foolishness? Thatha! Why are you silent? Won't you tell us your opinion?' Karikalan said.

'My child! The waves of the sea are howling into my ears. Your friend Parthibendran seeks to outshout them. What can I possibly say that will cut through these two soundtracks? Age has made me tire easily,' said Malayaman Milaadudaiyar.

'Parthibendra! Hold your peace for a while. Let thatha voice his opinion,' Aditya Karikalan said.

'Here, I have clamped my mouth shut. Poor thatha, he's taken the immense trouble of getting down from the hill fort and coming all this way at such an advanced age. God forbid that I should open my mouth in his presence! The sea is devoid of all intelligence, and howls ceaselessly into his ears. There is no one to tame it. It appears Samudra Raja isn't the least afraid of our King of the Hills!' Parthibendran said.

'Thambi! Parthibendra! There was a time, there was a time—a time when the very name "Tirukkovaloor Malayaman" would induce terror, why, *tremors* in every king in the entire world. The Chalukyars of Irattai Mandalam, the Vaana Kovarayars of Vallams, the Vaidumbarayars, the Gangars and Kongars would, like a snake that has heard thunder, slither into their pits and hide from the storm when they heard my name. Samudra Raja, too, conducted himself with deference. But as this body has bowed with age, insubordination has become the norm. I belong to a clan that has ruled for a thousand years. The Pazhuvettaraiyars, who have swept in from the west just now, seek to destroy me. That will never happen! Karikala! You said a short while ago that you didn't know what those Pazhuvettaraiyar brothers had in mind. Let me tell you what they have in mind. They want to weaken you and your brother, divide you and isolate you and drain you. Your brother Arulmozhi must be defeated in Lanka, and broken by the terrible ignominy of it. This wasted effort must fill you with rage against your brother. The two of you must be at each other's throats. This old man must look on and lose heart. This is what they have in mind if you look into ...' Milaadudaiyar was in the middle of this outpouring when his grandson interrupted.

'This plan of theirs will never succeed, thatha! No one can cause a rift between my brother and me, or make us go at each other's throats. I would give up my very life for Arulmozhi. Every moment, I'm tempted to board a ship and set sail for Lanka. What travails he must be facing there, while I live a regal life! My sword and spear have begun to rust. Every passing second is as an age to me. I cannot bear to stay here any longer. Thatha! Tell me, shall I board one of these frigates and set sail for Lanka?' Karikalan asked.

'My lord! This is an excellent idea! You have given voice to the thoughts that have raged in my head for months. Let us go. Come! There is no point in asking thatha what his opinion is. He will advise us to hold our horses. Let us set sail tomorrow. We will take half the army from Thondai Mandalam. Once we're finished with the war in Lanka, we will arrive at Nagapattinam, and then head for Thanjai, where we'll show the Pazhuvettaraiyars what we're about!' Parthibendran foamed and frothed.

'Karikala! Do you see for yourself? What did I tell you? I said I would not speak unless your friend kept his mouth shut, didn't I?'

'Here, I will keep my mouth shut, thatha! Do finish saying all you have to say!' Parthibendran said, and dramatically raised his hands to his mouth, clamping his palms together over his lips.

'Karikala! You're among the bravest of warriors. Not even this great land of Tamizhagam has produced many men of your ilk through the centuries. In my eighty years, I have seen many, many battlefields. But nowhere have I come across a soldier like you, who will throw himself into the middle of an enemy formation all alone and decimate them. You were not even sixteen years old when you took part in the great battle of Sevoor. The speed with which you ran into the midst of the enemy troops, the speed with which your sword flashed in every direction, the speed with which the heads of the enemy rolled … I have never seen that before. The scene is so vivid to me, I can conjure it before my eyes this very minute. Your friend Parthibendra is like you, too—the bravest of warriors. But the two of you are impulsive, short-tempered. This blurs your clarity of thought. You're tempted to do the very opposite of what should be done …'

'Thatha! You have said this many times before.'

'I have. But it has served little purpose, you say? Are you asking me to stop talking and go back to my hill fort?'

'No, no! Tell us what we should do.'

'You must bring your brother Arulmozhi here right away. The two of you should never be apart.'

'Thatha! What a notion! If Arulmozhi were to come here, what would become of the war in Lanka?'

'That war has reached a stalemate. They have captured Anuradhapuram. Now, the monsoon has begun. For the next four months, the army can't really march forward. All they must do is ensure that their gains are not lost. The commanders can see to this. It is crucial that Arulmozhi be here, Karikala! What is the point in hiding the truth? This is a time of terrible danger. The clan of Vijayalaya Chozhar and the empire he established are in peril. You and yours must gather at one place and exercise the greatest caution at all times. We must gather our strength too, and ramp it up. One can never tell when or from where the next threat will come ...'

'Thatha! Why are you scaring me like this? Why must I fear anything when I have a sword in hand? Why does it matter when or where the next threat comes from? I will handle it all alone. I will destroy it all alone. It is not my wont to fear any sort of peril ...'

'Son! Do you need to tell me how intrepid you are? But you must keep in mind what Tiruvalluvar Perumaan[1] has said too:

> *Not to fear what must be feared is foolish; the wise are*
> *Wont to fear what must be feared.*

'One must not be afraid when one is on the battlefield, facing enemies in direct combat. A man who shows fear under such circumstances is a coward. If a child who is wont to fear the battlefield is ever born into my dynasty, I will cut him to pieces with my very own gnarled and knotted and enfeebled hands.

'But one *must* fear clandestine conspiracies and plots hatched behind closed doors and perils that are invisible to the eye. This fear must induce the taking of precautions. Those who are born into royal families and are heirs to the throne cannot afford to be careless. Or the land itself will go to ruin.'

'Thatha! What clandestine conspiracies and invisible dangers do you fear? We can't watch out for something whose form we don't know. Unless you tell us …'

'I am coming to that. Some days ago, there was a midnight conference at Kadambur Sambuvarayar's palace. Periya Pazhuvettaraiyar was there. Thennavan Mazhuvarayar, Kunrathoor Kizhaar, Vanangaamudi Munaiarayar, Anjaada Singamutharayar, Irattai Kudai Rajaliyar, they were all there too. These are just the names that I was given. There could have been many others too …'

'So let them be. What of it? They must have watched the dance and drama until midnight, filled their stomachs to bursting, choked themselves on alcohol and fallen asleep. Why does this matter to us? What would all these ancient relics you've mentioned confer about? What could such doddering old men set in motion anyway?'

'What's the point of my saying anything when this

is your opinion of old men? I'm a more ancient relic than any of them, aren't I? More doddering than all those old men?'

'Thatha! There is no need for you to take offence. Would I speak of you in the same breath as those old codgers who can't lift a finger without help? All right, what happened next, tell me?'

'There you go again, speaking of old codgers who can't lift a finger without help. Don't forget that the leader of those old men wed only recently. And understand that when an old man weds a nubile young woman, no valiant young warrior could be as dangerous as this newly energised old codger!'

This talk of old men and weddings had wrought a strange change in Aditya Karikalan's countenance. His eyes were bloodshot all of a sudden. They seemed to stare and scream like those of a Shudra Goddess[2] who was baying for sacrificial blood. His lips trembled. He ground his teeth. Malayaman did not notice any of this. But Parthibendran did.

'Why talk of weddings now, aiya? Tell us what happened in the Sambuvarayar palace after?' the Pallava scion asked.

'I was coming to that, but I'm getting on in years. My mind tends to stray, and I take off on tangents. Karikala! Parthibendra! I want the two of you to listen carefully. That midnight conference did not comprise your old codgers alone. There were some youngsters too. One was Sambuvarayan's son Kandamaaran. The other ...'

As his grandfather hesitated, Karikalan prompted him, 'Who, thatha? Who was the other?'

'Your great-uncle Kandaradityar's son, your uncle—Madurantaka Devan himself!'

At this, Aditya Karikalan and Parthibendran howled with laughter.

'What is the meaning of this laughter? How is this funny? Are you mocking me again?' Milaadudaiyar demanded.

'No, thatha! No! What we found funny was that you referred to Madurantakan as a "youngster". That's why we're laughing. He is the oldest of the codgers, the most venerable of the veterans … he's taken to Shiva Gnanam, hasn't he?' Aditya Karikalan said.

'Haven't you heard that old men can rediscover their youth? Madurantakan, too, has found new vigour after he wed. He was all set to become an ascetic who would worship Shiva all day. And, now he's finding new brides everywhere he goes. One, two, three … he's in the midst of a series of matrimonial matches …' said Miḷaadudaiyar.

'Let him marry. Let him find many more brides. What of it?'

'Thambi! These matrimonial matches are no ordinary marriages. They are royal alliances. They have been forged in order for the Pazhuvettaraiyars to set their clandestine conspiracies in motion!'

'Thatha! Why are you still talking in riddles? Speak openly. What is it that the Pazhuvettaraiyars want?

What are they seeking to do by going from place to place and calling conferences? What do they intend to do by marrying off Madurantakan into all these families?' Aditya Karikalan asked.

'Nothing but this: They want to ensure you and your brother are divested of your titles and inheritance, and that Madurantakan is seated on the Chozha throne. It is in order to get your father's consent for this that they have kept him as if in prison at the Thanjai fort,' said Milaadudaiyar.

25

MALAYAMAN IN A FRENZY

Upon hearing those words from the venerable Tirukkovaloor Malayaman, whose skill was complemented by intelligence and whose intelligence was compounded by experience, Aditya Karikalan stopped just short of fainting.

He stood stunned, unable to move a muscle for some time.

Parthibendran could find no words.

Even the sea sounded subdued. The wind froze, and the 'Ele-lo!' of the labourers loading their goods from the boats to the ships and lowering goods from the frigates to the boats no longer carried to them.

Finally, Aditya Karikalan, embarrassed at having allowed his surprise to show, looked his grandfather right in the eye and said, 'Thatha! I have heard people gossiping in this vein. But I figured those were baseless rumours. Yet, you seem absolutely certain? Do you know something that has led you to believe this could happen? Surely, it is impossible!'

'Why is it impossible? Before your grandfather was crowned king, your great-uncle, his older brother Kandaraditya Devar ruled Chozha Naadu. Doesn't his son have a greater claim on the throne than the rest of you?' Malayaman Milaadudaiyar asked.

'No, not at all! That nincompoop, who can't string a sentence together, who has no idea how to hold a sword, who should have been born a woman but was born a man by error … how can he have a claim to the throne? A greater claim than Aditya Karikalar, who rode into the battlefield at the age of twelve when he was yet to leave his childhood behind, the lion who beheaded Veerapandiyan, the bravest of warriors who has never tasted defeat? Aiya! Milaadudaiyare! Have you lost your mind in your dotage?' Parthibendran seethed.

Aditya Karikalan had to calm him down before turning to his grandfather to say, 'Thatha! This empire means nothing to me. I can rely on my sword to win myself ten empires, each larger than this one. But how is any of this fair? If it had been determined earlier that Madurantakan was the heir to the empire, I would not have stood in his way. But I have been declared the crown prince and a Yuvaraja Pattabhishekam was held for all the land and all its peoples to know. How can such a decision be withdrawn? Do you agree that Madurantakan should be the heir?'

'No, I don't. Never will I agree to that. If you were to accept that Madurantakan is the heir to this empire and step aside to give it to him, I would first cut you to pieces with my sword, and then stab your mother who bore you in her womb for ten months with it, and then fall on it myself for the sin of having brought her into this world. For as long as I have breath in my body, I will never allow the Chozha empire to be wrenched away from you!' roared the old man. His eyes, grown dim with age, were now afire. His body shook with emotion.

'Well said, thatha, well said!' cried Parthibendran. He ran up to throw his arms around Malayaman, tears in his eyes.

Aditya Karikalan was staring into the depths of the sea. After a while, he turned to his grandfather and said, 'Thatha! If this is your opinion, what are we waiting for? Let us gather an army and march on Thanjai. Let us dispose of the Pazhuvettaraiyars and their allies Mazhuvarayar, Sambuvarayar, Muththarayar, Munaiarayar and the lot once and for all. We will capture the fort, and throw Madurantakan in prison. We will free the emperor. All we need is your blessing and your consent. Parthibendran and I will join forces and rout them out. Who can possibly defeat us?'

'There is no one who can defeat you on the battlefield, true. But how will you wage war against conspiracies and palace intrigues? Even as you approach Thanjai with your army, they will have word out that you're marching on your father's fort to usurp his throne! They will claim that the humiliation was more than your father could bear, and that the emperor is dead. There will be those who believe this, won't there? What will you do in the face of this, my child? Won't you lose heart? Would you ever be able to bear the accusation that you are your father's usurper?'

Aditya Karikalan rammed his hands against his ears and cried, 'Shiva-Shiva! I can't bear to hear the words!'

'This is why I said right at the beginning that we are surrounded by danger.'

'What is your counsel, thatha, what is your counsel?'

'First, you must send someone trustworthy to Lanka. You must have him bring Arulmozhi back here with him. It won't be easy to tear that boy away from the battlefield, from the men he commands. You must send someone who is capable of persuading Arulmozhi, of making him change his mind ...'

Parthibendran interjected at this point to say, 'Aiya! If you consent, I will go myself and bring him.'

'I leave the decision to Karikalan, and to you. But whoever goes must not poke his nose in something that is none of his business, as is Vandiyadevan's wont ...'

'You see? Didn't I tell you?' Parthibendran said.

'Have you heard something about Vandiyadevan that makes you speak of him like this, thatha?' Aditya Karikalan asked.

'I had my suspicions about him once. I wondered whether he had joined forces with our enemies. But then, I realised I'd been wrong.'

'You see, Parthibendra?' Aditya Karikalan said.

'Let thatha finish what he was saying. Why are you cutting him short? Aiya! What prompted your suspicions about Vandiyadevan?'

'I learnt that he was at the Sambuvarayar palace on the day of the secret conference. But I later found out that he had no part in the plot.'

'Thatha! How did you learn of this?'

'I was not invited to the feast at the Kadambur palace. That made me suspect something was afoot. Then, I had Kunrathoor Kizhaar apprehended on his way back from Kadambur and imprisoned at my hill fort. I learnt every detail of what had happened from him. Apparently, Vandiyadevan is a friend of Sambuvarayar's son ...'

'Yes, the two of them served together in our army. They were in the border patrol along Vada Pennai. They've been close friends since. I've known this for a while,' Aditya Karikalan said.

'That's as may be. But that day, Vandiyadevan was in the palace. I wasn't able to determine whether he was part of the conference, and therefore the conspiracy. From Kunrathoor Kizhaar's account, it was all clear. Once I learnt that Vandiyadevan had stabbed Kandamaaran in the back at the Thanjai fort and made his escape ...'

'Thatha! I will never believe such a thing. Vandiyadevan might be capable of just about anything else, but he would never ever stab someone in the back. And he is certainly not such a lowlife as to stab his own friend in the back …'

'But what if he were to learn that this friend was involved in a conspiracy against his ejamaan[1]? And perhaps that friend had tried to draw him into it too?'

'Whatever it is, he would challenge his opponent to a fair fight. He would never blindside someone with a stab in the back!'

'Your faith in your friend is quite incredible, thambi! Well, we don't know what exactly happened, but the Pazhuvettaraiyars have announced that it was Vandiyadevan who stabbed Kandamaaran in the back and are hunting him down for the crime. This is all I know. Clearly, Vandiyadevan and Kandamaaran must have fallen out at some point. Isn't it obvious, then, that Vandiyadevan could not have been involved in this conspiracy against you?'

'I need no such evidence. If Vandiyadevan were to join forces with our enemies, the entire world would turn topsy-turvy. The oceans would dry up. The sky would shatter. The sun would rise at night. The Chozha dynasty would run to ruin …' Aditya Karikalan said.

'I second what the prince says. Vandiyadevan would never ever betray us and join forces with our enemies. My only quarrel with him is this incurable flaw of his—all it will take to turn his head is a face coated with turmeric paste.[2] He simply cannot think straight in the presence of a woman.'

Aditya Karikalan smiled. 'It is with that flaw in mind that I have charged him to go meet Ilaiya Piraatti once he has delivered the olai to my father. Once he lays eyes on the princess, he will have no hope of escape. He will be her slave forever.'

'Oho?' said Milaadudaiyar at once. 'So this is your plan for Vandiyadevan, is it? It escaped me entirely! Have you had any news of him since he left Thanjavur? Or has word come in from Ilaiya Piraatti at least?'

'I'm expecting word at any moment. But no news has reached me yet.'

'Once Arulmozhi arrives, you must bring your sister here too. Then, all our worries will be at an end. We can leave everything to Ilaiya Piraatti. She will know exactly how to deal with this. All we must do is put her words into action.'

'Thatha! It appears you're even worse than Vandiyadevan where Ilaiya Piraatti is concerned.'

'Yes, Karikala! When your sister was a toddler of two, she took the kodungol[3] in hand. Your grandmother and I, your mother and your father, were all putty in her hands. I, at least, remain so. Her word is law to me. Karikala! My speaking thus of your sister takes nothing away from you. You must, in fact, take pride in having such a sister. There is and has never been a man or woman who is her equal in brains or beauty. You know what sort of man our prime minister Aniruddha Brahmarayar is, don't you? If even he consults Ilaiya Piraatti on all matters, what remains to be said?' Milaadudaiyar spoke with fervour.

Parthibendran, whose rivalry with Vandiyadevan tended to get the better of him, said, 'Well, no one can argue with all this. But what if Vandiyadevan has fallen for the charms of another beauty even before he has had a chance to meet Ilaiya Piraatti? For instance, what if he has chanced upon that stunner of a woman, Pazhuvoor Ilaiya Rani ...?'

He had lowered his voice while speaking the last line, and the older man didn't hear the words. But Aditya Karikalan did, and he swung round and glared at Parthibendran with a fury that came as a shock to the Pallava scion.

Malayaman raised himself from his seat and said, 'Parthibendra! You're leaving for Lanka tomorrow, aren't you? You youngsters must have a lot to discuss. I'm an old man. I'll make my slow way back to the palace now. You boys take your time.'

Once he was some distance away, Parthibendran turned to Aditya Karikalan and said, 'Arase![4] My prince! My commander! I can see something is troubling you. A pain seems to gnaw at your heart. I know it has to do with the Pazhuvoor Ilaiya Rani. Every time the subject of Periya Pazhuvettaraiyar's marriage comes up, your entire mien changes. Your eyes turn red. You burn with rage. For how long will you keep this hurt to yourself? You've told me a thousand times that I'm as dear to you as life itself, that I am your most trusted friend. Won't you open your heart to me? Can you not share your hurt with me, and give me an opportunity to find the salve for your suffering? How long can I watch in silence as you writhe in pain?'

Aditya Karikalan let out a long sigh. 'My friend! My suffering is ceaseless. It will only end with my life. There is no salve for it. But there is no reason for me to keep it from you. I will tell you tonight. Now, we must accompany the old man to the palace. It isn't good form to let him go alone.'

With those words, he rose from his seat.

26

'NO VENOM MORE VICIOUS, NOR POISON MORE POTENT'

The three warriors stayed the night at one of the palaces of the erstwhile Pallava emperors. After dinner, Malayaman left to watch the enactment of Aravan's story, which he had heard was being staged by the Aindu Ratham—Five Chariots. Aditya Karikalan and Parthibendran headed for one of the higher terraces of the palace.

Aditya Karikalan took in the cityscape by night. Little spots of light from deepams shone brightly, like stars scattered on earth. Silence prevailed in the streets. The final puja of the day was done, and the doors of the many temples were being drawn shut for the night. The ocean's waves kept up a melancholy lament, 'Ooooooo'. By the Five Chariots, a villupaattu[1] stalwart was singing the story of Aravan, accompanied by his troupe. The members of their audience, silhouetted against the flares that lit the makeshift stage, appeared as shadows.

'Look, the old man has found the energy to go listen to a storytelling session at his age! Say what you will, but the kings of his generation were true kings. Who has their physical strength and mental fortitude these days?' Aditya Karikalan said.

'Arase! Have you too begun to speak of the "good old days"? What have the kings of yesteryear achieved that we haven't in our time? There is no record, not even in our epics, of someone who went to battle at as young an age as you did!' Parthibendran said.

'Parthiba! I know all too well that your heart is true, that you're incapable of thinking one thing and saying another. Or I would suspect that you're not my closest friend, but a dangerous enemy in disguise. The extent to which you flatter me! Nothing will ensure a man's descent into the netherworld as fast as flattery!' Aditya Karikalan said.

'Aiya! If one were to voice untruths about a man from vested interest, in order to win him over and put him to use, that would count as flattery. If I were to go up to that man whom the Pazhuvettaraiyars have enslaved in Thanjavur, Madurantakan, and say, "You're the bravest of brave warriors," that would qualify as flattery. If you ever come to know that I have done such a thing, cut me down with the sword in your scabbard. I have said nothing about you that strays from, or even exaggerates, the truth. Which hero of yore or lore has ever wrought the deeds you have on the battlefield, at such a young age too? Perhaps your great-uncle, Yaanai Mel Thunjiya Rajadityar, was your equal in valour. One can't claim he did more than you ...'

'Enough, Parthiba, that's enough! How can you speak of Rajadityar and me in the same breath? He took on the enormous armies of the Rashtrakutas, who came swelling down the battlefield like wave upon wave, with a handful of men at his command, and yet decimated them before ascending to the heavens! We are not even qualified to speak of Rajadityar, let alone draw a comparison between him and ourselves! Let's leave aside the Chozha clan. Look at the Pallava clan into which you were born. What incredible men that dynasty has produced! Will we ever see the likes of Mahendra Varmar or Mamallar in this land? Look at Narasimhar, who defeated Pulikesi—the ruler of the entire swathe of land between River Tungabhadra in the south and River Narmada in the north—and destroyed Vatapi, and raised the flag of victory. How do you and I fare by comparison to him? Could anyone so much as imagine, let alone create, a city like Mamallapuram, this place which looks like it belongs in a dream? ... Adada! Look around you, look in all four directions, just once, Parthiba! You see where the villupaattu is being staged? Look closely. Could anyone have glanced upon that rock and seen five such incredible chariots hidden inside, waiting for a sculptor to excavate them? Are they ordinary mortals who saw such a thing? Just the thought of how a newly-created

Mamallapuram must have looked, three hundred and fifty years ago, makes my hair stand on end, gives me goosebumps. Does it not evoke such emotions in you? Doesn't this work of your ancestors make you hold your head higher and your shoulders broader?'

'Arase! You said some time ago that I was flattering you. But you seem to have forgotten that it also falls to me to point out your flaws. This madness of wasting away one's life on painting and sculpture and art seems to be engulfing you too. It is from this madness that my ancestors lost everything they had. Once Mamallar returned from Vatapi, having raised the victory flag, what did he do of note? Dug up rocks and scooped out stones! What purpose did that achieve? It allowed the Chalukyas to gather an army and come back for revenge. They destroyed Kanchi and Uraiyur. They went right up to Madurai. If Nedumara Pandiyan hadn't stopped the Chalukyas at Nelveli, they would have captured the entire peninsula! We would still be under their rule!'

'No, Parthiba, no! No royal dynasty has ever ruled any land forever. Even the Ishkvaku dynasty into which Lord Rama was born came to an end at some point. The Irattai Mandalaththaar eventually defeated the Chalukyas. The rise and fall of kingdoms is but natural. Empires which stretch across vast territories over decades may disappear without a trace. Look at my ancestors! Chozha kings like Karikaal Valavan and Killivalavan are said to have presided over a golden age. But what do we know of them or their time? We only know their names through the songs composed by poets of their era. Then again, we don't know whether these songs tell the truth or whether they were the products of minds intoxicated with alcohol and ardour. But this dreamland conjured by Mahendra Pallavar and Mamallar will survive the test of time. It will tell their story and write them into the history books, millennium after millennium. What have you or I achieved that could be compared to their work? We have killed thousands of men and made mountains of corpses on the battlefield. We have irrigated the earth with rivers of blood. For what else will we be remembered?'

Parthibedran was stunned into silence for some time. His expression suggested he couldn't believe it was Aditya Karikalan who had spoken as he had. Then, he said with a heavy sigh, 'Arase! When you yourself speak of war and valour in this manner, what could I possibly say? I can see your mind is troubled. You're not your usual self today. That is why you're saying these things. Aiya! Can you not tell me what is eating away at you? May I not share some of your burden? Won't you open your heart of gold and show me what is within?'

'Parthiba! If I were to tear open my heart, what or who do you think you will find within?'

'It is that very thing I wish to know, swami!'

'You won't see the mother and father who

birthed me, nor my sister and brother who are dearer than life to me, nor even my closest friends—you and Vandiyadevan—within. You will see a woman who is the very vision of vengeance, the supreme personification of sin. You will see the Pazhuvoor Ilaiya Rani, than whom there exists no venom more vicious, nor poison more potent. You will see Nandini, of whose place in my heart and the torment this place has caused me I have never spoken to a living soul before you!'

Parthibendran heard the words as through a mist of hot smoke from burning coals. 'Arase! I had figured some of this out for myself. Every time talk of the Pazhuvoor Ilaiya Rani comes up, your face darkens and your eyes turn fiery. Your body grows heavy with unspeakable sorrow. I have noticed all this. But how did such a base desire find place in your heart? You come from a culture which accords even women who are strangers to one the status of mother. Pazhuvettaraiyar is a long-time relative by marriage of your clan. He is a venerable old man. He might be our enemy today, but there was a time when it wasn't so. Your father and grandfather felt and showed the deepest respect for him. This is a woman whom he has wed following all the old traditions, with agni sakshi—the holy fire as witness. However vile she may be … how could you possibly allow yourself to even feel desire for her? How could you allow her to live in a chamber of your heart?'

'I should not, Parthiba, I should not! Don't I know it? It is because I know this is terribly wrong that I am so tormented. But my desire for her, my according her a place in my heart ... these precede her wedding to Pazhuvettaraiyar. A long, long, long time ago, this poison—this pining for her—seeped inside me. I have tried my best to draw it out, and I haven't been able to. I speak as if it were all her fault. Only God knows with whom the blame lies. Well, if you look at it, the blame lies with the God who created the two of us. Or with the fate which wrought a meeting of our souls and then a separation!'

'Arase! Did you know Nandini before she became the Pazhuvoor Ilaiya Rani? Where did you meet her? When? How?'

'That is a long story. Do you wish to hear it today?'

'Yes, I certainly do. My mind won't be at peace unless I do. You have commanded me to set sail for Lanka tomorrow. I will not be able to carry out my duties diligently. My heart can only rest once I have heard it all from you, and offered you comfort and solace.'

'My friend! You wish to offer me comfort and solace? I will find neither in this birth. I doubt I will, even in the next one. But I will tell you, so your mind will find peace and your heart rest. You won't have to leave for Lanka thinking I have kept a secret from you.'

Having said this, Aditya Karikalan stood silent for a time. Then, he heaved a great sigh and began his story.

27

NANDINI'S BELOVED

'I met Nandini for the first time when I was around twelve years old. One day, my siblings and I were playing in the lake at the back of our palace. We'd gone boating. We had just returned and were making our way back to the palace through the flower garden, when we heard our Periya Piraatti, Sembiyan Mahadevi's voice. All three of us had grown up in her loving care. When we heard her call us, we rushed towards the arbour where she sat, eager to tell her about our games. Once we went in, we saw that there were three others with her. One was a girl about our age. The others appeared to be her parents. They were telling Mahadevi Adigal[1] something about the girl. When the three of us walked into the arbour, everyone inside turned to us. But all I could see was the little girl's large eyes widening in surprise. I can see them today too, in my mind's eye ...'

With that, Aditya Karikalan looked skywards, his

gaze distant. He fell silent. Perhaps he saw the little girl's face in the nebulous clouds that floated gently above.

'Aiya! Go on!' said Parthibendran.

Aditya Karikalan came back to earth, and resumed his story. 'It was Kundavai who told our grandmother all about our adventures in the lake. Mahadevi Adigal heard her out, and then said, "My darling! Do you see this little girl? How radiant she is! This family has come from Pandiya Naadu to see our Eesanya Bhattar. They will be here for a while. This girl's name is Nandini. Let her join in your games too. She will make you a good companion!"

'But I learnt that this did not appeal to my sister. As the three of us left for the palace, Kundavai turned to me and said, "Anna! That girl there, did you notice how awful she looked? Why, her face reminds me of an owl! Our grandmother asks me to play with her! But how will I stop myself from laughing when I see that horrendous face? What do I do?"

'When she spoke these words, this interesting and important truth dawned on me—jealousy in women is congenital. They are born with envy in their hearts. However beautiful a woman is, she cannot bear to so much as see another beautiful woman. My sister was known for her good looks. It was said no one as lovely had ever been born into our dynasty. And yet, she could not stand to be in the presence of another beautiful girl. Why else would she speak about her so disparagingly?

'I didn't give my sister an easy time of it. I said emphatically that the other girl was stunning, just to annoy Kundavai. We would argue over this rather often. Our brother Arulmozhi would blink and stare, not understanding what our quarrel was about. Not long after, my father set off to join the war against the Pandiyas. I went with him. We beat back the Pandiya army, and the army the Lankan king had sent to aid them. Eventually, we figured that Veerapandiyan had either fled and gone into hiding, or had been felled in a battle somewhere. He had disappeared. With this, the Lankan army beat a hasty retreat. We chased them up to Sethukarai. Most of them were killed. The survivors boarded a ship and escaped.

'My father wanted to teach the Lankan king, who sent his army to the Pandiyas' rescue every so often, a lesson he wouldn't forget in a hurry. He decided to send a large army to Lanka under the command of Kodumbalur Siriya Velaar. It took us a while to gather the ships, equipment, ammunition and other amenities we would need for battle. But we didn't return to Chozha Naadu until we had seen our forces off, and then received confirmation that they had made a safe landing at Mathottam.

'By the time I reached Pazhaiyarai, over two years had passed since my departure. I had forgotten the priest's daughter who had come to our kingdom from somewhere near Madurai. When I arrived at the palace, I saw that this girl and my sister had both grown up in my absence and changed beyond recognition. They had become close friends too. Nandini had not simply grown up, but looked more radiant than ever in her royal finery. It was my sister who had chosen her clothes and jewellery.

'Nandini's demeanour around me was different too. She was shy. She wouldn't meet my eyes, or speak to me as she used to earlier. I did my best to scrape away this shyness. Talking to her, spending time with her, gave me a joy unlike any I had known before. I can't tell you what a surprise that discovery was. I felt emotions I had never imagined I could. My heart would swell like the Kaveri in spate after the first flood, every time I met Nandini … why, every time I laid eyes on her.

'But it didn't take long for me to learn that no one was happy about this. After my return, Kundavai began to show a sudden animosity towards Nandini. One day, our grandmother Mahadevi Adigal sent for me and said, "Nandini is from a family of priests. You are a prince. Both of you have grown up. It isn't good form for the two of you to spend time with each other."

'I, who had thus far treated Periya Piraatti pretty much as divinity and obeyed her every command implicitly, was now infuriated by her words. I paid them no heed. I flouted her wishes, and sought Nandini out in plain sight of everyone. But this didn't last long. One fine day, I learnt that Nandini and her parents had left for their hometown in Pandiya Naadu. I was overwhelmed with sorrow and overrun by rage. I let the sorrow fester within, and took my rage out on my sister. Thankfully, I was sent northwards soon after with the Chozha army assigned to beat back the Rashtrakutas, who were lording it over Tirumunaippaadi and Thondai Mandalam. That was when you and I met, and became close friends.

'With King Malayaman's help, you and I took on the Rashtrakuta forces. We chased them north of the Palaru and conquered Kanchi. Just then, we had bad news from Lanka—that our troops had been pushed back, and that Kodumbalur Siriya Velaar had been killed. Having got wind of this, Veerapandiyan—who had been hiding in a desert cave until then—slithered out like a snake from its anthill, gathered an army and recaptured Madurai. To celebrate the victory, he raised his fish standard.

'Do you remember what a frenzy this sent us into? We rushed to Pazhaiyarai. My father's health was already on the decline at the time. His legs had grown weak. And yet, the emperor was ready to head for the battlefield. I stopped him, and promised I would not return to Chozha Naadu without having brought Madurai under our rule and Veerapandiyan's head under my arm. You were with me all through. My father heard my oath, and gave us his blessing to join the army against Pandiya Naadu. The army was under the command of Kodumbalur Boothi

Vikramakesari, and the emperor asked that we serve the commander. We agreed to this and left. We met Periya Pazhuvettaraiyar on our way, remember? He was unhappy that the Kodumbalur king had been given command of the army and that he himself had been overlooked for the post.

'When Boothi Vikramakesari saw our hunger for battle, he handed over the command of the army to us. My friend, it wouldn't be wrong for us to speak with pride of our bravery on that battlefield. We defeated the Pandiya army and won Madurai back. But that was not enough. We wanted to make sure we had reduced that army to dust, so they would never be able to fight us again. They broke ranks and scattered, but we bade our soldiers chase them down and finish off every last one of them, while we took a sizeable army with us and focused on hunting down Veerapandiyan himself.

'The fish standard gave away his location. We found him soon enough. But he was protected by his elite army, the Abathuthavigal, who surrounded his camp like a fortress wall. The Abathuthavigal of Pandiya Naadu stand a rung higher than our Velakkaara Army in the ladder of heroism. They take an oath that they will never retreat in the face of an enemy. They will protect the Pandiya king with their lives, failing which they will behead themselves on the sacrificial slab.

'Those heroic men did their duty that day. Not one was left standing. We killed them all, and made a mountain of their corpses. But we did not find Veerapandiyan in the camp. The flag had fooled us. A lone elephant stood bearing the standard. The Pandiya king was missing. He was, after all, an escape artist with much experience in fleeing battlefields. We split our army into four factions, and sent one in each direction to scour him out.

'You and your men raced down either bank of the Vaigai River. I got into the river and headed south. I saw the hoofmarks of a single horse at spots along the bank. There were bloodstains along the way too. I followed these tracks, and eventually saw a beautifully tended garden that appeared as an island in the middle of the river. There was a Tirumaal temple on the island, with a couple of priests' houses nearby. Flowers that would be used in the puja blossomed in the garden. There was a little lotus pond too.

'My friend! Perhaps you remember. Some days before, I had pointed to that island and issued strict instructions that none of our men must venture on to it. The reason for this was not simply that I did not want to cause any disturbance to those who looked after the temple, or to the pujas that were held within. It was that the queen among women, who had stolen my heart and built a temple for herself within, lived there. I'd chanced upon Nandini sometime earlier, as I was exploring the island. Her appearance had undergone a slight change. She wore her hair in a bun to the front, like Andal, and a string of flowers around the bun. She wore a garland of the same flowers.

'"To what do we owe this bizarre look?" I asked.

'She told me that after she had been forcefully separated from me, she had determined that she would never marry another man. Her husband was Lord Krishna, she said. This sounded like madness to me. A mortal woman marrying a God? But I had no wish to hold a debate on the matter just then. I decided I would sort this out after the war. I asked her if she needed any help.

'"Please see that none of your soldiers comes here,' she said. 'Only my old parents live in this house. They have both lost their eyesight. I have an older brother, who is a bit unpredictable. He is on a pilgrimage to Tirupati at the moment," she said.

'I promised her I would ensure that no one would intrude on the island. I went to visit her a couple of times after. My old flame was now rekindled. My love for her grew tenfold. But I forced myself to stay patient. I would focus on doing what I had to do. I would return to Pazhaiyarai carrying Veerapandiyan's head. Then, I would ask my father for permission to marry this woman. He could not possibly refuse after I had brought him the enemy's head.

'It was after all this that I spotted the horse's tracks on the island. It stunned and enraged me. I followed the tracks, and saw a horse tied to a large tree trunk. So, the rider must be in one of those houses. I went to Nandini's house and looked in through the window. My friend! What I saw inside tore through my heart like freshly-forged iron. Veerapandiyan was lying on an old rope cot. Nandini was feeding him water, her face glowing with a concern I had never seen before. Tears had gathered as two large drops in the corners of her eyes.

'I was consumed by fury. I kicked the door open. Padaar! I was inside. Nandini, who was bandaging the man's wounds, stopped when she saw me. She stood up, approached me and then fell at my feet. She rose and said, her hands folded in a plea, "Aiya! I beg you, in the name of the love you once felt for me, not to harm him. Please don't kill him, he who is so badly wounded, with your own hands."

'I could barely speak. I somehow found the words to stammer, "What is your connection to this man? Why are you asking me to spare his life?"

'"He is my beloved. He is my God. He is the very embodiment of generosity, who has consented to marry me," she said.

'The slight compassion I had begun to feel for Veerapandiyan, who lay badly wounded and barely conscious, melted away from me. This paadagan, this wretch, this sandaalan! What revenge he had wrought on me! He could have taken away my entire kingdom, and it would not have hurt. But to steal away this queen among women whom I had enshrined in my heart! How could I show him compassion? Never!

'I kicked Nandini aside and took one leap on to the bed. One swing of my sword, and it was all over.

Veerapandiyan's head was severed. It rolled onto the floor. It fills me with shame to think of this terrible act now. But at the time, my fury from the battle and my fury at Nandini's revelation had bound themselves together to drive me into a frenzy.

'As I left, I turned to look at Nandini. She met my eyes, unblinking. I have never, ever seen such an expression in anyone's eyes before or since. Her eyes were as fire, radiating kama, krodha, lobha, moha, mada, matsarya[2] all at once. I have wondered over and over again what that look portended, but I still haven't figured it out.

'By this time, you and many others had come looking for me. When you saw Veerapandiyan's headless body and his bleeding head, you all broke into cries of victory. But my heart was heavy with burden. It was as if the Vindhya mountains themselves had been lifted on to my chest and were pressing down on me!'

28

THAT DAY, IN THE ANTAPURAM

Centuries ago, when Mahendra Pallava Chakravarti ruled from Kanchi, he made arrangements for stories from the Mahabharata to be narrated and staged across the land. He felt this would rekindle the valour and battle-readiness of a people who had lost their martial spirit and embraced the love of peace and compassion preached by Buddhism and Jainism, which had gained currency in Tamizhagam. He built Bharata mandapams for the exclusive purpose of reciting these tales. This tradition continued without pause after his time in some places, such as Thondai Mandalam. People would gather either in halls or open spaces where stages were improvised, to listen or watch the performances. Troupes that specialised in narrating the Mahabharata or spin-off stories from it, through various theatrical and folk forms, had cropped up.

One of the most popular stories was that of Aravan.

While on his tirth yatra, the Pandava prince Arjuna was resting in a forest on the outskirts of Manipur, when he chanced upon Chitrangi, the Manipuri princess. They fell in love, and had a son called Aravan. Born of a union between the crown princess of this mountainous land and the great warrior Arjuna, Aravan turned out to be a skilled fighter and astute strategist. When preparations were being made for the Kurukshetra war, he sought his father out and offered to fight on behalf of the Pandavas. On an auspicious day before the war, as talk was on about how their efforts would be helped by a human sacrifice, Aravan said, 'Here I am. Let me be the human sacrifice.' There was no warrior braver or stronger than he in the entire Pandava army. He had volunteered himself for the sacrifice, and so it was determined that he would be the chosen one.[1]

The story of Aravan, who gave up his life for the benefit of the side to which he had pledged his allegiance, stole the hearts of the Tamil people. They built temples for Aravan by every Draupadi temple, and conducted a Tiruvizha[2] in his honour.

The performance of his story that was being staged that night by the Aindu Ratham of Mamallapuram was winding up.

'Long live Sundara Chozha Chakravarti, ruler of all three worlds!'

'Long live Kopparakesari Aditya Karikalar!'

The echoes of the assembly's chants floated

through the air to the terrace where Aditya Karikalan and Parthibendran stood. They could see the crowd beginning to disperse.

'The narration is over. Malayaman will return in a bit,' Aditya Karikalan said.

'The narration of Aravan's story is over. But the story you were narrating to me hasn't reached its conclusion yet, has it?' Parthibendran said.

'Can you believe how strong Malayaman's mind is at this age? He's able to will himself to stay awake past the midnight hour to listen to a story!' Aditya Karikalan said.

'Is it such a great wonder to live to an old age? The town is teeming with old men who can't sleep and must pass the time listening to stories ...'

'Would you equate Tirukkovaloor Malayaman with such ordinary old men? How many battles he has seen! I doubt we'll so much as *live* to his age. Even if we do, we certainly won't have his strength and steadfastness!'

'Arase! There's a reason for the men of his generation being as strong and steadfast as they are ...'

'What is that reason?'

'They didn't get themselves caught in the honeytraps of women. They didn't fall for the daughter of a priest, of all things, and ruin their lives pining for her. If they did ache for a woman, they simply dragged her by the hair, threw her into the antapuram and went about their work.'

'Parthiba! Nandini is not really the daughter of a

priest. There must be some mystery, some truth we don't know about her birth.'

'What does it matter whose daughter she is? She could be the daughter of a priest or a prince, or an orphan for all I care. Look at that other relic, Periya Pazhuvettaraiyar. He's chanced upon her somewhere. He's brought her along and shut her inside the antapuram along with all his other wives.'

'My friend! That does strike me as bizarre.'

'What does? That the old man was caught in her web?'

'No, no! This woman who once said she loved me, and then said she was going to marry Veerapandiyan … how did she agree to marry this old man? This is what seems bizarre to me.'

'That doesn't strike me as bizarre in the least, aiya! It is your actions which seem bizarre to me. This woman had been tending to that sworn enemy of the Chozha clan, Pandiyan … that cowardliest of cowards who would flee at the very hint of defeat but had the temerity to style himself "Veerapandiyan" … and she begged you to spare his life. You left without doing her any harm. It is this I find most bizarre. You should have either felled her right there with your sword, or bound her arms and legs and thrown her into prison! You did neither of those, and let her stay on there as if she had done nothing wrong!

'I remember now. You emerged from the hut with Veerapandiyan's lifeless body and threw it to the ground. We all screamed and cheered like men possessed. Through all this, I heard sobs from within the hut. I asked you who was inside. You said, "Oh, some women from the priests' families. They're already terrified and distraught. Don't any of you go inside and scare them now!" We were so buoyed by this final victory that we didn't pay those sobs much attention. We left as a group with Veerapandiyan's head for a trophy. You came with us. But you didn't take part in our celebrations. You seemed low on energy. I asked you what had happened, and you shrugged it off. I remember now, I was worried you'd been wounded badly and were keeping it from us,' Parthibendran said.

'There was no wound on my body, Parthiba! But my heart had been inflicted a wound that would never heal. I can never forget the sight of her bending low and folding her hands, standing between me and the cot on which Veerapandiyan lay, begging me for mercy. "Aiyo! I didn't grant that one wish of hers!" my heart screamed. If only I could have brought Veerapandiyan back to life by giving up my own, I would have done it for her. But that wasn't possible, and I felt helpless for it. Parthiba! We think so highly of our strength. We thump our chests and say nothing is beyond us. We read the inscriptions that say kings are descended from divinity, that we have the characteristics of Mahavishnu, and buy into this ourselves. Yet, do we have the means to restore a life that has left a body?

Does any royal from anywhere have this gift? We can only take life. No human can give life ...'

'And a good thing, too. If you had had this gift, what a terrible thing would have happened! You would have restored Pandiyan's life. He would have gone and found another cave for himself. The war with the Pandiyas would have, in all likelihood, been ongoing. All this for the crocodile tears of a woman!'

'Pallava! You have the misfortune of being a misogynist—you hate all womankind and have no idea what love is. It is this that makes you speak thus!'

'True. I haven't been trapped in the web of a woman's bewitching eyes. But then, your dear friend Vandiyadevan has but to glance upon a pretty face, and he'll fall head over heels in love. That is why he is dearer to you than I am! Isn't that so, arase?'

'Aha! You've managed to bring in Vandiyadevan here too. I was wondering how you'd let so much time go without disparaging him.'

'Yes, any truth I tell you about him will strike you as bitter. So, I'll stop now. What happened next, arase? Did you not meet Nandini again? Did you not ask how she, who was weeping and wailing for Veerapandiyan, had gone on to wed this old man?'

'The night Veerapandiyan was killed, after the victory celebrations, the rest of you collapsed into sleep at the army camp. I couldn't sleep. Every nerve in my body ached to see her again. *I must meet her, and I must console her somehow*, I thought. *I must beg her forgiveness*. There was another part of me that wanted to vent its fury against her too. But, one way or another, I simply had to see her. My mind could not be at rest unless I did. I could not return to Chozha Naadu without meeting her once more. So, in the middle of the night, I slipped out of the army camp. None of you heard me leave or mount my horse. I made my way to that island in the middle of the Vaigai River. My heart was beating erratically. My entire body trembled. My legs felt numb. I got off my horse, and made my slow way to the Perumaal temple ... only to find that all the huts in its vicinity had been burnt and reduced to ashes. An elderly couple was sitting by the debris of one such house and weeping. When I went closer, I realised they were the very couple who had first brought Nandini to Pazhaiyarai. When they saw me, their sorrow and terror seemed to multiply many times over.

'For a while, they couldn't speak a word. I spent some time reassuring them that they were safe. I asked them gently what had happened. It took me a good while before I could get a word out of them. They finally told me that their elder daughter lived in a village on the other side of the river. They had come to know she was about to deliver a baby, and had wanted to be with her. Nandini had refused to accompany them. She was used to following her heart, and would brook no instructions. They had seen little point in trying to convince her, and had left her behind to visit their other daughter.

'On their way back, they had seen a group of thugs dragging a girl, her hands and feet tied, towards a pyre of some sort. Such things were bound to happen at wartime, they'd thought. Afraid to approach the thugs, they'd hurried on to their home. When they'd arrived, they'd discovered it had been burnt down. There was no sign of Nandini.

'After telling me all this, the old man and his wife looked at me and wailed, "Ilavarase![3] Where is our daughter? Where is our darling little girl?"

'I'd already suspected that they could not be Nandini's real parents. Now, I knew for certain. Would anyone leave a young woman, a child born of their bodies, all alone and traipse off by themselves? I felt no sympathy or compassion for them. Nandini's fate filled my heart with unspeakable grief.

'"Go find the pyre on to which your daughter was thrown, jump into it yourselves and die!" I cursed them and left. I reached the camp well before sunrise. The rest of you were still asleep. None of you knew of my going or coming back.'

'Yes, Ilavarase! We did not know. I can't believe you have kept this grief all to yourself since. I never dreamt that you would flout the fundamental rules of friendship as you have. In your place, I would never have kept such a thing from you,' Parthibendran said.

'But you are not in my place, Parthiba! No one in this world could ever have been in my place. Who can tell how you would have acted had you truly been in my place?' Aditya Karikalan said.

'Arase! Let us not argue over water under the bridge. What happened after? When did you see Nandini next? Was it after she had become the Ilaiya Rani of Pazhuvoor, or before?'

'If only I had seen her before, she would never have become the Ilaiya Rani of Pazhuvoor. Neither you nor I were in town for Periya Pazhuvettaraiyar's wedding. You remember how disgusted we were when we came to know he'd married at this age? Soon after, my Yuvaraja Pattabhishekam ceremony was held. It was to avoid all conjecture and controversy about the heir to the throne that my father, grandmother and other elders decided to make a public announcement. Perhaps they suspected that someone would instigate Madurantakan into staking his claim. Along with the title of crown prince, I was given the title of "Parakesari" as well as the right to issue decrees and have inscriptions carved on my authority.

'My beloved father said, his heart and soul filled with joy, "From this day forward, the responsibility of ruling this Chozha empire rests entirely with you."

'The ministers, courtiers, commanders and commonfolk cheered at this announcement, expressing their consent and contentment. In the commotion, I had forgotten all about Nandini. But soon after the rituals of the pattabhishekam were finished, something happened that ensured I would not forget her until my dying day.

'My father placed the ancient Chozha crown on

my head, and ushered me to the antapuram, so I could seek the blessings of my mother, grandmother and the other women of the royal household. My brother, the prime minister and the Pazhuvettaraiyar brothers accompanied us.

'Along with the older women, my sister, her friends and companions and several other young women were waiting for me in the antapuram. They had all dressed up for the occasion, and their faces were beaming in anticipation of receiving me.

'But I had eyes for only one among all these faces, and that was Nandini's. The goddess who ruled over my heart, the woman I believed had been burnt to ashes, now stood before me! How had she landed up at the antapuram? How had she gone from wearing those simple clothes and flower garlands to adopting this avatar, resplendent in silk and jewellery? How had she found a place among the queens of the antapuram? And what a bewitching smile she had! How had her beauty, already unrivalled, grown tenfold?

'In a matter of moments, I had built castles in the air. Was this day, the day I had been declared the crown prince, going to be the best day of my life? Was it going to be the auspicious day on which the woman who had claimed my heart would claim the title of royal wife? Had some magic occurred that would change the course of my life?

'As these thoughts crowded my head, my mother Vaanamahadevi stepped forward.

'"My child!" she said, as I sought her blessings. She kissed my forehead.

'Just then, something happened that no one had foreseen. My father shouted, "Aaaah!" and collapsed on the floor. He had lost consciousness. There was mayhem. As several of us rushed to lift the emperor off the floor and revive him, all the women save my mother and grandmother Sembiyan Mahadevi disappeared into their quarters. My father regained his consciousness fairly soon.

'I sought my sister Kundavai out, took her aside and asked, "How did Nandini land up here?"

'My sister told me that Nandini had wed Periya Pazhuvettaraiyar and was now the Pazhuvoor Ilaiya Rani. It was as if a spear had been thrust into my heart. My friend! I have been wounded on several battlefields. But the wound caused by Kundavai's words, "Nandini is now the Pazhuvoor Ilaiya Rani" has never healed!'

With that, Aditya Karikalan pressed a hand to his heart. The hurt that throbbed within was palpable.

29

MAYA MOHINI

All this while, Parthibendran had been listening to his friend's story without much empathy. But upon hearing that last line and looking at Aditya Karikalan's expression, Parthibendran could not be unmoved. His heart melted and his eyes welled up.

Wiping away his tears, he said, 'Arase! I never dreamt that love of a woman could throw one into such depths of misery! None of us knew that you were in such pain on the day of the Yuvaraja Pattabhishekam. Your listlessness on that day left us surprised. We tried our best to cheer you up with jokes and light conversation ...'

'Yes. I remember. You and the others tried everything. You teased and joked, you spoke of the wonders I would work for Chozha Naadu when I became the emperor. That very day, you changed the map of the land, so it stretched from Lanka to the Himalayas! Then, you crossed the oceans and conquered the territories that lay beyond for me. I remember every word, and I remember how much hurt I felt at each one … I could not find it in myself to share the joy.

'Not long after, Nandini invited me to the Pazhuvoor palace. I wasn't sure whether to accept the invitation. Eventually, I decided to go. I had to talk things over with her. I needed answers to my questions, I needed my doubts cleared. I wanted to know the truth about her origins. There was also a slight suspicion in my mind that my father's sudden loss of consciousness on the day of the pattabhishekam had something to do with Nandini's presence in the antapuram. He was revived fairly quickly, but he never fully regained his health after, as you know.

'I had an instinct that speaking to her would unravel something … some sort of mystery would be solved that day. I came up with plenty of excuses for going to the palace. But the truth was that I couldn't resist her magnetic power. I was fooling myself with all sorts of pretexts so I could go. That day, Pazhuvettaraiyar was not in town. No one stopped me at his palace. No one there knew of my old ties with Nandini. They assumed the crown prince had come to meet the queens of Pazhuvoor to seek their blessings and good wishes.

'I met Nandini at the lata mandapam of the palace garden. Parthiba! You've heard the stories of seafarers, haven't you? They speak of maelstroms and vortices in the ocean, which have unbelievable powers of suction and force. The grandest of ships can break into pieces if caught in one of these whirlpools. In Nandini's presence, I was as a ship caught in a whirlpool. My heart, body and soul were in tatters. My mouth had a mind of its own. My words took me by surprise. Even as my brain wondered, "Why on earth am I saying such things?", my tongue spouted stupid lines. Nandini congratulated me on my elevation to crown prince, and said she had been most pleased to hear.

'"I take no pleasure in that," I said.

'"Why?" she asked.

'"What sort of question is that? How could anything give me any pleasure? You have gone and done such a terrible thing."

'She made out that she didn't understand what I was on about. Things went on in this vein. I accused her of betraying me and choosing Veerapandiyan instead. I spoke mockingly of her marriage to this old man, Pazhuvettaraiyar.

'"Ilavarase!" she said. "First, you killed my love. Then, you killed the man who loved me, before my very eyes. It appears you won't be appeased until you have killed me too. My being alive is not to your taste. Well, then … why don't you kill me and fulfil your desires?"

'With those words, she reached for a pen knife tucked into her waist and held it out to me.

'"Why would I kill you?" I said. "It is you who are skinning me alive. You're torturing me to death."

'I ended up speaking words that make me cringe even at the memory.

'"Not all is lost," I said. "In fact, nothing is lost yet. Just say the word. Say you will leave this old man and come with me. I will give up my empire for you. We will board a ship and set sail for some distant land!"

'That sent Nandini into paroxysms of laughter. My skin crawls when I think back to that moment. Do you know what she said next?

'"And what do you propose we do on this distant land? Cut firewood and sell it for a living? Or plant groves of banana trees and live off the yield?"

'"I don't expect such things to appeal to you. You were born and raised in a poor priest's household, and have now climbed the ranks to become the Pazhuvoor Rani, haven't you?" I said.

'"Oh, I don't intend to stop here," she said. "I plan to sit on the throne of the Chozha empire, as the chakravartini, the empress of this land. Tell me if you're willing. Are you willing to kill the Pazhuvettaraiyar brothers, throw Sundara Chozhar in jail, take over the mantle of emperor and make me your wife?"

'"Aiyo! How can you speak so callously?" I asked.

'"Why, was it not callous to kill a wounded man who was confined to his bed before my eyes?" she said.

'My anger got the better of me. I spoke words no man should speak to a woman, and stormed off having vented all my rage on her. But she had a parting shot for me.

'"Ilavarase!" she called as I was leaving. "If you ever change your mind, come back to me. When your heart makes place for my being chakravartini, come back to me!"

'That was the last time I saw her.'

Parthibendran was overcome with horror and terror. 'Arase!' he said. 'Can such a rakshashi live in this world of humans? It's a good thing you haven't met her again!' He sighed.

'Well, it's true that I haven't been to meet her. But she hasn't left me alone. She haunts me day and night. She comes as memories in daytime, and dreams at night. Sometimes, she comes smiling to throw her arms around me and kiss me. At other times, she comes with a dagger in hand to stab me to death. Sometimes, she comes sobbing. At others, she comes with her hair loose, her eyes wild, her nails tearing scratches into her cheeks, wailing and beating her breasts. She comes laughing like a madwoman, she comes like a nurturing caregiver, she whispers words of solace into my ears, she hisses accusations at me ... God! I can't tell you how that paadagi[1] torments me. Do you remember what thatha said this evening? Why don't I go to Thanjai, he asked. Truth be told, the reason I want my father to come to Kanchi rather than go to Thanjai myself is Nandini.'

'Arase! Is it for a woman, of all things, that you baulk at going to Thanjai? What will she do to you that makes you so afraid? Do you think she might try to poison your food?'

'No, Parthiba, no! You haven't yet understood me well enough. I am not afraid of her killing me. I'm afraid of her bending me to her will. If that Maya Mohini were to say, "Throw your father into prison!" or "Banish your sister from the empire!" or "Kill this old man and seat me on your throne!" once more, I might be tempted to do as she says. My friend! There are only three options—Nandini must die, or I must die, or the both of us must die. Unless one of these comes to pass, I will never know peace!' Aditya Karikalan said.

'Arase! What sort of talk is this? Why should you die? Say the word. I'll postpone my trip to Lanka and set off for Thanjavur right away. I'll kill her and return. I don't mind if I'm cursed for my streehatya[2].'

'If you do this, I will consider you my worst enemy,' Aditya Karikalan said. 'If Nandini must be killed, I will kill her with my own hands. And then I will kill myself. If anyone else so much as thinks about harming the nail of her little finger, I cannot bear it! My friend! Forget Nandini. Forget all I have said about her. Sail for Lanka tomorrow, as thatha said. Find a way to convince my brother Arulmozhi to leave, and bring him here. We'll get him to stay here. Let grandfather and grandson do what they will. You and I will go to Lanka. We'll gather a large army again and sail eastwards. We will conquer Savagam[3] and Pushpakam and Kadaram[4]. We will then head westwards and conquer Arabia and Persia and Egypt.

The tiger flag will fly over all these lands. Parthiba! Do you know those kingdoms are not bound by the rules of chastity we follow here? The king can point at any woman he likes, and have her thrown into the antapuram!'

Before Parthibendran could respond, Tirukkovaloor Malayaman entered.

'There is no story quite as astounding as that of Aravan in this entire world,' he said. 'Not in any of the lands of which you spoke just now. But I see the two of you are still wide awake, talking! Parthibendra, have you forgotten that you must leave for Lanka tomorrow?'

'That is why we're wide awake and talking. We were discussing my mission,' Parthibendran said.

The story continues in

BOOK 3

RIVER PRINCE

An Extract

THE HALLUCINATIONS OF SUNDARA CHOZHAR

The next morning, Sundara Chozha Chakravarti sent for his beloved daughter. He ordered the servants, helpers, physicians and everyone else attending on him to keep their distance, and bade Kundavai sit close to him. He stroked her back affectionately. She intuited that he was aching to tell her something, but was struggling to put it into words.

'Appa ... are you angry with me?' she asked.

Sundara Chozhar's eyes brimmed with tears.

'Why would I be angry with you, amma?' he asked.

'Why else? For flouting your orders and coming to Thanjai!'

'Yes. You ought not to have flouted my orders and come here. The Thanjavur palace is no place for young women. You must have deduced this already from last night's incident.'

'To which incident are you referring, Appa?'

'I'm speaking about that girl from Kodumbalur having a fainting fit. How is she doing now?'

'There's nothing the matter with her today, Appa. She was given to fainting fits in Pazhaiyarai too. She always recovers shortly after.'

'Did you speak to her, amma? Didn't she tell you anything about what she might have seen or heard in the palace last night?'

Kundavai thought for some time and said, 'Yes, Appa. When the rest of us were away at the Durga temple, she had tried to go to the terrace all by herself. On her way, she apparently heard someone lamenting pitifully. She says it frightened her out of her wits.'

'I thought as much. Do you see at least now, my child? This palace is haunted. A ghost wanders through it. Please don't stay here. You young girls should all leave!' Sundara Chozhar said.

Kundavai noticed that he was trembling. His eyes, burning and bloodshot, stared into nothingness.

'Appa, why must *you* stay on, then? Why must Amma stay here? Let us all return to Pazhaiyarai. Your move here seems to have done nothing for your health. You haven't recovered,' Kundavai said.

The emperor said with a bitter laugh, 'Where is the question of my recovering anymore? I have absolutely no hope of it. I've given up.'

'Appa! Why must you be so forlorn? The chief physician at Pazhaiyarai is confident he can cure you.'

'Yes, I heard that you believed him and sent someone to Lanka to fetch herbs. My daughter! This is evidence of your deep affection for me.'

'Is it wrong for a daughter to nurse deep affection for her father, Appa?'

'No, of course not. It is my great fortune that I have a daughter capable of such love. It wasn't wrong for you to have sent someone to Lanka to fetch the herbs, either. But whether you bring me herbs from Lanka or Savagam Island[1], or even nectar from Devalokam itself, this body will not heal in this birth ...'

'Aiyayo! Don't say such things.'

'You've come here, even flouting my orders, amma ... this truly fills my heart with joy. I'd been wanting to sit you down one day and tell you everything, to make a clean breast of it all. The opportunity has arisen now. Listen to me! Ailments of the body might be cured by medicinal herbs. But mine is an ailment of the mind. Which herb can tackle that?'

'Appa, what could ail the mind of the emperor who rules the three worlds?'

'You too have imbibed the hyperbolic imagination of the poets, my child! I'm not the ruler of the three worlds. I'm not the ruler of even one whole world. My kingdom is a little patch of land in one corner of one world. I'm barely able to bear the burden of even this ...'

'Why must you bear the burden, Appa? Is there no one you deem worthy of bearing the burden of governance? You have two gems for sons. Each was born a lion cub, each is a warrior among warriors, each is capable of bearing the heaviest burden one could place on ...'

'My daughter, it is this which makes my heart stop. Both your brothers are heroes without parallel. I've raised them as I have raised you, dearer to me than my two eyes. But I wonder whether I would be doing the right thing in handing over the kingdom to them. Would you say it would be right to bequeath a kingdom along with a curse to my sons?'

'What sort of curse could this kingdom carry? Our ancestors include Sibi, who gave of his own flesh to save the life of a dove,[2] and Manuneeti Chozhar, who sacrificed his son as penance for a calf.[3] Karikaal Valavar and Perunarkilli have ruled this very kingdom. Vijayalaya Chozhar, who bore six and ninety battle scars on his body, has sat on this very throne. Aditya Chozhar, who erected a hundred and eight temples along the banks of the Kaveri, and Parantakar, who donated a golden roof to the Chitrambalam, have expanded the realm. Kandaradityar, whose motto was "Anbe Shivam"[4] and who embodied both love and divinity, has ruled this land. What sort of curse could such a kingdom carry? Appa! You're labouring under some sort of delusion. If only you would leave this Thanjavur fort and ...'

'If I were to leave this place ... oh my dear girl, you don't know what hell would break loose the next moment! Do you think I have traded the beauty of Pazhaiyarai for this gilded cage, this Thanjai prison, for my own pleasure? Kundavai, my presence here is simply to stop the Chozha empire from breaking into pieces. Think back to what happened when the play was being staged yesterday. I was observing it all from the nilamaadam[5]. I even wondered whether I should put a stop to it in the middle ...'

'Appa! What are you talking about? The play was quite wonderful. My heart was bursting with pride, thinking of the greatness of the Chozha clan! Why did you want to stop it in the middle? Which part of the play did you find unsavoury?'

'The play was wonderful, yes, my child. I saw no flaw in it. I'm speaking about the audience's reaction to the play. Did you not notice the undercurrents of rivalry between the Kodumbalur faction and the Pazhuvoor faction flowing through the audience?'

'I did, Appa!'

'If this was how they behaved when I was right here, think what would happen if I were to leave Thanjavur. The very next moment, war would break out between the two factions. There would be a massacre like that which broke out in the clan of Krishna Paramatma,[6] and our empire would be destroyed even as they destroy each other ...'

'Appa! You are the emperor. Your word is law. The Pazhuvettaraiyars and Kodumbalur Velir are both bound to your every whim and wish. If they cross a line, they're essentially asking for their own destruction and nothing else. Why must it worry you?'

'My daughter, over the last century, these two clans have rendered invaluable service to the Chozha empire. Would we have expanded as we have without their help? Wouldn't their destruction be the death knell for the empire too?'

'Appa ... if you were to come to know that one of those two factions comprises traitors who are conspiring against you ...?'

Sundara Chozhar stared at Kundavai in surprise and said, 'What are you saying, my girl? A conspiracy against me? Who is hatching such a plot?'

'Appa, people who are pretending to be your faithful allies are secretly plotting against you. They're scheming to deny your sons the title, and hand the kingdom over to someone else ...'

'To whom? To whom, my daughter? Whom are they going to crown king instead of your brothers?' Sundara Chozha Chakravarti asked almost eagerly.

Kundavai said softly, 'Chithappa[7] Madurantakan, Appa! Even as you lie in your sickbed, these people have been plotting such a betrayal.'

Sundara Chozhar sat up to the extent he could, and said, 'Aha! If only their efforts were to bear fruit, how wonderful it would be!'

Kundavai nearly jumped out of her skin.

'Appa! What is this! You speak like an enemy of the very sons you have birthed!'

'No, I'm no enemy of theirs. I wish to do them good and nothing else. Let this cursed kingdom not go to them. If only Madurantakan would consent ...'

'If only Chithappa would consent! He has consented with all his heart. He is ready to be crowned king right away. Is this what you're going to do? Don't you need my older brother's consent? The heir's consent?'

'Yes. I'll have to ask Aditya Karikalan. And not just him. Your Periya Paatti[8] must consent too ...'

'Would a mother refuse to consent to her son inheriting a kingdom?'

'Why ever not? Don't you know your Periya Paatti even after all these years? I sat on the throne at Sembiyan Mahadevi's behest. It was she who persuaded me to become king, and later to make Aditya Karikalan the official crown prince. Kundavai, your Periya Paatti loves you very much. You must speak to her and persuade her to let Madurantakan become my heir.'

Kundavai was stunned into silence.

'After that, you must go to Kanchi. Go speak to your brother Aditya Karikalan and convince him to say he doesn't want this accursed kingdom. We will crown Madurantakan king. And then we will be able to live in peace, freed from this curse,' the emperor said.

'Appa, you speak of a curse over and over again. What is this curse?' Kundavai asked.

'My daughter, do you believe in the idea of rebirth? They say memories of our previous births can persist in our current births. Do you think this could be true?'

'Appa! What do I know of these things? They are grand philosophical conundrums.'

'They speak of the ten avatars of Mahavishnu. They say the Buddha took on many avatars before his last one. There are some quite beautiful stories about each of those births …'

'I've heard those, Appa.'

'If the gods and holy men are subject to rebirth, can ordinary mortals be exempt?'

'Maybe not, Appa.'

'Sometimes, I am visited by memories from my previous births, my daughter. I haven't spoken of them to a single soul. Even if I did, no one would believe me. They wouldn't understand, either. They will say I've lost my mind along with my body. As if it weren't enough to harass me with physicians, they would throw tantriks and mantravadis at me too.'

'Oh, yes, Appa! There are already those who say this—your ailments will not be cured by physicians. It is tantriks who must be called …'

'You see? You won't think this too, will you? You won't laugh at me when you hear what I have you say, will you?' the emperor said.

'Need you ask, Appa? Don't I know just how heavy your heart is? Would I think to laugh at you?' Kundavai said. Her eyes were bright with tears.

'I know, my daughter. That is why I'm trusting you with that which I have not told anyone else. Let me tell you my memories from another birth. Listen …,' Sundara Chozhar said.

NOTES

1. 'A ROYAL GUEST'

1 A reference to the legend of Satyavan and Savitri, where the wife tricks Yama into returning the life of her husband, thereby becoming an epitome of spousal devotion.

2 'Pillaai' is a form of address, which extends the vowel in 'pillai', meaning boy or son. The closest translation of this sentence might be an avuncular 'O son, don't worry'.

3 Literally 'young king', this Tamil word means 'prince', and is typically used while referring to a younger brother either to the king or to his heir.

2. THE CHITRA MANDAPAM

1 Meaning 'Elder', and a reference to Periya Pazhuvettaraiyar

2 Palm leaves on which letters and messages were traditionally written.

3 The six tastes, or arusuvai, are—inippu (sweet), pulippu (sour), kaarppu (spicy), uvarppu (salty), tuvarppu (tart) and kasappu (bitter).

5. A WOMAN ON A TREE

1 Trumpets used in a particular form of folk music.
2 Drums used as an accompaniment to folk music.

7. THE MANTRAVADI

1 One of the twelve Vaishnavite poet-saints known as Azhvars, and the only woman among them. Believed to have lived in the seventh or eighth century, she has been credited with writing the works *Tiruppaavai and Nachiyar Tirumozhi*. She is said to have attained salvation through marriage with Lord Krishna in the form of Ranganatha.
2 Flattery.
3 One of Kalki's puns—'kavi' means both poet and monkey.
4 The God of Love, an equivalent of Cupid in Indian mythology, he is described as so handsome that those who laid eyes upon him became intoxicated simply by breathing in the beauty emanating from him.
5 'Selvam' literally means 'wealth'. But 'selvan' and 'selvi' are also used to refer to one's son and daughter respectively. The word 'selvam' is corrupted to 'chellam' and used as an endearment in Tamil and Malayalam, meaning 'darling' or 'beloved'. This is why 'Ponniyin Selvan' is variously interpreted as referring to Ponni's wealth, her son, and her beloved.

8. 'DO YOU REMEMBER ...?'

1 There is a Tamil adage that goes 'Pennbudhi pinnbudhi'. 'Pennbudhi' means 'a woman's intelligence' and 'pinnbudhi' is hindsight. The implication is that women

only understand things in retrospective and regret the errors they have made.

9. THE LIONS CLASHED

1 The asura brothers from the legend of the Varaha and Narasimha avatars of Lord Vishnu.

2 A reference to Sundan and Upasundan, who were inseparable until the devas sent down the apsara Tilottama to create a rift between them and thwart their ambitions of conquering the three worlds. Interestingly, this is the only set among the brothers mentioned who were driven apart by a beautiful woman.

3 An ancient measure of time, estimated to work out to around twenty-four minutes.

13. THE CRYPT

1 The nine divine treasures that are in the possession of Lord Kubera in Indian mythology—padmaraga (ruby), mahapadma (lotus), shankha (conch), makara (crocodile), kacchapa (tortoise), mukunda (jasmine), nanda (delight), nila (sapphire) and kharva (so massive as to be uncountable). Scholars have been befuddled by the symbolism that this odd mixture of gems, emotions, animals and things carries.

14. 'IS THIS YOUR IDEA OF FRIENDSHIP?'

1 A man whose hands reach his knee, considered a great hero since it must have taken years of pulling a bowstring from a tender age for the bones to grow in this manner.

2 The destruction of these gardens is described in most

versions of the Ramayana. Ravana's Ashoka Vanam was destroyed by Hanuman on his mission to meet and rescue Sita in Lanka. The Madhu Vanam was a garden dear to Sugriva, and guarded by his uncle Dadhimukha. The Vanaras, led by Angada, were ecstatic upon receiving news of Sita being found alive and safe in Lanka and celebrated by raiding the honey and fruits of the Madhu Vanam. Sugriva usually punished trespassers with death, but in the case of his son and the other marauding Vanaras, he understood their joy and its significance and forgave them.

3 A raised platform on the verandahs of traditional Tamil homes that serves as a resting place for travellers or members of the household who do not wish to disturb those inside with untimely arrivals or departures.

4 Pejorative term that means 'mute'.

5 'Pinam', usually corrupted to 'ponam', literally means 'corpse'. In connotation, it may come closest to 'bloody' or 'useless', and is used as an angry curse.

6 A reference to Lord Shanishwara, who is believed to visit misfortune upon those whose lives he enters. It is often used as a curse, as if to say someone brings ill luck.

15. PAZHAIYARAI

1 'Padi', pronounced with a short 'a' and soft 'd' sound, refers to a place that is associated in some manner with any of the ten avatars of Lord Vishnu.

2 Literally 'Mother Tamil', this is the personification of the land as a woman of pulchritude, intelligence, skill and compassion.

3 Contrary to popular belief, it appears Krishna did not break pots of butter from a pathological craving for destruction or dairy, but to protest the raising of taxes by his uncle King Kanśa, which had forced the villagers to use their cattle as curd- and butter-producing machines. The story goes that on one particular day, when the villagers were journeying to Mathura to pay their taxes in kind—carrying butter and curd and milk in clay pots known as 'uri' in Tamil—Krishna and his friends broke the pots so the taxes would not reach the king, and ate the goods that fell to the ground. This is celebrated as Uriyadi Tirunaal—literally, 'The holy day on which the pots were broken'.

4 Tamil devotional poems often envision the god in whose praise they are sung as a mother, a child or a lover. The changed gender is a deliberate device that indicates that the lord is responsible for the conception, nourishment and safety of the poet, who is seen as the child.

16. 'THIS IS ALL HER DOING!'

1 The Tamil name of Mahabalipuram.

2 'Annai' means 'mother' and 'annaye' is a respectful form of address to an older woman.

17. THE DELINQUENT SPY

1 Literally, 'Old Kaveri'.

2 Literally, 'New Kaveri'.

3 Another way of referring to Tamizhagam, or the Tamil lands.

4 Literally meaning 'female thief', this is an affectionate term for a woman who is mischievous or clever.

5 A reference to Ravana's son, known variously as Meghnad, Ravani and Inderjit.

18. THE DISCONTENT OF THE PEOPLE

1 Literally meaning 'The Three'—it is a reference to the three most prominent Shaivite saints, Appar, Sundarar and Tirugnanasambandar.

2 Pasurams are verses in the praise of a particular god, which lend themselves to various tunes. Azhvars would typically sing the praises of Tirumaal, as they call Lord Vishnu.

3 Kanyakumari.

4 Tirupati.

5 Although 'Devar' and 'Varmar' could refer to any man of the royal dynasty, in this case it refers to Madurantaka Devar.

6 The native town of Andal; the temple where she is said to have prayed still stands, a small one famed for the hundreds of parrots in its trees and the garden from which she is said to have gathered flowers.

7 A 'maadam' is a large mansion with several stories and terraces on various levels. Temples were typically surrounded by these rich households, which is why the four streets around the temple ponds are usually called North Maada, South Maada, East Maada and West Maada streets, even today.

8 Ayarpadi is literally where the cowherds live—a reference here to the places where Krishna lived as a child.

19. EESANYA SHIVA BHATTAR

1 A Shiva devotee who is often depicted as a dwarpalak holding an axe, Chandeshwara Nayanar is the subject of an interesting legend. Born into a poor Brahmin family, it was his wont to create a Shiva lingam from sand and then worship the lingam with an offering of milk. His father saw this as a waste of good milk. Once, he saw his son meditating before a sand lingam doused with milk. Enraged, he kicked the lingam. At this, his son hit his father's leg with a staff, which—as is befitting of legend—turned into an axe and severed the leg. There was a happy ending, thanks to a timely appearance by Lord Shiva, who restored the damaged limb to normalcy, and then put Chandeshwara Nayanar in charge of protecting temples. It is customary for devotees to clap their hands before the idol of Chandeshwara to prove that they are leaving empty-handed, since it is not likely the deity will have as much sympathy for thieving devotees as for maimed fathers.

20. OF WHIRLPOOLS AND WOMEN'S EYES

1 In Tamil, the idiom goes, 'Vedaalathukku vaazhkkai pattu murunga maraththil era maatten enraal, mudigira kaaranamaa?' 'Vedaalam' is Tamil for 'Betaal'. 'Vazhkkai pattu' typically refers to marriage. So, essentially, the proverb translates literally into, 'If one were to say, after being given in marriage to Betaal, "I won't climb the peepul tree", is it a feasible proposition?' The idiom is typically used in everyday contexts, such as having to run an errand for a boss. The hilarity derives from the vision of the victim as Betaal's bride and

the perpetrator as Betaal. Our strapping Vandiyadevan doesn't quite fit the image of a blushing bride hesitating to climb the peepul tree.

2 A mythological king who would, to his own detriment, never tell a lie. As is typical of such legends, this cost him his kingdom, wife, son and personal freedom, but as is also typical of legends, it all turned out to be a test and every character in the story was eventually either returned to life and freedom, or escorted to Heaven with a red carpet rolled out.

3 A legend in which the elephant Gajendra was saved from the clutches of a crocodile and from the cycle of death and rebirth, thanks to a timely appearance by Lord Vishnu.

4 Tamil for 'carp', the kayal is said to be the ideal shape of a woman's eyes. The name 'Kayalvizhi' is a common Tamil one, a near translation of 'Meenakshi'.

5 This is an allusion to the story of Vatsasura, one of the demons who was sent by Kansa to kill a teenage Krishna. The asura took on the form of a calf and joined the herd Krishna was tending. Krishna recognised the asura, walked up nonchalantly to the calf whose form he had taken and then hurled the calf at a wood apple tree. The asura came crashing to the ground, along with all the wood apples of the tree.

6 The kurundu tree is believed to have medicinal properties. Its leaves and flowers are used in ayurvedic preparations. It is also believed to bring good luck, and it is customary for those in distress to plant one in their homes.

21. WONDER OF WONDERS

1 A reference to the mythological Vamana avatar, in which Lord Vishnu asks King Mahabali for land he can cover in three paces, and upon being granted the request, assumes such mammoth proportions that two steps encompass the netherworld, the earth and the heavens.

2 This is a reference to an incident in the Mahabharata, when Krishna volunteered to go as a Pandava envoy to meet Duryodhana and negotiate for peace before the Kurukshetra war.

3 Tamil for the sonpatta or the bidi leaf, once a symbol of royalty.

4 An ancient Tamil text, written by various poets, which contains verses sung in praise of the Chera, Chozha and Pandiya kings. 'Muththollaayiram' is an amalgam of 'moonru' (three) and 'thollaayiram' (nine hundred). It comprises nine hundred verses about each clan, making for a total of two thousand seven hundred verses.

22. THE PARANTAKAR AADURASALAI

1 'Aadurasalai' literally means 'centre for the aadura', where 'aadura' could refer to someone who is physically ill, mentally ill or homeless. It could be roughly translated as 'infirmary' or 'sanatorium', but the concept of an aadurasalai was a uniquely Chozha one, and its history is interesting. At first, the Chozha kings introduced aadurasalais in the temples. There was a room where physicians would tend to the wounded or sick. Eventually, aadurasalais were established as large centres dedicated to healing. The king was expected

to donate land for the establishment of the aadurasalai as well as for the physicians employed there.

2 A traditional martial art whose invention is credited to the sage Agastya, the art finds mention in ancient literature from the Sangam era, dating back to the third century BCE. The word 'silambam' derives from 'silambambu'. 'Silam' is an old Tamil word for 'hill' and 'silambambu' is a particular type of bamboo found in the Kurinji hills in present-day Kerala. The armies of some kings included dedicated silambam regiments.

3 Kalki Krishnamurthy used the royal 'we' rather often while speaking of the story, the readers and the characters. This is likely because the 'our' refers to the team running the magazine *Kalki*, in which *Ponniyin Selvan* was first serialised.

4 Healer or doctor.

5 A 'thaazhvaaram' is a verandah with a sloping roof, typically at the front of a house, or in the inner quarters surrounding the courtyard.

6 The designation for this post is Tirumantra Olai Adhikari—it was a position of great esteem, an official selected by the king to oversee all the letters sent out on the ancient version of a royal letterhead, a *seppedu* or copper plate.

7 The word literally means 'female thief', but is used in the same manner as 'rascal' or 'badmaash'.

23. MAMALLAPURAM

1 The agglutinative Tamil corruption of 'Vishnu Griham'

24. WHEN AN OLD MAN WEDS

1 'Perumaan' typically refers to a deity. But if one looks at the etymology of the word, it could be said to come from 'peru', which means 'great' and 'mahan' which means 'great man'. So, the word could be broken down to mean 'the greatest of the great'.

2 Although the term is no longer politically correct, I have retained Kalki's use of 'Shudra Goddess', because the phrase continues to be used in Tamil. It is considered that the gods have a caste system too, and there are deities who are offered meat and alcohol as prasad. These are the lesser gods, the Shudras among them. They, and the practices involved in their worship, are considered less refined than the temple gods and rituals. Typically, they are worshipped in open spaces and the idols are cruder. The priests who officiate at such rituals are of lower castes.

25. MALAYAMAN IN A FRENZY

1 This word could mean 'employer', 'boss', 'master', 'ruler' or 'landlord'.

2 It was customary for (usually unmarried) women to coat their faces in turmeric, which served the purpose of sunscreen and bleach. Typically, the women would stop using turmeric after marriage, but not always.

3 In this context, 'kodungol' means 'sceptre'—essentially, the reins of the kingdom. Later, 'kodungol' came to be associated with unjust rule, since this was a curved sceptre, but it appears there is no such connotation here.

4 'Arasu' can be loosely translated into 'royal' in

this context, although nowadays it is used to mean 'government'. The 'e' at the end indicates it is a form of address. A rough translation would be 'Your Royal Highness'. Although Parthibendran and Aditya Karikalan are close friends, they do observe a hierarchy of rank. Parthibendran uses the respectful plural while addressing Aditya Karikalan, whereas the latter uses the informal singular. Parthibendran tends to use Aditya Karikalan's title rather than his name.

26. 'NO VENOM MORE VICIOUS, NOR POISON MORE POTENT'

1 An ancient folk tradition practised in present-day Tamil Nadu, Kerala and parts of Sri Lanka, where a bow—'villu' in Tamil and Malayalam—is used as a musical instrument and the narration, in song, is interspersed with musical interludes.

27. NANDINI'S BELOVED

1 A term of respect, a rough if more ardent equivalent of the Hindi "ji".

2 In Hindu theology, these are the arishadvarga, the six forbidden passions—kama (lust or desire), krodha (anger), lobha (greed), moha (attachment), mada (sense of putting oneself before all others), matsarya (prejudice or partiality)—that stand in the way of one attaining moksha.

28. THAT DAY, IN THE ANTAPURAM

1 I could find no version of the Aravan story in which he is the son of the princess of Manipur—known more popularly as Chitrangada—who had been raised as a

warrior and fell in love for the first and last time with Arjuna. Their short-lived relationship did yield a son, but this does not seem to be Aravan. In all the versions I could find, Aravan is the son of the Naga princess Ulupi. Some versions interpret the word 'Naga' as suggesting she was from present-day Nagaland, but most see her as a serpent princess. Chitrangada's son is not known to have ever met his father, perhaps the chief reason he wasn't killed in the Kurukshetra war. Aravan, in some versions of the tale, is said to have volunteered himself as a sacrifice. In most, it was Krishna who put his name forward. The others who qualified for the sacrifice were Yudhisthira, Arjuna and Krishna himself, all of whom were deemed less dispensable than Aravan. Due to the consummation of his one-day marriage with Mohini, the female avatar of Lord Vishnu, Aravan is worshipped by transgender women of Tamil Nadu, who celebrate wedding festivities and then observe mourning rituals the next day at a grand annual celebration in Koovagam. In a separate Draupadi tradition, the head of Aravan which was offered as sacrifice is seen as a symbol of fertility and believed to grant progeny to the childless. Kalki Krishnamurthy appears to have heard, probably through an oral tradition, a mixed-up version of these two stories. The most popular story of Aravan is heart-breaking—it is said he was strong enough to decimate the Kaurava army all on his own, and end the war before it could even begin. Krishna felt compelled to get him out of the way so that the war between good and evil could unfold as it did. Saddest of all is the idea that Aravan had gone to seek his father out because his maternal uncle despised Arjuna and Aravan was keen to broker peace between them. So, the first time he met his father, he was asked to lay down his life.

2 An annual temple festival, celebrated by the entire village.

3 Tamil for 'Oh, Prince!'

29. MAYA MOHINI

1 'Paadagi' literally translates into 'traitor', used with the feminine ending. It could refer to any form of treachery.

2 The murder of a woman, forbidden to a soldier.

3 Present-day Java.

4 Present-day Kedah.

THE HALLUCINATIONS OF SUNDARA CHOZHAR

1 Modern-day Java.

2 As the gods were wont to when they were bored, Agni and Indra decided to put Sibi Chakravarti to the test. Agni took the form of a dove and Indra that of an eagle. The two descended on to a terrace of the palace and interrupted the king's navel-gazing to ask him for help. The dove asked for succour, shelter from the eagle who was all set to devour him. The eagle asked not to be denied his prey. Sibi offered to feed the eagle many times the weight of his prey. The eagle insisted nothing would be as tasty as the dove. The king said he could not let down a creature that had sought his protection, but could not let a subject go hungry, either. The eagle reluctantly agreed to trade

the dove for an equivalent in its weight of flesh cut out of the king's right thigh. The king began to cleave his thigh, but even when he had cut it right to the bone, the flesh weighed less than the dove. Finally, he sat on the balance, and learnt in the stupor of his blood loss that the entire exercise had been the entertainment of an evening for the gods. As some recompense for his trouble, he would go down in history as the king who had all but given up his life to save a dove.

3 Manuneeti Chozhar had arranged for a bell to be placed in the palace accessible to every subject. Anyone who wanted to complain to the king could ring the bell. One day, the bell was pealing madly. The king rushed to see what the matter was, and found a weeping cow pulling at the rope of the bell. Her calf had been run over by a chariot in the palace boulevard. The king, wracked by guilt, decided his punishment would be to experience the cow's own loss and suffering and had his son run over in the same boulevard. As is customary in such cases, a member of the divine pantheon appeared and restored to life both the calf and son.

4 'Anbe Shivam' translates literally into 'It is love that is divine', meaning that love—in this context, affection, care, concern and consideration—are the ultimate form of divinity.

5 A terrace lit by the moon.

6 A reference to the infighting among the Yadavas, the subject of the *Mausala Parva* and the reason the Pandava brothers gave their kingdom up and began their long walk to Heaven.

7 An uncle, either one's father's younger brother or

cousin—as in this case—or the husband of one's mother's younger sister or cousin.

8 Literally 'older grandmother' or 'senior grandmother'—the older sister of a grandmother, or the wife of a grandfather's older brother.